RA[illegible] KATHERINE COMPTON'S HISTORICAL ROMANCES

EDEN'S ANGEL

"PACKED WITH ADVENTURE.
LACED WITH HUMOR AND TENDERNESS.
DON'T MISS THIS ONE!"

Romantic Times

OUTLAW BRIDE

"POIGNANT AND SWEETLY SENSUAL . . .
A DELIGHTFUL ADVENTURE-FILLED TALE"

Affaire de Coeur

BLUE MOON BAYOU

"A FAST, INTRIGUING READ
WITH LOTS OF ADVENTURE
AND WONDERFUL CHARACTERS"

Rendezvous

THE LADY AND THE OUTLAW

"ABSOLUTELY DELICIOUS . . .
PERFECT . . . LOVED IT!"

Affaire de Coeur

Other **AVON ROMANCES**

Whispers in the Wind

Katherine Compton

AVON BOOKS NEW YORK

WHISPERS IN THE WIND is an original publication of Avon Books. This work has never before appeared in book form. This work is a novel. Any similarity to actual persons or events is purely coincidental.

AVON BOOKS
A division of
The Hearst Corporation
1350 Avenue of the Americas
New York, New York 10019

Inside cover author photo by Amanda Beth Tietze
Published by arrangement with the author
Library of Congress Catalog Card Number: 94-96262
ISBN: 0-380-77455-0

First Avon Books Printing: February 1995

Printed in the U.S.A.

RA 10 9 8 7 6 5 4 3 2 1

All glory be Thine.
And through me,
Let Thy light shine.
In every form and fashion,
To each word,
Lend Thy truth, peace, and passion.

Chapter 1

English countryside, 1886

In the dark swirling mists between slumber and awakening, Galilea heard the murmuring again. The softly spoken words, just beyond understanding, floated into her ears as if drifting upon the early autumn wind.

Was the voice whispering inside her head . . . her *own*? Galilea strained toward the unintelligible syllables in her groggy state.

No . . . not *her* voice. Someone else's—but a familiar, mellow voice she felt she should have known just as well.

Galilea blinked her eyes open, her body slightly tingling with the traces of deep sleep. A soft cushion of grass cradled her, the rich brown earth beneath it, warm. Bright spots of sunlight broke through the silhouettes of leaves dangling overhead. As the tree limbs rustled in the breeze, the muttering rushed through her mind one last time, then was gone—lost once again in the midst of a forgotten dream.

Galilea sat up slowly. A soft chill skimmed the surface of her skin as she glanced around the meadow. The tall grass dotted with wildflowers rippled in the wind. A flock of birds flew from the brush and fluttered across the sky. But as usual, she was all alone.

Combing her fingers through her hair, she frowned, then absently pushed the tangled blond strands from her face. She was well-accustomed to the voices and visions in her head. They were as much a part of her as the heart beating in her breast. But this whispering that had plagued her on the cusp of awakening for the past few mornings was new and foreign. The words, spoken like a secret, did not hold substance. Yet, the garbled message was always the same. And the voice was that of a child. Of that much, she was certain. But she'd been unable to follow the rambling—as if she wasn't meant to understand it.

Not yet, anyway. Only when the whisperer was ready for her to comprehend the words would she clearly understand their meaning. Even knowing this, she could not quiet her curiosity about the strange familiarity of the child's voice.

A screech came from a branch high above her head, calling Galilea's attention to the large black crow perched there.

"Good morning, Magus," she said. "Yes, I know, 'tis time to get up."

With a yawn, Galilea stretched her arms high over her head. Rising from her bed of grass, she brushed the twigs from her tattered skirt. It was a bright and sunny day—a rare occurrence in this part of England where the mornings were usually tinted with gray mists and fog. Galilea gazed at the pale blue sky and marveled at the color. It was sad how the beauty of the world was so often taken for granted by those too busy to notice.

On such a day, she swiftly decided, she would not waste another minute of the sunshine worrying about some faraway, unnamed voice—not when she had something much more pressing to attend to.

"Are you coming, Magus?" she asked, smiling up at the black bird.

The crow cawed and flapped his wings, then he glided from the tree branch and landed on Galilea's shoulder. Reaching up, she stroked his breast lightly with a fingertip. He tickled her ear with his beak. It was a simple exchange of affection, but one Galilea held dear. She preferred the company of God's lesser creatures to that of the human race. Animals were more accepting of her. And she was much more comfortable around them. The woodland beasts did not seem to notice that she was any different from anyone else—nor, she highly suspected, would they have cared even if they did.

With her first step, Magus took to the air, soaring several yards ahead of her, then circling back to assure she followed. Moving with haste, she made her way through the tall grass to the wall of trees that lined the other side of the meadow.

White Fern Forest, it was called, and, according to legend, haunted. Indeed, Galilea had noted the pitiful, wandering spirits from time to time—none truly malicious, merely lonesome for the lives they'd left behind.

But today there were no ghosts. Today, shafts of muted sunshine fell through the green canopies above, casting a white radiance over the woods.

Galilea inhaled the scent of pine with every breath she took. Pine needles and fallen leaves crunched beneath her feet as she wove between the trees, her mind deeply engaged with the task at hand.

The new master of the manor was arriving today, or so it was rumored. She had a need to see him at close range . . . to search the workings of his mind . . . to assess what sort of man he was. After all, he had the authority to evict her from Luxley lands if he so desired. And that would never do.

This special place had become her haven from the world for nearly a year. The meadow and forest had nourished her with a plentiful supply of nuts and berries. The standing walls of the castle ruins had shielded her from the cold northern winds. The tall grass growing on the hillside had provided her with a bed. The leaves on the forest floor had been her blanket. 'Twas her home now.

Galilea nibbled her lower lip. She did so hate probing into others' thoughts uninvited. It was rude and rather like eavesdropping, although sometimes it simply happened against her will. Then again, there were times when no matter how hard she tried, she could not guess what another might be thinking. More often than not, the voices came in droves, sometimes one overlapping the other. Although that generally only happened when she was in a crowd. Which was another reason she kept to the meadow.

Magus sailed above her as she stepped from the thicket of trees and started over the hill toward the old castle ruins. Sunlight illuminated the deteriorating pillars of stone. Galilea steered away from the once mighty fortress, now decaying with age.

Generations upon generations of ancient phantoms still dwelled within the castle, and carried on as if their lives had never ended. Often, Galilea would sit upon the crumbling walls, watching and listening to them as they moved about. She heard the laughter, the agony, the triumphs . . . the sweet pledges of love and honor. At times, she pitied those earthbound souls forever locked in time. At other times, she had envied them.

But she would not allow the old ones to detour her today.

Magus filled the air with a soft mournful cry, making her suspect once more that he was one of them—a roaming spirit who had made his home inside a crow. He landed on the remains of a turret and called to her again, flapping his black wings in a fussy fashion. Still, she would not be swayed. Ignoring the bird, she walked past the castle, gathering wildflowers all the way down the hill.

Galilea settled beside the trunk of one of the many elms that lined the road to Luxley Manor. Hidden from passersby, she folded her feet beneath her and dropped her bouquet in her lap. As she waited for a glimpse of the new lord, she split the stems with her thumbnail, stringing one flower through the next, and stared across the road into the distance.

The gables of Luxley Manor were barely visible above the treetops. Once, she had stood on the edge of the wood that surrounded the house and viewed the magnificent structure in all its glory. She had tried to visualize the interior of the house but could picture nothing in her mind's eye. She had considered peeking through the windows at night, though she'd never quite summoned the courage to follow through with such an idea.

She'd always been afraid to venture too close to the house. It was as if she and the old Lord Luxley had had an unspoken agreement. He would not banish her from his lands as long as she stayed out of sight and did not make a spectacle of herself. She had sometimes wondered whether the remaining inhabitants of the manor were even aware of her existence. They had not made any attempt to drive her away since old Lord Luxley's death—nigh eight months ago now.

But the family must have known she was there. All the tenants knew. Everyone in the nearby village knew. She had overheard them discussing her and read their thoughts as they'd passed along the road. She knew the tales they told about the mad woman who lived in the meadow—a witch, some even called her.

Galilea glanced down at the wreath she was making. Perhaps she *was* mad. Ollie had once told her that madness, like beauty, was often in the eye of the beholder. But she was no witch standing over a cauldron peering at images in the smoke. She was as human as any of the rest of them. Although few had ever treated her as such.

Only Ollie had understood her. Ollie had said she was special. He had assured her that her power of perception was a divine gift. The "knowing" he had termed it.

All the same, Galilea wasn't always so sure the "knowing" was a *gift* exactly. There were times when she saw things and heard things that weren't so divine.

Galilea lifted the ring of flowers and placed them on her head, remembering when Ollie had first shown her how to weave a wreath. Her heart constricted a little at the thought of him. A whole year had passed, and still she grieved. She missed him sorely. He had taught her so many things—about nature and science, about the constellation. How she had loved those evenings when he'd pointed out the stars in the night sky, naming them one by one.

Oliver Jones had meant the world and all

to her. A tinker who'd been traveling this very road when she'd been an infant; shoved into his arms, he'd been a father to her . . . a tutor . . . her friend.

Together, they had journeyed throughout the countryside in their little wagon, peddling pots and pans and household goods—singing bawdy songs, discussing philosophy, touching upon near every subject under the sun.

But those merry days were finished now.

A warm tear trickled down Galilea's cheek, unnoticed until it fell upon her thigh. She watched the dark wet spot seep into the threadbare fabric of her skirt . . . felt the dampness against her skin.

After Ollie had died, the creditors had come, like vultures flocking to a corpse. They had taken everything: the horse, the wagon, the wares, Ollie's books. They had wiped away all evidence that such a magnificent man had ever existed. Galilea had been left with not even the means for a proper burial, and Oliver Jones, to whom a shrine should have been built, had been laid to rest in a shallow unmarked grave alongside paupers and thieves.

Galilea took a deep shuddering breath, holding back the next wave of pain. Ollie had made her promise not to weep for him—a promise she hadn't kept very well. He had looked upon death not as an exit from this world but rather an entrance into another. A place much grander than one could imagine, he had told her, where the sun shone all the time, where birds sang, and church bells chimed. Even on his deathbed, he had spoken of what a great adventure it would be to converse with the angels of heaven.

Closing her eyes, Galilea fastened her mind on his face at the moment of his passing: the bright gleam in his pale blue eyes, the serene smile pasted upon his lips. The vision flooded into her heart, filling the empty aching space . . . reminding her that a special part of Ollie would forever live on in her cherished memories.

The method eased the vacant spot inside her chest, as it always did. Day by day, she was getting better at living life alone. But in the beginning, she'd been lost without Ollie. Like a babe abandoned in the woods, she had wandered aimlessly. Until she had awakened one morning in the meadow.

Here, on Luxley land, she felt a peace she had never before experienced. She sensed she belonged here among the ghosts and ghouls of the castle ruins and White Fern Forest.

The new owner of the manor had *to let her stay.*

Galilea wiped the wetness from her cheek with the back of her hand. She leaned her head against the tree trunk and gazed down the length of the dirt road. Not a soul was coming and the sun was rising higher. She fell into a trance listening for the sound of an approaching coach.

Her thoughts drifted over what she had learned of the new master. It was very little. The villagers claimed he had swindled old

Lord Luxley out of the estate in a card game in London. *Such a man might lack compassion.*

That notion echoed over and over in Galilea's mind as the shadows of the trees stretched across the road. The ground grew hard beneath her still form. Life stirred all around her. Squirrels scurried about collecting their nuts. Rabbits popped in and out of the brier bushes. Chirping birds skipped from limb to limb in the branches high above. The blue of the sky slowly deepened to violet.

When at last dusk cast a lavender haze over the countryside, Galilea came to a sad realization.

He's not coming, a voice murmured inside her head, though she could not determine whether this bit of wisdom came from the workings of her own logic or from some other unnatural source. It mattered not, she supposed. No one traveled these roads after dark. If the present master of Luxley Manor had stopped at the village this late in the day, he'd no doubt been detained. The widespread tales of headless knights in armor and countless other demons were sure to delay his journey until the morning light.

Galilea rose, unfolding her cramped muscles, and started up the hill. A chill was in the air, but she did not dwell on it. Instead, she focused on the perfect cure for her disappointment.

Tiny stars were beginning to blink in the darkening sky as if lanterns were being lit one by one in the dome of heaven. The castle ruins silhouetted on the horizon looked almost habitable in the waning light. Magus would be roosting in one of the turrets.

Galilea inhaled deeply, taking the cool crisp breaths of the season into her lungs. She made her way up the steep incline, thinking of the time Ollie had taken her to the ballet in London.

An old friend of Ollie's had worked the curtains in the London Pavilion. Galilea had been allowed to watch the performance from the wings. She'd been mesmerized by the lithe beauty of the dancers, dazzled by the costumes. The entire troupe of dancers had passed right by her when they'd exited the stage, and the prima ballerina's netted skirt had brushed her arm.

Galilea now walked with purpose toward the castle ruins. She sensed the spirits of old were sleeping as she stepped through the crumbling, arched entryway and stooped just inside. Her fingers were numb with cold as she pried the loose rock from the bailey. Reaching into the dark cavity, her hand glided over the contents: a cluster of dried four-leaf clover, a bird's nest filled with turquoise bits of a robin's broken egg shell, a shiny brass button, a tattered satin ribbon she'd found on the road . . .

In the farthest corner of the cramped space, Galilea grasped what she was looking for.

She removed the small, tin, heart-shaped box with utmost care, and stood, admiring the way the pale moonlight glinted on the intricate stamped design on top. Ollie had given her the memento one year on the feast of Saint Stephen. The creditors had considered it worthless. But to Galilea, the little music box was the most precious treasure in the whole world.

Tucking her prized possession into her pocket, Galilea climbed up the time-battled wall surrounding the castle. Once she reached the top of the parapet, she retrieved the tin, set it in a safe place between two rocks on the ledge, and opened the lid.

A sweet, tinkling melody rose from the box, an enchanting sound that washed over the hillside chasing away the dreariness.

Galilea positioned herself at one end of the narrow wall. As the tune chimed out a short introduction, she reached up and straightened the crown of flowers upon her head. Then she closed her eyes and ran her hands down her bodice, feeling the frayed fabric turn into silk beneath her touch.

And the magic began.

The stone ledge, cold and hard beneath her bare feet, suddenly transformed into the London Pavilion stage. The full moon shining bright in the evening sky became her spotlight. And a silent audience of long dead souls gathered in the courtyard below.

The wind whisked through the trees that lined the road, making a mournful sound.

Collin MacLaine turned his coat collar up against the sudden chill and urged his skittish mount onward. The plow horse that the innkeeper had lent him for a tidy fee was direly obstinate and challenged his every command. It did not help matters that Collin was no accomplished horseman. He'd never had the means for such frivolous luxuries as riding lessons, and was unprepared to handle the stubborn animal.

The horse's hooves clipped in the silence, striking the hard cold ground with a hollow note. A night such as this was the stuff of which ghost stories were made, Collin declared, watching a thick white fog form and hover above the road.

A blast of wind jerked a lock of long dark hair from the thong at the nape of his neck and whipped it across his eyes. Collin shoved the hair from his face and frowned, recalling the innkeeper's warnings.

The squat, balding man had done his best to persuade him to wait until morning to continue on to Luxley Manor. No doubt the old fool had thought to scare Collin into a night's fare by stammering out such dark and gruesome tales.

Collin straightened in his saddle and pulled his cloak tighter around him. He prided himself on being a scholar and above silly folklore. He pitied these poor countryfolk. What nonsense they had been raised to believe.

Indeed, the wind *did* make an eerie noise hereabouts. But there was a perfectly logical explanation for the moaning sounds. The road cut through a dale with hills flanking both sides. The wind merely grazed the treetops, whistling and whining through the leaves.

Collin narrowed his eyes on the dark horizon in the distance, observing the silhouette of the castle set against the purple sky. The way the full moon hung above the crumbling towers truly did present what some might call a frightful picture. Once the old fortress surely rose on the hill in all its glory. Now it stood as a constant reminder that *nothing* lasted forever. He could understand this small country community's fear in that concept.

But for the villagers to honestly believe that the old ruins and nearby woods were haunted was utterly ridiculous. It was a widely known fact that anything you could not see, hear, smell, weigh, or measure, simply did not exist.

Collin shook his head, considering the notion that it would be useless to try to convince the locals that the grim tales told by their ancestors were merely fables, no doubt fabricated to hasten naughty children home before dark.

Suddenly, the unruly horse reared up on hind legs, bucking frantically.

Caught off guard, Collin toppled from the saddle. His backside slammed hard against the cold ground, jarring his entire system. In the moments it took him to recover, he watched the wicked beast of a horse gallop off in the direction of the village inn.

Cursing beneath his breath, Collin remained seated whilst he gathered his dignity.

The horse's uncooperative disposition was another in the long list of encumbrances he had had to deal with since his journey's start.

First the latch on his secondhand trunk had given way, spilling the contents all over the sidewalk outside his London apartment. Before he'd had a chance to gather his belongings, some dirty little vagrant had snatched his best hat and gloves and taken off with them. Then the coach had lost a wheel. Now the damned horse had left him stranded in the middle of the road.

Collin glanced around and found himself positioned at the base of the hilltop castle. According to the directions he'd been given, he shouldn't be far from the manor. It couldn't be more than a short walk.

With a disgusted grunt, he pushed off the ground, rubbed his sore hip, then attempted to dust himself off. He was thinking that *surely* no further catastrophes could delay him at this point, when a strange tinkling sound reached his ear.

On the tail of the howling wind, he could barely make out . . . a faint, hauntingly beautiful tune. He lifted his gaze once more to the long ago deserted castle, from whence the music appeared to come.

There was a movement on the bailey—a shadow skittering back and forth.

Collin set his mouth in a hard line. He was of a mind someone was playing a nasty trick on him. Perhaps the innkeeper had hired some young scamp to set the skeptical new resident of Luxley Manor back on his heels.

Well, no lad wearing a sheet was going to frighten Collin MacLaine away. He had come to stay, and stay he would. And the sooner these countryfolk realized he was here for the duration, the better they would all get along.

With a sharp tug on his lapels, Collin started up the hill, noting the tinkling melody grew more distinct with his ascent. It was not without effort that he made his way over the steep incline. Flat rocks jutted from the grassy slope, probably planted there by past inhabitants to slow the progress of would-be conquerors. Further hampering his climb, the tall grass whipped his knee-high boots and tangled around his ankles.

His annoyance with the situation—with the whole damn wretched day, in fact—reached its peak when he stumbled, tore his trousers, and scraped a knee. Grabbing a nearby stick, he righted himself and pressed onward in a dour mood, bent on pouring out a good earful on whoever was up to these absurd shenanigans.

As he rose over the last ridge of strategically placed rocks, Collin squinted at the dark figure. At this distance, he could assuredly see the creature was quite human. Breathing hard from the climb, he tossed the stick aside and picked up his stride.

A few yards from the main bailey, his footsteps dragged to a stop.

The form on the wall glided into a ray of

moonlight, taking on the shape of a small-statured woman . . . the very picture of a fairy-queen he'd once seen in a child's story book.

Her hair fell well below her waist, gleaming silver in the wan light. To the tune of a tinny-sounding music box somewhere hidden from sight, she danced along the narrow walkway of deteriorating stones with the grace of a winged angel. The outline of her slim figure was visible beneath the thin, almost transparent fabric of her white gown. Upon her head she wore a wreath of common wildflowers—blossoming weeds of the same kind found in nearby fields.

With her arms arched high above her head as if she gave homage to the starlit sky, she balanced on one foot and did a pirouette.

Collin's jaw fell slack as he watched her performance. It was mystifying—the grace with which she danced . . . her foolish bravery. The woman's exquisite beauty, not only in the physical form, but in every lithe movement of her body, held him breathless.

A cold blast of October wind slashed at his cloak and set his shoulder length hair free and flying behind him. It was as if his surroundings attempted to steal his sense of time—as if the ground beneath him was pulling him into some myth from the Middle Ages.

He could not move. He could merely stand there and stare, feeling his pulse beat hard at the base of his throat . . . feeling fear grip him at the thought of the lovely creature crashing onto the rocks that cascaded down the hillside. Such a fall would most certainly be fatal. 'Twas sheer folly to dance along such a dangerous ledge. Only a fool or a *madwoman* . . .

The notion that the dainty fairy-like woman might be shallow-witted had no sooner formed in his mind when she dashed toward a crevice in the bailey where missing stones left a wide gap.

Collin's heart lurched as he witnessed the impossible leap across the broad *V* in the wall. The woman glided over the opening in slow motion, the moonlight seemingly following her, and glowing a bit brighter when she landed in perfect balance on the opposite ledge.

As she continued her dance, a trickle of sweat dripped from Collin's brow. A sudden anger swallowed his relief that she'd somehow miraculously managed not to kill herself.

Ironically, the daft woman had frightened him like no ghost ever could.

The blood warming in Collin's veins brought him home to his own sensible self, and he stepped forward, briskly moving toward the bailey wall.

"You there! Woman! Hold where you are!"

Chapter 2

Galilea froze on the ledge. As the shout reached her ears, a warm, radiant glow filled her heart, spreading outward, seeping into her limbs. She turned her head and observed a tall, dark figure below.

Emotions of a mysterious nature ran amok within her breast, within her brain, though fear was not among them. She could not sort the strange string of chaos that assaulted her as she looked down upon the strong, moonlit features.

The man did not appear transparent, as a specter would, but neither did he seem quite real with his cloak billowing out behind him and his hair fluttering wildly about his shoulders.

How peculiar that she'd not sensed the stranger standing there until he'd spoken. Was he a vision then, she wondered—a figment of her imagination? Rarely, did any individual, spirit or otherwise, approach her without a tingling sensation shimmying up her spine.

Granted, she'd been lost in her dance.

Dancing always closed her off from the world, freed her for a brief spell from the voices in her head. Still, she'd never failed to feel an immediate warning whenever someone ventured too close.

The tune of the tin music box pinged out the last few notes of its sweet melody, leaving only the whispering wind rushing through the silence of the night.

As the tune ended, the peeved expression the intruder wore flattened as if he'd forgotten what it was that he was so angry about.

Then quite suddenly he seemed to remember and frowned again.

"Come off that wall before you break your silly neck," he yelled.

When he spoke again, Galilea was certain he was no phantom. His voice was too clear, too forceful to be that of a spirit.

The notion that he was indeed flesh and blood made her insides quake. She was accustomed to the visitations of ghosts. To have a living soul come calling was an entirely different matter.

He stepped forward.

She took a step back, edging closer to the ledge.

"Are you deaf?" he asked, his tone only slightly kinder.

Galilea was overwhelmed—not by the question, but rather by his attempt to converse with her. No one hereabouts dared talk to the "madwoman of the meadow."

Then again, he was obviously not from the

village. His attire, while somber and not nearly as fine as the garments worn by a country squire, looked to be the clothes of a gentleman. Galilea tried to focus on the workings of his mind, but it was as if a heavy black curtain hid his thoughts from view.

Could he be the new vicar she heard had just arrived—come to save the local madwoman from possession?

Nay. Not even one bound by the vows of the church would venture up the hill to the castle this time of night . . . for surely he'd been warned about the provincial ghosts and goblins.

And if not the new vicar, then . . . the stranger below could only be—

"Very well then." He called louder this time, cupping his mouth with his hands. "If you'll not come down of your own accord, I'll come up and fetch you myself." With that, he strode to the wall, braced a boot at the base and grasped the stone above his head.

Moved by sheer terror, Galilea ran with the speed of a rabbit across the top of the bailey. Leaping from one stone to the next, she skittered down the far side of the wall, dashed across the courtyard, and ducked into a dark alcove.

She placed a hand upon her breast, feeling her pulse pump hard against her palm . . . hoping the new proprietor of Luxley Manor, or whoever he was, might give up trying to scale the wall and simply go away and leave her be.

A string of deep curses echoed throughout the fortress.

Galilea peered around the pile of rocks that partially blocked the opening and saw the man drop from the bailey into the cobbled courtyard. As she watched him stalk forward in her direction, her breathing grew so loud in her own ears that she feared he might hear her.

No more than ten yards from the alcove, he paused and slowly turned in a circle. "Did the innkeeper pay you well to pull off this charade?" he called into the night.

Galilea retreated a little further into the dark recess, but not so far that she couldn't survey his every move. Her gift, as Ollie had called it, appeared useless against this man. She could perceive no small measure of what he may be thinking as he stood anchored in the center of the courtyard intensely scanning his surroundings.

Try as she would, Galilea could gain no more knowledge of him than her mortal eyes could assess. So she took in his physical attributes, which alone, she decided, were indeed impressive.

He towered well above six feet in height, presenting a tall masterful persona. His features were nicely placed, not too large nor too small, although quite severely broody, she determined. He might have been truly handsome had he worn a halfway pleasant expression.

"Answer me, damn you," he whispered

harshly. "I know you're here." Folding his arms across his chest, he planted his feet wide, and once again the wind set his cloak and tousled hair dancing. The effect made him seem to possess an almost demon-like disposition, which distracted Galilea from his looks.

"Yes, I know you're here somewhere." He began to stroll about, ducking down and peering into the shadows along the outlying walls.

As his search brought him nearer to the alcove, Galilea pressed her spine against the inner wall and closed her eyes in a desperate attempt to become invisible.

His boot heels clicked loudly against the paved cobblestones.

Galilea's heart pounded against her breastbone, picking up pace as his footsteps moved closer and closer.

"I *will* find you, fair lady. And when I do—"

A jagged streak of lightning split the sky and clap of thunder shook the earth, cutting Collin's threat short. He stopped in mid-stride and looked up to find clouds rolling overhead, fast and furiously.

A huge raindrop promptly plopped down and splattered in the center of his forehead. Lightning illuminated the whole landscape for a split second, then left him blinded in complete darkness.

He heard a shuffling noise in the pitch-black shroud that claimed the castle . . . and the strange, sweet scent of wildflowers rushed by him.

Collin snapped his head in the direction of the sound . . . then recognized the pitter-patter of soft footsteps. Lightning flashed again, preceding another rumble of thunder. In the instant of radiant brightness, he glimpsed the fairy-like creature disappearing through a hole in the wall of the ancient ruins.

The droplets of rain swiftly accelerated, turning into bucketsful washing over the countryside.

Wrapping his cloak tighter around him, Collin hastened from the dilapidated castle.

He made his way down the hill, stumbling and sliding along the muddy slope . . . and ardently swearing to wring the woman's neck if ever he saw her again.

After one of the longest hours of his life, Collin approached Luxley Manor—at least he hoped the large home belonged to the Luxley estate. He'd passed no other dwelling along the road.

In any event, he didn't intend to walk any further in the downpour. His hair was plastered to his head. His drenched cloak weighed heavily upon his shoulders. He was cold and tired, and for the last mile or so, his scraped knee had started to sting.

The rusted wrought iron gate creaked in protest as he worked it open just wide enough to squeeze through. As he trudged up the overgrown path, lightning cracked the sky behind the mansion, creating a dim view of the place.

The poor condition of the estate struck him at once. Even in the stormy denseness the neglect was obvious. When he neared the gabled mansion, he noted the shutters hung loosely by the hinges, banging without mercy against the side of the house. The flower bed in front of the rutted, half-circle drive was filled with weeds, and the cherub statue in the center of it was badly chipped and missing one arm.

Collin climbed the wide steps, his boots dripping mud. It was well past any decent calling hour, he knew. Nevertheless, he wasted no time in putting the brass door knocker to good use.

" 'Ear now, wots all this noise about?" came a shrill voice as the door finally opened a few inches, and a miniature, middle-aged woman wearing a nightcap poked her head out.

Collin straightened to his full height and attempted to smile, but he feared the smile didn't fare well enough to hide his misery.

"Good evening, madam," he began, his voice weary in spite of his effort to sound mildly pleasant. "Might I inquire if this would be Luxley Manor."

"You might, and it 'tis." The woman tucked her chin and frowned, emphasizing the legion of wrinkles around her mouth. "But everyone's retired for the evenin', they have. So whatever business you 'ave 'ear will 'ave t' wait till the morrow."

When she proceeded to slam the door, Collin flattened his palm against it.

The woman squeaked at the insult, then narrowed her wide eyes into slits. "Now you see 'ear, mister—"

"Collin MacLaine."

"Collin . . . MacLaine?" The woman echoed an octave higher. She blinked twice. Then her face lit with acknowledgment. Skittering backward, she pulled the door wide. "Lud, do come in, sir."

Collin walked into the soft yellow illumination provided by the single candle she held in her free hand.

"Oh lud," she repeated, then shut the door and rushed to set her candle on a small table in the foyer. "Let me be takin' that wet cloak for you, sir."

As the little woman fussily stripped him of the outer garment, Collin took in the faded, flowered wallpaper alongside the wide, curved staircase that stretched up into obscurity. Darkness concealed whatever lay beyond the grandfather clock, on past the ring of flickering candlelight, limiting the initial view of his new home.

A musty odor assaulted him upon his next breath and before he could place a finger beneath his nose, he sneezed.

"Oh, you poor thing, bless ya. Yor bound t' catch yor death out and about in such weather. I'll 'ave old Winston light a fire in the study and we'll get a good 'ot cup o' tea down you straight—"

"Fanny!" The woman flinched at the harsh whisper coming from the darkness.

"What on earth are you doing opening the door to a stranger at this ungodly hour?"

A tall white-haired man strode into the orb of light, appearing stiff and staunch even in the long white nightshift he wore.

" 'Tis 'im, Winston," Fanny whispered. " 'E's come at last. 'Tis Master Collin MacLaine, it 'tis."

Winston lifted his chin and peered down his long pointed nose at Collin. "The Scotchman?" he asked, placing a definite sniff at the end of the question.

Collin took offense at the man's tone, an obvious testament to his feelings for the Scottish.

"My father was Scottish," Collin replied, elevating his own chin to an equal level. Then, for good measure, he tacked on, "My mother was Cheyenne Indian. Now . . . might I inquire as to *your* position here, sir?"

The older man blinked rapidly. Though his face flushed notably in the wan light, he recovered rather quickly. With a roll of his shoulders, he fixed his features in an unreadable, yet quite distinguished fashion.

"Winston, sir—the butler, to be precise," he stated crisply, then clasped his hands at his waist and cleared his throat. "I've been in the Luxley's service for forty years."

"I see." Collin observed the butler with a critical eye. As he did so, he noticed Winston maintained an impressive amount of dignity.

Despite the old bugger's disrespect for Scotsmen, Collin found himself admiring the man's spunk. He and the ancient Winston would get on well once they understood each other, he decided.

"Forty years, you say?" Collin commented as he peeled off his damp gloves and stretched them forth. "With such a commendable show of loyalty, you shall be with us for a good many more years, I hope."

Winston's mouth tightened at the corners. He dipped his silver gaze to the gloves, and after a slight hesitation, snatched them from Collin's grasp.

"I'll see they're properly cleaned, sir," he said, each word fairly quivering.

"Very good, Winston, you do that." Collin turned his attention to Fanny, who had stood by wringing her hands and watching the exchange. "Dear lady, you did mention a cup of hot tea, did you not?"

"Oh, aye, sir, I did, sir. And I'll be seeing to it straight—"

"Fanny? Winston?" A masculine voice floated over the banister at the top of the stairs. "Is something amiss down there?"

Heavy footsteps thumped upon the carpeted steps, making the boards groan and creak.

Collin squinted into the darkness and observed one obscure figure following another down the stairs. As the two emerged from the shadows, they took the form of a tall gentleman and a willowy woman near equal in height—both, Collin would guess, close to his same age and in their mid-thirties.

The man shoved a hand through his sandy, tousled hair and frowned at the butler and Fanny, then settled a cool gaze on Collin.

"I demand an explanation for being rousted from my sleep in the middle of the night." His words were bitten off and bore evidence of upper-class British breeding. Behind him, his lady clutched her chenille robe closed and peered warily over his shoulder at Collin. "Well?" he said, using the tone of a child who usually got what he wanted with the stamp of a foot.

" 'Tis Master Collin MacLaine," Fanny the informer supplied. " 'E's come, just like they told us 'e would."

A half-dozen expressions moved over the gentleman's features within the space of a few flickers of the candle flame, before he fixed his mouth in a subtle smile—a smile that didn't quite reach his deep-set eyes.

"Collin MacLaine. Of course." Stepping forward, he extended his hand. "We expected you several months ago. Since we'd not had word from you . . . well, naturally we thought perhaps—" Cutting his sentence short, he pressed his lips into a tight line.

Collin grasped the man's hand and shook it firmly. "You seem to have me at a disadvantage, sir," he commented, then furrowed his brow. "I was told the house would be empty save the presence of a few caretakers."

"And so it shall be soon," the fair-haired

man replied. His palm felt cold and clammy against Collin's own. "You're tired, I can see, Mr. MacLaine. I'm sure the Widow Luxley will explain everything to your satisfaction in the morning. But I do forget my manners. I am Roland Cameron. And might I present my wife, Elenore—the late Lord Luxley's daughter."

He released Collin's hand to tug the woman forward.

Elenore stared openly at Collin for a moment or two, her expression bland. Then she glanced at her husband, as if seeking his approval, before she spoke.

"Welcome to Luxley Manor, Mr. MacLaine," she said in a soft gentle voice. The timid smile she offered transformed her rather common features, giving off the serene, quiet beauty of a Renaissance painting. "I apologize for any inconvenience you've suffered this evening. The solicitor told us . . . well, you see, it's been months . . . and well, quite frankly, we'd almost given up on—"

"Mummy?" A plump boy of ten or so lumbered forward from the base of the stairs, rubbing one eye with a fist.

Elenore hastened to the child. Stooping in front of him, she caught his elbows and looked lovingly into his chubby face. " 'Tis all right, dearheart, Mummy's here."

"Go back to bed, Phillip," Roland commanded with a stern frown in the direction of mother and child.

"But I'm not sleepy."

"You heard me. Go back to your bed!"

Elenore hugged the boy and glared pointedly at Roland.

A wave of exhaustion washed over Collin. He'd not been prepared for an encounter with the late Lord Luxley's kinsfolk. Considering the situation, the unexpected event hadn't gone all that badly. At present though, he was certainly in no mood to stand witness to a family dispute.

His impatience must have caught Elenore's attention, for she straightened instantly, pulling the child close to her side.

"What must you think of us, Mr. MacLaine, to leave you standing there soaking wet?" Her demure voice took on the air of authority as she turned to the maid. "Fanny, do go and warm Mr. MacLaine a bit of the beef broth we had for supper, and see to it—"

"Madam, please," Collin interrupted. "I assure you there's no need for all this fuss on my account."

"Oh, but there is." Elenore's features moved into the same blank expression she had worn in the first few moments of their meeting. "We want you to feel welcome here. After all, 'tis *your* home now."

Collin didn't miss the slight strain in the way she'd pronounced the last four words. There'd been an underlying current of resentment in them that had crept under his skin, making him feel anything but *welcome.*

"Do as I say, Fanny." Elenore directed the maid with a delicate wave of her hand. "And take Phillip with you. Give him a tart and some warm milk before he goes back to bed. Then do hurry and ready our Mr. MacLaine a room."

Elenore ruffled the boy's blond hair before Fanny took the child in tow. Her lips lifted in a small smile once more as she watched the two leave the foyer.

She brightened the smile to an insincere degree when her gaze shifted to Collin again.

"Winston will see to your comfort, Mr. MacLaine, won't you, Winston?" She merely glanced in the butler's direction.

"Yes, madam," Winston replied, holding his stiff pose.

Sliding next to her husband, Elenore looped an arm around Roland's. "You will excuse us if we do not join you, Mr. MacLaine. My husband and I have been feeling a bit under the weather lately, haven't we dear?"

Roland's frown increased, then eased as he looked from his wife to Collin.

"Indeed," was all he said before his thoughts seemed to wander elsewhere.

"Let's do retire now, Roland." Elenore patted his arm, then addressed Collin once more. "We'll bid you good night, sir. My mother will wish to see you first off in the morning. I'm sure she's anxious to expound upon our predicament. Pray, sir, do be gentle with her. She *is* still in mourning for my father, you know."

"Of course," Collin agreed, although he

wasn't quite sure exactly what it was that he was agreeing to.

"Sleep well, Mr. MacLaine."

Elenore's parting words held the same tone she had used when assuring Collin of her desire for him to feel welcome at the manor. A sense of pending disaster lingered in the foyer, closing in on Collin while he watched the couple disappear into the shadows halfway up the stairs.

"If you will come with me, sir."

Collin's contemplation of the matter dwindled when he turned and found the butler looking down his nose at him again.

He studied the staunch, white-haired man for a long moment. "Winston . . . do you *never* take repose from that rigid posture?"

"Hardly ever, sir." Winston picked up the candle on the table. As the stiff-backed butler pivoted on his heel and strode off, leaving the new master of the manor to follow. Collin very plainly heard him murmur, "Most definitely not in the presence of a Scotsman."

Shortly later, Collin sat in a comfortable leather chair by a cozy fire in the study. With his boots drying nearby, he propped his bare feet on the hearth. Then he reached for the brandy Winston had cordially, if not quite cheerfully, left on the table next to him. A few minutes before, the old butler had deserted him, mumbling some phrase that had ended with "damned Scots." And Collin was not at all displeased to see him go.

Alone at last, Collin focused on the bright golden flames licking upward toward the blackened chimney. The warm yellow glow filling the spacious room welcomed him in a way none of the residents of the manor had. He inhaled deeply, noting how the fragrance of burning wood chased away the stale, unused odor that had permeated the air when the room was first opened.

He had liked the library the instant he'd stepped through the wide double doors. While Winston had gone about the business of lighting a fire, Collin had been drawn to the bookshelves lining the walls at either end of the room. As he'd browsed through Lord Luxley's accumulation of leatherbound literature, his fingers had left trails in the dust. The room could most definitely use a thorough cleaning. Still, it would be a perfect place for him to work.

Collin took a sip of brandy, letting the liquid heat trickle down inside him. The blazing fire crackled in the serene silence, and a smile creased his lips. Contentment. Sweet contentment. *This was what a home should feel like,* he mused.

Here, in the peaceful countryside . . . here, in this very room, he would write his masterpiece. A brilliant composition of poetry that would be quoted time and again for ages to come . . . an outstanding, *ingenious* collection of poems no London publisher could call "too shallow" . . . or "ordinary".

In this sanctuary, he could concentrate, dig

deeper for the "feeling" all the editors had claimed his previous efforts had lacked.

There would be no more babies wailing or shouting matches seeping through thin apartment walls. No more venders harking their wares in the streets, nor barroom brawls beneath his windows at night. Nothing to distract him.

Nothing . . . but the entire Luxley brood . . . a squawking maid . . . and a grumpy old butler with a grudge against Scotland.

Collin straightened in his chair, downed his brandy, and set the glass on the table. Staring hard into the fire, he braced his elbows on his knees and steepled his fingers against his lips.

He could live with the butler and the maid, he supposed. Those two should be no more difficult to handle than the spoiled sons of aristocrats he had tutored for the past ten years. Granted, he'd had no experience in dealing with servants heretofore. Still in all, as a schoolmaster, he had learned very successfully how to exercise his authority.

The Luxleys, however, were another story. Needless to say, having had the run of the manor for so long, the family would no doubt feel free to invade his privacy whenever they wished. They would have to go.

When he met with the Widow Luxley in the morning, regardless of their *predicament,* as Elenore had put it, he would simply tell the widow that she and her kin must take their leave as soon as humanly possible. Of course, he would approach the matter with the utmost of care, taking into consideration the grieving woman's sensibilities. After all, he was not completely heartless.

Collin breathed a sigh of relief, eased back in his chair, and clasped his hands behind his head. Having made his decision, he closed his eyes, and attempted to set the day's trying events behind him.

Yet, an uninvited vision of the nymph dancing on the castle wall loomed in his mind.

What a pity such a fair-faced lass should be *non compos mentis*.

Collin frowned and shifted uncomfortably in his seat. Upon second thought, the idea of having a madwoman running about the countryside distressed him greatly. The shallow-witted woman might very well distract him from his work in days to come. Surely . . . there must be something that could be done about the fairy-queen creature . . . some *place* she could be taken. Bedlam, perhaps, or another sanitarium in the general vicinity—

A rush of cold air swooped across Collin's face with a startling effect. His eyes flew open. In the same instant, the fire fluttered and grew suddenly dim.

Collin twisted in his chair and peered over his shoulder, expecting someone's entrance into the room to be responsible for the draft.

But the double doors to the library were still closed. And, as Collin recalled, the hinges had creaked quite distinctly when Winston had left the room shutting the doors behind him.

Collin's gaze drifted slowly around the study, stalling on the dark corners where the soft orange glow from the fireplace could not reach. His skin prickled with the strangest sensation—as if someone watched him through an opera glass from afar.

A small cynical laugh escaped him. He reached for the brandy and filled his glass again. His nerves had been put to the test this evening. He'd probably drifted off into light sleep, let the fire die down, and dreamed the blast of air that had—

The sound was faint at first, yet prominent enough in the stillness of the night to catch Collin's ear.

He set his drink aside and sat upright in his chair, listening.

Nothing. For a long moment, an absolute silence claimed the room.

Then, a pronounced giggling circled around him—at a speed that was impossible for him to follow with the turn of his head. As the laughter echoed on, rising in volume, Collin realized the tone was that of a child.

Fury and frustration launched him from his chair. Once he came to his feet, the taunting laughter ceased abruptly.

Collin curled his fingers into fists at his sides, and scanned the dark recesses of the library once more. For all appearances, he was alone in the room, yet . . .

Elenore's cherub-faced son promptly came

to mind. *Boys would be boys*—wasn't that the saying? Naturally, the child had somehow slipped into the study. Old houses such as these had been known to harbor secret passageways—perchance the bookcases hid a concealed exit of sorts.

Collin focused on the bookshelves at the farthest end of the room, and tucked his chin. "All right, lad," he said, his voice vibrant with irritation. "You've had your fun. Show yourself this instant."

A burst of giggles bubbled forth, seemingly coming from the very spot where Collin had fastened his gaze. Though there was no one there that he could see, he started forward, but halted in mid-stride when the laughter moved as if by magic to the other end of the room.

"That's quite enough, young man!" Collin pivoted and stormed in the opposite direction. In his haste, he stubbed his toe on the leg of the desk. With an ardent curse, he limped onward, only to have the childish chuckling change positions once again.

Abandoning pursuit, he stopped in a broad stance and braced his hands on his hips. "I am not in the least amused by your little game, lad. And when I get my hands on you, you'll damn well be sorry you ever—"

The rattle of the brass doorknob grasped Collin's attention. The laughter trailed off just as the library door squeaked open.

Fanny paused on the threshold, balancing a silver tray against her hip. She craned her neck and peered warily into the room. "Was that *you* I 'eard hollering just now, sir?"

A stab pierced Collin's temples. He pointed his frown directly at the maid. "Elenore's son . . . what's-his-name?"

"D' you mean Phillip, sir?" Fanny scurried forth, the dishes rattling on the tray.

"Aye, Phillip." Collin returned to his chair, plopped into the seat, and massaged the bridge of his nose. "That dreadful boy was just in here annoying me."

"*Phillip,* sir? In *'ear,* sir?" The maid straightened after setting Collin's light supper on the table next to him. She clasped her hands at her waist and wrinkled her nose. "Nay, you must be mistaken, sir. I've just left Master Phillip in the kitchen. A mess, 'e was, too. Blueberry tart all over 'is—"

"Are you disputing my word?" Collin glared at the woman from beneath his lowered brow. "I distinctly heard a child laughing—only moments before you entered this room."

Fanny's eyes widened. Glancing about the study, she slid a hand up her bodice and clutched her robe closed at the throat. " 'Eaven preserve us," she murmured, then settled her gaze on Collin again. " 'Twas not the boy, sir. Aye, 'e's been known to be a nuisance, he 'as. But the mischief this evenin' was not 'is doin', I fear. 'Twas . . . Wee Lizzie, I'd be thinkin'."

"Wee Lizzie?"

The woman looked over her shoulder, then

edged closer and whispered, "Elizabeth Luxley, sir."

Collin grimaced at the thought of another child under foot in the house. He sighed deeply, and running a hand over his chin, stared into the dying fire.

"From hence forward, Fanny, you're to see to it that those children come no where near me. Do you understand?"

When the maid made no reply, Collin looked up to find an expression of dismay etched upon her face.

"Fanny? Did you hear me? I said—"

"Oh, I 'eard you well enough, sir. And I'll give me word little Phillip'll cause you no grief—not if I've any 'and in it." Fanny nibbled her lower lip and glanced to one side. "But there's naught I can do about Lizzie. She's a mind of her own, she has. At times, for days on end, we'll not 'ear a peep outta 'er. Then of a sudden like, she's up to 'er old tricks again."

"Come now, Fanny." Collin cocked his head and studied the distressed woman. "You seem quite capable of governing a misbehaving lass."

Once again the maid's gaze roved over the room in a leery fashion. "Wee Lizzie's no ordinary lass, sir. She's—" Fanny clamped her lips, and viewed Collin as if trying to decide whether to continue or not. After a short deliberation, she stooped close to his ear. " 'Tis a *spook*, I'm speakin' of, sir. Not a child in the flesh."

Chapter 3

At dawn the next morning, Galilea stood beside the huge oak tree where she'd spent the whole day before awaiting Luxley Manor's new master. Magus fluttered about squawking on the branch above her head, trying desperately to gain her attention.

"Hush, Magus. I'm thinking."

Barely sparing the crow an upward glance, she concentrated on the gables peeking above the distant treetops across the road. The roof of the grand old house was prominent against the pink and gray streaked sky.

It was him—the new master of Luxley Manor—the angry man she'd seen at the castle last night.

How unfortunate that he'd seen her as well.

Galilea ran a hand over her cheek and let it drift downward over her tattered bodice. He would believe all they said about her now. She was fully aware her midnight dance was unconventional. Witnessing such an act could only stand to prove to one, she supposed, that she was indeed quite insane.

And the new master of the manor had not

appeared to be a man who would tolerate harboring a madwoman on his lands.

A wave of dizziness floated over Galilea. She wrapped her arms around the tree, digging her fingers into the bark. As she shut her eyes, his moonlit features materialized behind her closed lids.

Once again, a strange glow filled her—the very sensation she'd experienced when she'd stood on the castle wall looking down at him. 'Twas a potent feeling she could not name—warm and powerful, yet . . . *frightening* all in the same breath.

Hugging the tree tighter, Galilea willed his face and the bizzare response accompanying the image to be gone from her mind.

Her limbs quivered. Perspiration formed on her upper lip. Her heart pounded harder and harder . . . until, at last, the vision broke into pieces and faded away, releasing her.

Weak, and troubled by a worrisome premonition of the days to come, she pushed away from the tree. As she turned from the sight of Luxley Manor and walked unsteadily up the hill, Magus soared in the air above her. The black bird's sorrowful caw echoed off the crumbling towers of the old castle, and the cry intensified Galilea's anxiety.

Collin awakened tossing from side to side. When he cracked his eyes open, it took him a long moment to remember where he was.

Struggling free of the tangled sheets, he

propped himself against the headboard and glanced around the sparsely furnished room.

He'd been too tired to take much notice of the poorly lit chamber when he'd entered. Now, the shaft of dust-moted sunshine breaking through the split in the red velvet drapes illuminated what shadows had hidden the previous night.

Dark wood-paneled walls gave the room a wholly masculine appearance. While the heavy carved dresser, bed, and washstand suited Collin well enough, the noticeable lack of personal items reminded him to send someone to collect his trunk at the inn.

Feeling the result of one too many glasses of brandy, Collin combed his fingers through his hair. His hand stalled on the top of his head as the vivid dream he'd had during the night came back to him in full force.

The fairy-queen had stood on the castle wall beckoning him forward, her silver hair floating about her. Lifted by the wind, he had moved on air toward her . . . with no will of his own. She had opened her mouth, but rather than words, the tinkling sound of a music box had flowed from her parted lips. Unable to stop himself, when she'd stretched out her arms, he had reached for her in return. Just short of their fingers touching, she had smiled a wicked smile . . . and he had suddenly lost his weightlessness . . . and fallen.

Collin's chest tightened with a rush of the intense fear he'd experienced in the middle of the night—*during the dream.* He recalled the terrible sensation of endlessly falling . . . constantly waiting to hit the ground.

Collin blinked, let his breath out slowly, then frowned.

Dream? More a *nightmare,* he'd say.

Flinging back the coverlet, he swung his legs over the side of the bed. Instead of rising straight away, he propped his elbows on his knees, held the weight of his head between his hands, and stared at the floor.

He had expected the country to be a quiet, peaceful place for him to work. He had counted on the sunshine and fresh air to inspire him.

So far, his quest for serenity had turned out to be an exhibition of madness.

Collin studied the frayed carpet beneath his feet. The alluring fairy-queen came to mind, stretching her arms toward him in a wistful, wanton fashion . . .

He frowned, though the very act made his head ache even more. Shoving the intruding thought aside, he centered on his current qualm, and the fact that his surroundings were not quite as redeeming as he had hoped they would be.

Collin allowed himself a moment of disappointment. A moment, no more.

Still in all, he would not concede he had made a mistake in coming to the manor. He had left a life of little worth behind. The decision to leave London had been easy. He neither missed his shabby apartment nor the commotion of the city. He harbored no regrets about giving up his post teaching spoiled, arrogant boys—who thought they already knew everything there was to know.

Perhaps he'd been too hasty in his opinion of the celebrated English countryside. Maybe, he had expected too much, too soon. *Maybe,* he merely needed to take charge and—

A sharp rap on the door disrupted the unfinished rationalization.

Slipping on the dressing robe the butler had loaned him, Collin moved to the door and opened it.

Fanny stood in the corridor, hands clasped demurely at her waist. Although she held her chin high, she kept her eyes downcast and pursed her lips slightly before speaking.

"Breakfast, sir," she said in a snippy tone that matched her pose. "They're all down in th' dinin' hall waitin' for you. The widow bid me t' ask you t' join them as soon as you'd wish."

"Thank you, Fanny. You may tell the widow I'll be down shortly."

Collin didn't miss the glare the maid shot him as she spun on her heel and hustled off. Closing the door, he lifted an eyebrow. She no doubt thought him harsh after he'd chastised her last evening for telling ghost stories. At least now, she understood that he would not tolerate her covering for young Phillip.

And young Phillip would be advised, as well. Right after breakfast, Collin decided then and there, he would let the boy know he'd stand for no more pranks.

Collin dressed hastily and with little care. He tied his hair at the nape with a leather thong then started to exit the room. Upon catching his reflection in the looking glass as he passed, he stopped and took a step backward.

The sight of his image in the mirror gave him the impression that the madness in the area must be contagious.

He looked absolutely dreadful. A dark stubble covered his jaw. Purple shadows circled his eyes. Since his trunk had not yet arrived, he had had no choice but to wear the clothes he'd worn the day before. He had opted not to don his wrinkled jacket or cravat, and left his shirt open at the throat. Indeed, he appeared quite the madman.

Collin ran a hand over his whiskered chin, and a smile lifted one corner of his mouth. What would it hurt if the Luxleys thought him of unsound mind? Perhaps they might be all the more easily convinced to take their leave promptly.

Collin quit the room upon that note, not bothering to smooth the stray lock of hair that fell across his brow. After all, he was not attending breakfast to gain the family's adoration. Their swift departure, however, was another matter altogether.

Following the sound of hushed chattering, Collin found his way to the dining hall with no trouble. As he approached the doorway, Elenore's soft voice lifted slightly above the others.

"Well, there's naught we can do about it, is there? Insomuch, we must all trust he will be charitable and—"

"Good morning." Collin's greeting put an instant stop to the discussion. He entered the room favoring his scraped knee and paused behind the empty chair at the head of the long table.

Looking past the gaping faces turned his way, his gaze traveled briefly over the dining hall. It was a most magnificent room. The three huge cross-paned windows at the far end served the dual purpose of filling the hall with sunshine and providing a grand view of the rear gardens—which if attended properly might have been lovely this time of year.

Collin brought his attention back to his breakfast companions. So still and quiet, they put him in mind of wooden puppets. Elenore was seated to his left halfway down the table. Roland sat directly across from his wife. And at the far end near the windows was Widow Luxley, he presumed.

Collin gave them all a cordial smile, then seated himself at the head of the table. As he picked up his napkin and shook out the fold, he tried his salutation once more.

"Splendid morning, wouldn't you say?"

Silence prevailed for another awkward moment before the well-fed, black-clad woman at the far end of the table shifted heavily in her chair.

"Splendid, humph. 'Tis rather nippy, if you ask me. Indeed, the chill makes my bones ache. And 'tis much too bright a day for my taste. Splendid morning, humph." The woman mumbled her opinion, pinning Collin with a hard cold stare. Without warning, she snatched a small bell next to her plate and rang it viciously. "Fanny! We'll be having our breakfast now," she screeched. "And don't you dare dawdle, you worthless—"

"Mother, please." Elenore intervened in a soothing tone—a sharp contrast to the one the widow had used. A ray of sunshine slanted across Elenore's face as she turned to Collin, making her features appear almost angelic. "Mr. MacLaine, may I present my mother, Lady Lux—"

"Oh, Elenore, let's not be pretentious." Lady Luxley's dark eyes pierced Collin again. "He knows who I am. And I know who he is." Leaning slightly forward, she raised one dark eyebrow in an exaggerated fashion. "He's the rake that swindled my poor Charles. And now he's come to throw a poor widow and her children out on their ears."

Collin was jolted slightly by the woman's brusqueness. Then again, he hadn't expected this confrontation to be pleasant.

Remaining calm despite the heat scaling the back of his neck, he gripped the arms of his chair and straightened his spine.

"Madam, I assure you, I took no advantage of your husband."

"The devil, you say." The widow elevated her beak-like nose, all but daring him outright to argue the point.

Collin felt a muscle in his jaw tighten. He was not obliged to explain himself. He was now the rightful owner of the manor and all therein. He would not offer an apology.

In the end, it was not the widow's glare that prompted him to expound upon the matter, but rather Elenore's large brown eyes. "The game was played fairly, Lady Luxley. I can produce witnesses who will attest to such. Lord Luxley offered the manor as his ante. And I won it honestly."

"Honestly, humph. I know your kind, Mr. MacLaine. You vile, despicable cheat—"

"Mother, that's quite enough!" Elenore's voice raised in a commanding tone. Clenching her fists against the edge of the table, Elenore lowered her head a moment in an apparent attempt to control her temper.

Across from her, Roland stopped stirring his tea and peered cautiously at his wife.

Lady Luxley pressed a hand to her heart and stared white-faced at her daughter.

Collin massaged the bridge of his nose. He was beginning to think this family bickering might be a common occurrence, and the notion was most wearing. He was about to say so, when Elenore scraped back her chair.

Rising with grace and complete composure, she moved to drape an arm around her mother's ample shoulders. "There, there," she said soothingly. " 'Tis most upsetting, this . . . this *situation.* Perhaps you and I should take our meal upstairs. You'd like that, wouldn't you, Mother, dear?"

The older woman made a rather pitiful face and nodded.

"You must forgive us, Mr. MacLaine," Elenore commented in passing as she guided Widow Luxley to the door. "I'm certain Roland shall explain our predicament quite satisfactorily."

There was that word again. *Predicament.* Collin didn't like the sound of it at all. He disliked the way Roland ducked his head even less.

Fanny bustled into the room as the two ladies were exiting. After exchanging a few whispered words in the doorway with Elenore, the maid hurried to the table to serve the gentlemen.

Collin waited with no small amount of impatience while Fanny filled the plates. Once she'd left the dining hall, he cocked his head and looked pointedly at Roland Cameron.

"About this . . . *predicament* of yours, as Elenore is wont to call it—"

Roland popped a bite into his mouth, and began waving his fork to ward off the inquiry. He chewed his food leisurely, then swallowed, and presented Collin with a wavering smile.

"Would you mind terribly if we ate before discussing the matter? I'm famished." Without waiting for an answer, Roland set his full attention on his meal.

For a matter of moments, Collin stared at the kidneys on his plate. The Luxleys were an odd lot, to say the least. Collin had to wonder again if there might be a bit of madness floating in the air hereabouts.

He eyed Roland from beneath his lowered brow. *Was it madness? Or sheer deviousness?* Either way, Collin decided he'd had enough of avoiding the issue.

"Aye. I *do* mind, Mr. Cameron," he said, pushing his plate aside. "I was promised an explanation for your presence here, and I'd like very much to hear it. *Now,* if you please."

Roland swallowed his mouthful whole. Coughing and sputtering, he picked up his napkin and dabbed his thin lips. After a quick sip of tea, he set his watery, red eyes on Collin.

"Of course, Mr. MacLaine," he said, his voice strained from the episode. "You do indeed have the right to know the manner of things." Clearing his throat, he straightened in his chair and glanced around the room. "I simply don't know where to begin. You see, it's a rather embarrassing situation for the family . . . and well, quite frankly, I find it extremely difficult to put into words."

"Try." Collin leaned back and folded his arms across his chest.

The bright sunlight cascading through the windows cast an ashen tint over Roland's features.

"Yes, well . . . as you've probably noticed, the manor . . . the grounds—" he waved a hand to indicate his surroundings— "are in a sad state of disrepair."

"Aye." Collin nodded. "I've noticed. Do, go on."

"I'm afraid Lord Luxley did not manage his lands favorably."

"That much is obvious," Collin agreed. "But what, pray tell, does that have to do with the family remaining here after the land has been legally titled to someone else?"

Roland fidgeted, clasping and unclasping his hands on the table in front of him. "Well, you see, what with his gambling debts, he left us near penniless. There is the townhouse in London, but it, too, I fear, has not been well kept. In fact, the condition of the property in London is much worse than the manor, if you can imagine."

Collin made no response. Weighing the course of the conversation, he merely waited for Roland to continue.

"We've invested all we have in restoring the townhouse to a livable state. And we fully intend to retire there after the repairs are made. But you understand these things take time and—"

Collin closed his eyes wearily. "How much time are we speaking of?"

"A month, perhaps."

Collin squinted one eye open. "A month?"

Roland shrugged. "Perhaps no more than a fortnight."

Collin began a slow shake of his head before the man had finished his sentence. "I came here for peace and quiet, Mr. Cameron. It is imperative that I am not disturbed during my work. Therefore, I can not possibly—"

"I assure you," Roland cut in, "if you'll allow us to stay, you'll never know we're here. Reconsider, I beg you—not for my sake alone, but for that of my family. We have nowhere else to go, Mr. MacLaine."

Collin assessed the man's appeal for a long moment. He was inclined to deny the request once and for all and be done with it. On the other hand, he had no desire to be known as an ogre.

His chest lifted and fell with a heavy breath. Then he focused on the kidneys on his plate again.

"Very well," he said quietly, then raised his gaze to Roland's. "You may stay. But only as long as my privacy is observed. And you'll see to that the lad, Phillip, steers clear of the library. Understood?"

Collin spent the rest of the day exploring his new domain. He toured the manor briefly, familiarizing himself with the layout of the house—what corridors led where, and so forth. Then he promptly escaped out of doors.

As he walked the grounds, breathing in the fresh fragrance of the country, he recalled how stale the air had been in London. With the noise of the city left far behind, he could appreciate the pleasant sounds of his surroundings. Birds chirped and sang cheerfully in the trees. Cows bellowed in the distance. Now and then, the baaing of a sheep reached his ears.

A supreme tranquility enveloped him, despite his constant discoveries of how severely the property had been neglected. The garden wall was crumbling. The hedges of a small maze at the rear of the house were overgrown. The sheep in a nearby field were in bad need of tending. The crops needed cutting. The list grew longer as the day wore on.

By evening, when Collin returned to the manor, his estimate of repairs was overwhelming. He opted not to think too much on the matter until he had a chance to go over the books in the morning. Instead of dining with the Luxleys, he had supper in his room then retired to the library in the hope his writing might temporarily whisk his worries away.

For the first part of the evening, he was successful. With a blazing fire roaring in the fireplace and a brandy at his side, he worked almost feverishly on his poetry. The words spilled onto the paper as if poured out by some divine source.

Collin was concentrating on the last line of his second poem when a strange sensation gripped him. The room took on a sudden chill.

He paused in his work, his pen poised above the paper, and glanced around the library. The flames in the fireplace were still bright and licking upward. There was no draft in the room or he would have surely felt it.

Yet . . . cold seeped into his bones to such a degree that he clamped his teeth to keep them from chattering.

Then his ink bottle began to rattle. Merely vibrating at first, it quickly progressed into a frenzied clattering against the desktop.

Collin tucked his chin and frowned. But just as he reached out to still the bottle, the ink toppled sideways, spilling over his newly finished poem.

He came to his feet with a curse, tugging a handkerchief from his pocket. When he leaned forward to wipe up the mess, however, the paper slid across the desk by its own accord.

Collin froze, trying desperately to absorb what had just happened. The paper could not have moved across the desk by itself. Yet, with his own eyes, he had just witnessed that very feat.

No, his logic protested. It was simply a trick of the light. Or . . . perhaps he'd bumped the desk when he'd stood up.

Collin ran a hand through the length of his hair and smiled at the absurd notion that had popped into his head only moments before. Imagine, material objects maneuvering about without aid. The very idea was preposterous.

With a shake of his head, he reached for the paper again. As his fingers brushed the ink stained parchment, the page quivered then coasted from beneath his touch. Fluttering upward, the paper hovered in midair above his desk and started to spin . . . slowly in the beginning, then faster and faster.

Collin stood watching, his brain rapidly calculating reasons for such a phenomenon—his mind discarding each explanation as soon as it came to him. For the page to be suspended by no visible means of support was virtually impossible.

The paper finally stopped whirling and suddenly fell like a rock to his desk. Several seconds lapsed before Collin picked up his ink pen and poked at it. Once satisfied the parchment was completely lifeless, he settled uneasily in his chair.

Sheer rationality made him instantly reject what he'd seen. He'd had a full day and was extremely weary, he told himself. His imagination had simply run away with him.

Collin attempted to work a bit longer, but his attention continuously strayed to the ink-blotted page. He kept expecting the paper to jump up and start dancing at any given moment.

After a good half hour of getting absolutely no work done, he capped his ink well and left the library. As he climbed the stairs to his bedchamber, he vowed not to dwell on the matter of flying pages. Any mention of the incident would only feed Fanny's ridiculous ghost stories—when in fact, the whole affair had probably been no more than a hallucination brought on by exhaustion.

By the time Collin nestled his head into his pillow and closed his eyes, he had quite convinced himself that a decent night's sleep would most certainly hold any further hallucinations at bay.

Chapter 4

Collin had fully intended to think no more of the strange occurrence in the library, but the event was only the first in a long line of bizarre happenings that week.

The next day, when he sat down at his desk to work, the giggling of an invisible child plagued him again—and all whilst the lad, Phillip, could be plainly seen through the library window, innocently playing on the lawn.

In the days that followed, various objects floated about the room, candles blinked on and off, the desk drawers opened and closed at will. More often than not, the actions were accompanied by a phantom voice of tender age chanting some nursery rhyme, humming, or laughing gaily. Indeed, each incident grew more spectacular than the last.

Collin ceased trying to grasp explanations for the odd disturbances. He attempted escaping to his private chambers to work, but was tormented there as well.

On the seventh evening, when books levitated from the bookcase and flew around him in a frenzied fashion, he finally reached his wit's end.

Slamming the library door behind him, he headed for the wine cellar.

Collin had visited the dark cavern beneath the manor only once when he'd initially explored the house. The well-stocked cellar was one place, it seemed, that hadn't been neglected. Obviously, Lord Luxley had been quite fond of his port.

Collin cupped his hand in front of the flickering candle flame as he descended the narrowly framed stairs. A cool, damp, musty smell stung his nostrils, but he pressed onward, bent on getting mindlessly drunk.

Toward the last step, he heard a faint groaning and paused to interpret the sound. It appeared to be a deep, grating voice singing an old English ballad.

As Collin made his way through the maze of wine racks, the soft yellow glow of candlelight came into view at the back of the cellar . . . and the words to the song rang clear.

O hooly, hooly rose she up,
To the place where he was lying,
And when she drew the curtain by,
"Young man, I think you're dying."

Rounding the corner, Collin was more than a bit startled by the sight of old Winston, the butler, waltzing about with an invisible partner.

Winston swirled to the tune, and upon facing Collin, his jaw went slack. His pretend partner disappeared as his arms fluttered downward and he clasped his hands together at his waist. With a lift of his chin, he squared his aging shoulders.

"Good evening, sir . . . I was just . . . just—"

"No need to apologize, Winston." Collin set his candlestick on a nearby shelf and studied the assortment of wine bottles.

"I wasn't apologizing, sir," Winston replied arrogantly, then hiccuped. "I was just . . . *leaving*."

As the butler turned on his heel, Collin reached out and caught his sleeve.

"Winston, wait," he said, snatching a bottle of wine and holding it up in invitation. "Stay and have a drink with me."

Winston peered indignantly down his nose at him. "I dare say, I don't generally drink with the likes of Scots, sir."

Collin smiled sardonically. "Tonight you shall make an exception. Sit down."

Collin settled on the cool stone floor and motioned with the bottle for the butler to do the same.

Winston complied after a moment's hesitation. With a frown, he watched Collin uncork the wine.

Taking a long sip of the sweet nectar, Collin eyed him as well. The butler had made himself scarce over the past week, turning up in Collin's presence only when absolutely necessary. Collin stretched the bottle toward him.

"Must you look so sour, Winston? I haven't

asked you to kill anyone, you know. 'Tis a simple drink, no more."

Winston grunted, but he took his turn at the offer of wine.

They exchanged the bottle several times withoutspeaking, neither really acknowledging the other, each lost in his own thoughts.

"Wasn't that the old tune, 'Bonny Barbara Allan' you were singing when I came in?" Collin's voice echoed softly against the cold stone walls.

"Aye, it was," answered Winston. " 'Tis a favorite of mine."

For a short span, they both stared at the flickering candle flame. Then Collin picked up the familiar song where the butler had left off. After the first few notes, Winston joined in.

In Collin's opinion, they harmonized quite nicely together. They broke into three more ballads, the last a bawdy tune that had them chuckling before they finished.

As the song trailed to an end, Winston turned to Collin with a bright sparkle in his old eyes.

"You don't talk like a Scotchman," he said bluntly, then hiccuped again.

Feeling warmed by the port, Collin smiled lazily. "And why should I? I was raised in London." He took a long draw from the bottle and handed it to the butler. "Lived there all my life."

Winston frowned thoughtfully. "I don't care for Scotchmen, you know."

Collin nodded. "And I'm not all that fond of butlers."

From there on, with their distaste for each other out in the open, they got along fairly well. Collin popped the cork on three more bottles. Winston's staunchness wilted somewhat, and Collin's frustration faded with the liberal consumption of wine.

"Winston, tell me," Collin commented as he squinted at the candlelight through the end of an empty bottle like a pirate with a spyglass. "What's truly going on here?"

"Going on, sir?"

Collin lowered the bottle from his eye and met the butler's glassy gaze. " 'Tis the boy, isn't it? The lad, Phillip—he's a genius, am I right? And he's invented some device to make things float about in the library."

"Phillip? A genius?" Winston laughed and shook his head. "Oh, no sir. To be quite honest, the boy's a bit on the dim side, if you know what I mean."

Collin furrowed his brow. Even as the befuddled thought had entered his wine-soaked brain, he had known the theory wouldn't hold water. Hadn't he himself checked the room for gadgets and strings?

"But what other explanation could there possibly be," he muttered, thinking outloud, "for objects to be flying around the library by themselves?"

Winston sighed and fingered the edge of his crumpled coat tail. "You wouldn't believe me if I told you, sir. I can hardly believe it myself at times."

Collin searched the butler's serious expression. "Winston, you aren't about to go sputtering some wild tale about ghosts, are you?"

Winston snatched the half full bottle from the floor in front of him. He took a hearty drink, then wrist-wiped his mouth.

" 'Tis no bloody tale. 'Tis God's own truth. Whether you or I want to believe it or not, little Lizzie's lost soul walks the corridors of this house."

Collin closed his eyes and cradled his forehead in his hand. "Winston, there is no such thing as ghosts. When someone dies, they're gone. They cannot possibly come back to—"

"Elizabeth Luxley haunts this house, I tell you," Winston interrupted on a defiant note. " 'Twas in the tunnel beneath the old castle ruins they found the poor lass." The butler paused and shook his head. " 'Twas twelve years ago this summer solstice."

"Ah-ha!" Collin raised a finger and smiled. "Isn't it customarily alleged that a ghost will haunt the place of death? If so, and Elizabeth Luxley died in the tunnels, then she couldn't possibly be the one responsible for all the chaos in this house."

Winston lowered his white, bushy eyebrows. "Lizzie did not die in the tunnels, sir. She was very ill, and lived but a short time after we brought her home. 'Tis *her* haunting the manor, I say. I've seen her skipping down the stairs with my very own eyes."

Collin considered the matter rationally. "Perhaps you were mistaken. Perhaps . . . the young girl you saw was some lass who merely *looked* like Elizabeth Luxley—a playmate come to visit Phillip."

"In the middle of the night?" Winston tucked his chin. "I hardly think so. You're forgetting I was here when the child was born. I know what she looked like. 'Twas Wee Lizzie, and no other."

Winston's eyes took on a faraway glow as he focused on the flickering candle flame. "Such a pretty little thing, she was, sir. Hair so pale and fair . . . nigh the color of silver moonlight. And to come to such an awful end."

The butler's words trailed off, and Collin searched his face. "I suppose now you're waiting for me to inquire how she died," he commented dryly.

Winston shrugged. "Well, if you don't want to know, I shan't tell you."

Collin swallowed all logic with a sip of wine, and it took a moment to digest it.

"All right, then," he said, passing the bottle to the old butler. "Tell me."

Winston's eyes glimmered in the dimly lit cellar as he turned to Collin.

"Well, you see, sir, little Elizabeth was the product of a brief affair Lord Luxley had with a London actress. When the actress came to him with the news that she was with child, Lord Luxley boarded her in the hunting lodge, and provided a midwife to stay with her. The woman had no use for a child, and she said as much as soon as Lizzie was born. You can well imagine the position that put our lordship in—but when he viewed the babe, he vowed to keep little Lizzie and raise her himself, and since he and Lady Harriet had never conceived any children together—"

"Wait." Collin stopped the butler with a raised hand, catching a flaw in his story. "What about Elenore?"

"Elenore?" Winston appeared puzzled. "Why, didn't you know? She's Lady Harriet's daughter from a previous marriage. Oh, Lord Luxley loved her like his own. He even adopted Elenore, but 'twas Elizabeth he doted on. Like to have broke his Lordship's heart, it did, when our Lizzie went missing."

"Missing?"

"Aye." The butler sniffed, took a generous swallow of wine, then wiped his nose on his cuff. "Aye," he repeated, his voice low and solemn. "You never heard such screaming as the night our Lordship brought the baby to the manor. Lady Harriet wailed for days, but in the end, she reluctantly accepted the child into the household. Of course, Lady Luxley hated Lizzie. She made no pretense of that. His Lordship saw to it, though, that the lass was not subjected to Lady Harriet's wrath, and things went on well enough, until . . . "

Collin peered sideways at the old butler. Winston hung his head, seemingly about to nod off.

"Until what?" Collin prompted, his curiosity, by this time, getting the best of him. "Winston?"

Winston blinked, and Collin could have sworn he saw a slight glistening at the corner of the man's eye as he raised his head and stared off into the distance.

"We searched for Wee Lizzie for three whole days before we found the poor lass. 'Twas a terrible tragedy, that. And her only seven years of age." The butler ran a shaky hand over his chin. "I remember, Lord Luxley took to drinking and gambling quite liberally afterward. We were all so upset. We all cared deeply for the child, you see. Such a lovely little thing, she was, sir . . . so sweet and kind-hearted . . . always a smile for everyone."

A gap of silence followed, while Collin absorbed all Winston had told him. He sifted through the story again and again. Still, he could make no connection between Elizabeth Luxley's death and the disturbances in the library.

"A most unfortunate accident, indeed," he commented at last. "I cannot see though how a long-dead child could possibly cause the havoc I've experienced in the study this past week. The whole notion is simply preposterous."

Winston pressed his lips into a thin line. " 'Twas no accident, sir. I've always been of a mind that there was foul play done. And there's plenty that will agree with me."

"You mean to say, you think the girl was . . . *murdered*?"

Winston made no response other than a lift of his brow.

Collin frowned. "But who would harm a seven-year-old child?"

"I'm sure I wouldn't know," Winston replied. "Nothing was ever proven, you understand, but why else would Wee Lizzie haunt the manor—lest her soul was full of unrest?"

Collin shook his head slightly, unable to accept Winston's rendering of the situation, yet, at a loss to come up with any other explanation. While he had to admit the goings-on in the library were beyond strange, he could not grasp the concept that the roaming spirit of a dead child was to blame. There had to be another answer.

Regardless of why the bizarre disturbances persisted, the fact remained, they had to be stopped. His work was suffering. His health was suffering. His nerves had been stretched to the limit.

Collin ran a hand through his hair and pinned the butler with an earnest gaze.

"I came here to write, Winston. I resigned from a perfectly good teaching post at one of London's most prominent schools. I'm not certain what I shall do if I cannot make a go of it." Collin reached up and massaged his aching temple. "But, I simply cannot work under these dreadfully trying conditions."

Winston weighed the matter thoughtfully a moment. "Might I make a suggestion, sir?"

Collin glanced sideways, then nodded. "Please do."

"Well, sir, there is a woman in the meadow they claim has the knowing." The butler tapped a finger against his lips. "Perhaps she could be of help. I've heard she converses with the spirits of the castle ruins, and—"

"A woman in the meadow?"

"Aye, sir. Some call her a witch. Some say she's a fairy. Some swear they've seen her fly. While still others think her quite mad."

"Mad?" Collin narrowed his eyes on the butler. "Is this woman of small stature? With pale hair hanging to her waist?"

"Aye, 'tis the one I'm speaking of. You've seen her?"

Collin pushed up from the floor, strode a few feet away, then turned and gave the man a cynical smile. "Aye, I've had the pleasure, you could say. And I can assure you, the woman hasn't the sense to help us—much less herself."

"Ah well, there you're wrong, I'm thinking, sir. She talks to animals, and the creatures do her bidding. I've seen as much, and if she can communicate with animals, perhaps she can also convince little Lizzie to—"

"No." Collin folded his arms across his chest. "I'll not have a madwoman at the manor. Not if the house tumbles down around me. Not if thunder and lightning strike me. Not if—"

The ceiling-high wine rack next to Collin began to quake, rattling the bottles.

Winston scrambled to his feet and shook his finger accusingly. "Now you've done it, sir. You've gone and upset Wee Lizzie by something you said."

"What did I say?" Collin asked, glancing about as the other wine racks surrounding them started to vibrate as well.

Winston answered by moving past him and heading for the stairs. Collin grabbed the candlestick and quickly followed.

At the top of the stairwell, Collin looked back. From what he could see of the dark cellar, the commotion had ceased. The room was quiet again—but in the stillness, from some far corner, he distinctly heard the giggle of a child.

Collin could not leave the cellar fast enough. He nearly toppled Winston squeezing through the door. When the two of them stood huffing and puffing in the kitchen, he looked at the butler in grim resignation.

"Say I believed this nonsense about a ghost in the manor—which I don't, mind you—but just suppose I did?" Collin clamped his mouth shut. He strode halfway across the kitchen then turned on his heel, disbelieving he was having this conversation. "I mean . . . well, damn it all . . . where, precisely," he asked against his better judgment, "would we find this madwoman of the meadow?"

Galilea sat cross-legged in the middle of the meadow, absently petting the furry, gray rabbit curled in her lap. Deep in thought, she watched the muted morning sunlight creep across the tall grass. The wildflowers rippled in the slight breeze. Everything seemed so perfect, so peaceful.

She was happy here. Oh, she missed Ollie terribly from time to time. But in moments such as this, in the quiet beginning of each day, she harbored a very special sense of contentment. A sense of harmony. A sense of homecoming. She had everything she needed here . . . everything she could want. Her forest friends. Wild berries, nuts, and fresh herbs to make tea. Shelter from the rain in the castle ruins.

Galilea gently stroked the rabbit's ear. He cocked his head and looked up at her, then wiggling his nose farewell, hopped from her lap.

She had heard the whispering again upon awakening. Although the words had still been unclear, an explicit warning had sifted through.

He was coming, the master of the manor, to take her away from the meadow. How soon, she did not know. But he was coming. She could feel it in her bones.

Once more, the image of the man came vividly to mind; his long dark hair flying about his shoulders . . . his cloak billowing in the wind. The memory of the disturbing emotions he had evoked inside her returned with full force, and she hugged herself to keep from shivering.

She quickly closed herself to the vision, and came abruptly to her feet. Magus squawked from the limb of a nearby tree, aware of her sudden panic.

" 'Tis all right, Magus." She smiled up at the bird, trying to calm herself for his sake. "Come and walk with me. I grow weary of worrying, and shall fall prey to it no more this day. On the morrow, we shall decide what must be done. Today, we will carry on as usual."

The black crow sailed from the branch he perched on and landed like a hand of comfort upon her shoulder.

Galilea reached up and scratched his chest with a fingertip. He tickled her ear with his beak. And together they moved through the meadow toward White Fern Forest, where the extra nuts Galilea had gathered the day before would be equally distributed among the squirrels.

The quarter moon lent little light to the night. Collin craned his neck above the boulder set in the hillside and peered through the darkness at the castle ruins.

"Do get down, sir," Winston commanded, tugging at Collin's coat sleeve. " 'Tis a well known fact the lass is rather skittish. She's liable to bolt if she catches sight of us."

With a frown, Collin settled back on the cold, rocky ledge next to the butler, wondering how in Hades he'd allowed himself to be talked into this insane endeavor.

Wrapping his cloak more securely around him, he glared sideways at Winston. The old man obviously enjoyed issuing orders. Ever since the two of them had hatched this hair-brained scheme in their drunken stupor of the night before, Winston had taken it upon himself to be in charge of the stratagem.

All day long, the stiff-upper-lipped butler, who had previously avoided him for an entire week, had made a point of passing by Collin from time to time and giving him a conspiratorial wink.

Now, as a chill from the cold rock he sat upon seeped into his backside, Collin's doubts about this whole ridiculous venture surfaced once more.

"Are you certain she will be here?" he asked on a perturbed note.

"One can never be sure, sir," Winston answered with a lift of his bushy white eyebrows. "But, I'm told she oft appears to dance along the bailey wall at the bewitching hour. If she doesn't come tonight, we shall try again tomorrow evening, and—"

"We shall *not* try again tomorrow." Collin came abruptly to his feet, dusting his britches. "I must have temporarily lost my mind to have agreed—"

"Shhh!" Winston jerked him down behind the ledge. "Listen."

The tinny sound of a music box flowed softly into the stillness of the night.

Both men moved cautiously to the edge of the boulder and fastened their gazes on the ancient castle.

"Look," Winston whispered. "There on the bailey. There she is, sir."

In a moment of awed silence, they observed the woman's silhouette moving gracefully across the wall, swaying and swirling to the sweet tinkling melody.

Winston tugged Collin's coat sleeve again to gain his attention then motioned him down behind the ledge. Once concealed by the rocky bluff, the butler slid closer to Collin.

"Very well, sir," he said, taking on the tone of a captain speaking to a guardsman, "now here's how we shall go about it . . . "

A strange tingling gripped Galilea as she climbed the bailey. She paused in her ascent and searched the courtyard below.

It was as if the dark shadows lurking there had eyes. She'd often sensed someone watching her, but tonight, her perception was somehow different. She couldn't quite pinpoint the source of her uneasiness.

Of course, her innermost calm had been disturbed over the past few days, she reminded herself. Indeed, her emotions had been so unstable, her feelings so garbled, that she'd been leery of trusting her instincts lately.

Galilea battled with the odd sensation creeping up her spine for a moment longer, then she shoved it aside and continued climbing.

Dancing was the answer. The motion, the

music, would bring her balance and tranquillity.

Reaching the top of the wall, Galilea pulled the treasured music box from her pocket. She carefully braced it against a rock and opened the lid. And once again, the ancient dwelling became her stage.

For a time, she was lost to the feeling of freedom. Her body followed the chiming melody, her soul soared to the tune. Stars twinkled brightly in the sky above.

Then, of a sudden, a feeling as strong as a bolt of lightning struck her, causing her to stumble. She lost her foothold on the narrow wall.

Seized by the terror that she was falling, she dug her fingers into the rocky ledge. She clung to the crumbling wall, her legs dangling, her heart pounding hard in her throat.

Galilea's hands numbed around the cold stones. One of the rocks shifted slightly beneath her palm.

Somewhere amidst the amplified sound of her own heavy breathing, she heard what appeared to be boots clicking against the cobblestone in the courtyard. From the corner of her eye, she caught a movement in the shadows below.

Galilea twisted her head and glimpsed a tall dark figure moving to the wall directly beneath her. In that same instant, one of the rocks she held on to broke loose from the bailey. She plunged downward, debris from the ancient keep pelting her as she fell.

Time stretched into slow motion as she descended, intensifying the horror that she would hit the ground at any second. She imagined her bones cracking against the cobblestones. She saw her brief life pass before her . . . and her mind screamed, *"but, I'm not finished living—surely, there is something more significant I must do before I go!"*

When Galilea's body finally struck a solid surface, however, it was not the hard cobblestones she expected.

Opening her eyes, she found herself cradled safely—and in the arms of none other than the new master of Luxley Manor. She blinked twice, then stared wide-eyed at his handsome face.

He moved his mouth, apparently speaking to her, but an intense pain on the right side of her head drowned out his words. His features blurred and grew dim. Then everything went black.

Chapter 5

Somewhere in the countryside a rooster crowed. The first golden rays of sunshine poured through the leaded cross-paned window, casting a multitude of diamond-shaped patterns across the room.

Collin held his heavy eyelids open. He sat very still and quiet next to the bed, his gaze fastened on the pale, beautiful creature lying therein.

Winston's carefully laid excursion to the castle ruins the night before hadn't gone exactly as planned. It had ended most frightfully, in fact.

Of course, neither Collin nor the butler had anticipated startling the young woman to the point of causing her to fall from the bailey.

The bright idea had been to simply confront her after she had completed her dance and climbed down from the wall.

Collin's part in this brilliant plan had been to circle around behind the castle and block the little fairy-queen's escape. Fortunately, he had entered the courtyard in time to see her stumble. *Most fortunately*, he had been able to rush forth and catch her before she hit the cobblestone.

All the same, Collin felt completely miserable. He had contributed to the woman's present condition. True, she must have been mad to have climbed the bailey and performed such a stunt in the first place. And who was to say the little nymph wouldn't have fallen to her death if Collin and the butler had not been there to intervene?

Still, Collin had an inkling that he and Winston had somehow been responsible. It was an odd notion, he knew, to think the woman had miraculously sensed their presence—ridiculous, really—but Collin could not rid himself of the guilt that rubbed his conscience.

He shifted slightly in the chair, his muscles growing stiff. He had remained by the woman's side throughout the night, waiting, watching for some sign of recovery.

The bruise on her temple had gone from red to deep purple within those hours. She'd no doubt received the nasty bump from one of the pebbles that had rained down upon her when she'd fallen. Her breathing was so shallow, it could hardly be detected. Collin had leaned forward from time to time and held a hand-mirror in front of her mouth. He had sank back in relief when condensation had formed on the glass. Regardless, she had not moved since she'd been placed in the bed.

Running a hand through his hair, Collin let his gaze drift down the length of her frail body, barely visible beneath the coverlet. She'd felt weightless in his arms as he'd carried her to the manor. And now, she looked so small upon his massive mattress . . . so vulnerable.

The tempting notion of crawling into bed and wrapping himself around her blazed through his mind, through his loin.

Collin frowned instantly, both shocked and annoyed at his wayward hormones. To harbor such thoughts toward an injured, helpless guest in his home was unspeakable. Yet even as he chastised himself, his eyes roved over her once more, and the fire in his lower abdomen flamed higher, brighter.

Her face resembled that of a porcelain angel, quaint, peaceful, heart-shaped. Incredibly long eyelashes grazed her cheekbones. Her hair, the color of ripe wheat, splayed across his pillow and spilled over into waves against the linen sheets.

The woman's fairy-like beauty made her appear not quite real. In his weariness, Collin's better judgment drifted away, and he wondered if her skin would feel as smooth as it looked. He automatically curled his fingers into fists against the arms of the chair. He was of a strange frame of mind that touching her might cause the fairy-queen to vanish before his very eyes.

A tap-tap-tapping noise distracted Collin from his thoughts. He turned his head, tracking the sound to the window, and spied the source of irritation perched outside on the sill.

A huge black crow pecked repeatedly against the pane. Collin twisted in his seat and waved an arm toward the window.

Paying the gesture little heed, the obnoxious bird continued battering the glass with his beak.

Quite perturbed, Collin rose from the chair and moved to the window, making grand shooing motions.

The crow paused, cocked his head, and gave Collin what could only be termed *the evil eye,* then went on rapping on the glass.

Collin scowled. Not to be bested by a bird, he lifted the latch and swung the window wide, intending to chase the crow from the ledge once and for all.

The large black beast flapped his wings and did indeed fly from the sill—but only to circle round and sail through the open window into the room.

Collin whirled as the bird whisked past him.

At the same time, Fanny entered the chamber carrying a silver tray. "G'morin', sir. I thought you might like a bit of breakfa . . . aaah!"

The maid shrieked at the top of her lungs. The tray she held crashed against the floor.

The crow landed on the footboard of the bed. He ruffled his feathers then looked at both Collin and the maid as if trying to figure out what all the fuss was about.

Collin started forward slowly, his arms outstretched in preparation to snatch the bird as soon as he got close enough. But as he neared the bed, his gaze flickered to the fairy-queen, and he stopped in his tracks.

The young woman was sitting up, her long hair tumbling wildly over her shoulders . . . her crystal-clear green eyes wide and searching Collin's. She looked from him to the crow and back again.

Raising one slim arm, she spoke but a single word, "Magus"—a Latin derivative of *magic,* Collin noted.

The black bird flew from the end of the bed and perched on her arm as if by command.

Fanny gasped and slapped a hand over her mouth. " 'Tis a bad omen, a bird in the 'ouse," she murmured, backing toward the doorway. " 'Tis a sure sign someone 'ere'll be a-dyin'."

With that, the maid fled from the room wailing all the way down the hall.

Collin stood motionless near the foot of the bed, looking on as the young woman and the crow apparently exchanged some sort of silent greeting.

Collin blinked and cleared his throat, drawing the fairy-queen's attention.

"Are . . . are you feeling better?" he asked.

The woman set her large green eyes on him again. After a short spell, she nodded.

Her gaze followed him as Collin rounded the bed and eased back into his chair.

Collin stared at her in return. *Those eyes . . .*

so clear, yet utterly mystifying. A man could lose himself in them, Collin thought . . . and never find his way home.

The crow squawked, startling Collin, and leaped from the woman's arm onto the headboard where he began to parade back and forth.

Collin cleared his throat once more and closed his hands around the sides of the chair. "Um . . . so, you *can* hear and speak?"

"Of course, I can," Galilea replied, wrinkling her brow. The mere motion made her head hurt terribly. She was a bit dazed and quite disoriented. Scanning the room for some sign of where she was and how she'd gotten there, she reached up and gingerly touched a sore spot on her temple.

As if he'd read her mind, the gentleman next to the bed answered her unspoken question.

"I fear you acquired a rather nasty bump when you fell from the bailey last night. My manservant and I brought you to the manor in the hope that you'd soon recover."

"The manor? Do you mean Luxley Manor?"

"Aye. Luxley Manor."

Galilea studied the room more thoroughly. She couldn't count the times she'd wondered what lay within the walls of this house. Now here she was inside. She should have been excited, or at the very least, somewhat uncomfortable. Instead, an odd tranquillity enveloped her.

As her gaze wandered back to the gentleman, her memory flooded forth, and she suddenly recognized him. Blood drained from her face.

"And *you,*" she whispered hoarsely. "You're the new lord of the manor, are you not?"

"No lord, dear lady." He flashed a beautiful, albeit sardonic smile. "I'm a commoner." He made a mock bow from his sitting position. "Collin MacLaine, at your service, madam."

Galilea dropped her lashes and fiddled with the edge of the coverlet. He was most handsome—even with the shadow of dark bristles covering his chin and his long hair hanging in tangles about his face. He sat much too close and made her nervous. She absorbed strong, confusing emotions emanating from him. Yet, she also had a powerful sense that he was just as frightened of her as she was of him. She peered sideways at him, and he fidgeted in his chair.

"I . . . I should go," Galilea began, and attempted to rise from the bed. "'Twas very kind of you to come to my aide, and I—"

Collin rose from his seat and, gently grasping her shoulders, pushed her back onto the pillow.

"You should rest here for the time being," he said, tucking the covers beneath her chin. He glanced up and grimaced at the sight of Magus prancing along the headboard. "The bird, however, should go, I think."

Galilea looked from him to the crow and back again.

"Outside, Magus," she said softly, though her attention remained on the man bowing over her.

Magus ruffled his feathers and cawed loudly in protest, causing Collin to straighten abruptly.

Galilea tilted her head and frowned at the bird. "Outside, I said. *Now.* We shall discuss this later."

A disgruntled gurgle came from Magus's throat, then he flapped his wings and sailed out the window.

With a trace of amazement etching his features, Collin watched the crow fly off. Afterwards, he assessed Galilea for a long moment, then walked toward the door scratching his ear.

He paused and turned just short of exiting the room. Wearing an inquisitive expression, he raised one finger. He opened his mouth, then closed it, then opened it again.

"Your name?" He asked. "What is it they call you?"

" 'Tis Galilea."

"Galilea," he repeated, as if trying it on his tongue. For a few seconds he appeared to be struggling with indecision.

"I . . . I should like to discuss a matter of great importance with you later this afternoon, if I may." His pale gray gaze searched hers intently. "Rest, now," he added, then stepped into the hall and shut the door behind him.

His parting words left Galilea completely baffled. What possible "matter of great importance" could he mean? She pondered that absurd notion on and off for the remainder of the day—for she could not *rest* as he had suggested.

Once he had gone, she instantly climbed from the huge bed and went to the window. She had a decent view of the family cemetery, yet Magus was nowhere to be seen.

Galilea nibbled her lower lip, severely sorry that she'd been so stern with the bird. To call out for the crow would be useless at this point. Magus would pout for a while, as he always did, but in the end he'd come back, landing upon her shoulder out of the blue.

Galilea leaned further out the window and noted a trellis filled with ivy against the exterior wall nearby. The wooden meshwork looked sturdy, and the thought crossed her mind that she could easily climb down the lattice.

Pushing away from the sill, she turned and glanced about the bed chamber once more.

Truth be known, she didn't want to leave. Not just yet, anyway. This house and its hidden treasures had been veiled in secrecy much too long.

Galilea's spine tingled with a strange sensation. There *were* secrets here—something more than the four walls that kept her from running back to the meadow. Although she couldn't quite pinpoint what it was, she instinctively knew she was here in the manor for a specific reason.

Feeling certain some light would soon be shed on the matter, she strolled about the room, admiring the paintings of hunting dogs, trailing her fingers over the carved wood of the furniture. When she came to the dresser, she spied a lovely silver-handled brush.

Galilea clasped her hands behind her back, and lifted her gaze to the gilded looking-glass hanging above the bureau.

An awful sight greeted her. She walked forward and touched the mirror, disbelieving her own ragged appearance.

Reaching up, she rubbed a smudge of dirt from her cheek, then eyed a twig and bits of grass stuck in her matted hair.

It had been so long since she'd viewed her image in anything save a rippled stream. Now and then, she had raked a hand through her hair, but she'd lost all interest in herself after Ollie had died.

Her gaze drifted back to the brush on the dresser. She hesitated briefly before grasping the silver handle. Her eyes closed by their own accord with the first stroke through her hair.

Ollie had given her a brush, not near as elegant as the one she now held, though a fine brush all the same. He had combed out her tangles and plaited her hair every evening as they had sat by the fire, until she'd grown old enough to perform the task herself. Of course, the creditors had taken her beloved brush along with everything else.

Whereas sadness usually accompanied any memory of the creditors, at present her soul was soothed by the rhythm of the brush floating through her hair.

It took a good while to bring her wild tresses to order. Now and then, she would hear voices downstairs. Quickly setting the silver brush in its place upon the dresser, she would tiptoe to the door and open it a crack. Once assured no one was coming down the hall, she would return to the business of combing her disheveled locks.

Galilea made use of the pitcher of water left behind on the nightstand as well. And by the time the master of the manor came to call that afternoon, she had repaired herself to something at least resembling presentability.

Collin lost his nerve halfway down the hall. He halted, causing the butler trailing behind to bump into him.

"This is ridiculous, Winston," he said, aiming a frown over his shoulder. "The woman is strange. She talks to birds. But to think she's capable of a solution to our bizarre problem—"

"Not to worry, sir." The butler patted his arm as he moved past Collin and continued down the hall. " 'Tis quite understandable—your reluctance to approach such a delicate topic. Your colleagues would no doubt think you quite unstable if you brought up such a subject."

Winston knocked on the door of Collin's chamber, and hearing a soft invitation to enter, reached for the doorknob. Giving Collin a wink, and the knob a twist, he added, "Fortunately for you, sir, I shall handle everything."

Collin sighed and shook his head but was left with no other choice than to follow the butler into the room.

Galilea, or the fairy-queen, as Collin had come to think of her, stood by the window. Sunshine outlined her profile, casting her small frame in a rim of soft yellow light.

It was Winston this time that stopped in *Collin's* path. Collin fell short of running straight into the butler.

The woman turned and gave them a serene, heart-stirring smile.

Both Collin and Winston stood motionless and tongue-tied for a matter of moments.

With her hair brushed and her face washed, the fairy-queen was no longer merely pretty. She was exquisite, Collin noted.

He discreetly nudged Winston forward. The butler moved upon cue, though not before dousing Collin with a sour look.

"I am Winston, mistress." He approached the young woman wearing a charming expression. Taking her hand, he lifted it to his lips. "And you are?"

"Galilea," Collin supplied, rolling his eyes in the direction of the old fool.

Ignoring the obvious sarcasm in Collin's voice, Winston tucked Galilea's hand around his elbow and guided her to the chair. "Please do sit down, madam," he said, then seated himself on the edge of the bed. "I fear what I have to say may be rather lengthy."

Collin looked on as the butler expanded upon the situation. The fairy-queen listened to the ghost story without so much as batting a lash. Winston told the tale with grand gestures, prompting Collin to believe the butler was just as much a candidate for Bedlam as the madwoman he was conversing with.

". . . And so you see, madam, we are in dire need of your services," Winston explained in conclusion. "If you could persuade Wee Lizzie to refrain from her tricks, we would all be most grateful."

Galilea lowered her brow in concentration and clasped her hands in her lap. "You want me to try to contact the spirit," she commented rather than asked.

"Aye." Winston nodded, then looked to Collin for support. "Isn't that so, sir?"

Collin grimaced at the butler and folded his arms across his chest. "You should know that *I* personally do not believe a word of the hogwash Winston has just told you. There have, however, been several disturbing happenings going on in this house that I would be ever so grateful to see come to an end. Of course, we would completely understand, Mistress Galilea, if you were incapable of such a feat."

Galilea met Collin's gaze, her eyes wide and steady. "I can feel an unholy presence in this house, sir. Whether 'tis the ghost of Elizabeth Luxley, I cannot say at this point. But I do feel a great deal of despair and forlornness here. I do not know if the spirit lingering here will heed my words. Truth be known, the situation could get worse with my interference. But if I can help, I shall—for Elizabeth Luxley's sake, or whomever it may be, as well as yours."

"Splendid!" Winston chimed. With excitement shining in his old eyes, he leaned forward and grasped both the woman's hands in his. "You shall be duly compensated." The butler peered at Collin and lifted an eyebrow. "Won't she, sir?"

Collin twisted his mouth. "Well, there is the small matter of being able to afford her fee."

The fairy-queen glanced between the butler and Collin, appearing suddenly quite insulted. "There is no fee. 'Tis a gift I have. I do not peddle my ability to speak with spirits. I give it freely, as it has been given to me. Any reward I might receive shall come from knowing I've led a lost soul to the Light, most certainly *not* from earthly compensation."

An uncomfortable silence filled the room. Outside, in the distance, a crow cawed.

Winston cleared his throat. "Of course," he said patronizingly. "Of course, my dear, we shall respect your wishes. Won't we, Master Collin?"

Not waiting for Collin's response, the butler rose from his seat on the edge of the bed. "Well, it's all settled then. I shall go and tell Fanny to prepare a room for you. Are you hungry, my dear?"

"Famished," Galilea replied in earnest.

"Ah, good." The butler gave the woman a warm smile and she smiled at him in return. "You'll not deny our gratitude in the form of hospitality then. I'll have Fanny bring you up a tray."

Winston started for the door. "Are you coming, sir?" he inquired, obviously anxious to discuss the success of his mission with the skeptical master of the house.

"Aye," Collin answered, though he made no move to leave. For a long moment, he gazed at the beautiful fairy-queen sitting calmly in the chair. She gracefully endured his scrutiny. Her lovely face showed no signs of distress but, rather, a peacefulness that was entirely foreign to Collin.

He wanted to believe in her—*wanted* to believe she could accomplish the task she'd been given.

Faith, however, had never been one of Collin's greatest strengths.

"Sir?" Winston injected, poised in the doorway, his stiff expression rimmed with impatience. "If I might have a word with you?"

Collin blinked and slid his gaze to the butler. "Coming, Winston," he said, then followed the butler from the room.

After they had gone, Galilea sat very still and quiet in her chair, thinking. Mixed emotions and conflicting thoughts stirred inside her, bumping against each other.

She firmly believed fate had brought her to this destiny. She had a purpose to fulfill here, though she could not grasp the full extent of her mission. There was more to it—much more, she knew—than merely consorting with Lord Luxley's deceased daughter.

A vision of the new master of Luxley Manor came to mind, and a slight smile creased Galilea's lips. A strange warmth had circled her heart when she had awoken that morning and found him in the room. The warm feeling had come again when he had returned that afternoon with his manservant. Skepticism had been written all over Collin's handsome face whilst Winston had elaborated on his master's troublesome times with the ghost.

Most generally, Galilea would have felt ill at ease being in such close proximity with other human beings. Yet she had experienced little discomfort during her conversation with Collin MacLaine and his butler. Quite the contrary, she had been oddly tranquil in their presence . . . in this house.

Still, a disturbing sensation possessed her as well. *Sadness* . . . such sorrow, dwelled within the walls of the manor. Without a doubt, the source of grief was a restless spirit—and very probably, that of Elizabeth Luxley, from the sound of the woeful story the butler had told.

A sudden chill swept through the room. Galilea immediately sensed someone standing behind her. When she looked over her shoulder though, the feeling quickly vanished, and as she had suspected before she'd even turned her head, no one was there.

A gust of wind blew through the open window, lifting the curtain. Carried by the breeze, the faint, distant sound of a child weeping reached Galilea's ears . . . and without quite understanding why, tears filled her eyes.

The fairy-queen's agreement to aide Collin in his peculiar plight had left him with an unusual calming effect.

Once assured Winston was in the process of preparing accommodations for the strange and beautiful Galilea, Collin refused to listen to any more of the butler's boasting and escaped to the library.

He glanced warily around the room upon entering. When, after five full minutes at his desk, nothing out of the ordinary happened—no books flew about or anything—he settled down to work.

The moment he put his pen to the paper, his thoughts centered on the fairy-queen upstairs, and inspiration flowed forth in a steady stream of words.

The essence of Galilea dancing along the

bailey wall filled his prose. He wrote what he envisioned, about the moonlight gleaming silver in her hair and the gracefulness with which she moved.

The poem took on the finest form. The words held substance and strength. *Emotion,* the magic ingredient his work had heretofore lacked, appeared miraculously in every line.

Sweat beaded on Collin's brow. He drove his pen mercilessly, untaunted by Wee Lizzie or whatever else might be responsible for the unexplained events of past days—he still had trouble embracing the notion that the culprit was indeed a disgruntled spirit. As the task at hand completely absorbed him, the actual source of the pranks became less and less important. Collin was merely satisfied that he'd been given a rest from the torment for the moment.

Not two good hours after this wondrous surge of creativity, however, his concentration was once again shattered.

This time, though, the disruption came not from a specter he could not see but was rather instigated by the earthly bulk of Widow Luxley barging into the library uninvited.

The heavyset woman flung the double doors wide, startling Collin so that he nearly toppled his chair turning toward the commotion.

"Is it true?" the widow asked as she stopped beside the desk and peered down her nose at Collin.

Collin frowned, extremely displeased, to say the least, over her rude intrusion.

"Madam, can you not see that I am working? Perhaps I did not make myself clear. I agreed to allow you to stay here on the condition I would not be bothered whenever I was—"

"Fanny tells me you've brought that dreadful creature from the meadow into the house." Harriet Luxley folded her arms across her ample black-clad bosom and tapped her foot against the floor. "Lord Luxley, God rest his soul, would not hear of running that poor demented peasant off our lands. He claimed her loitering about in the meadow did no harm. After his death, I respected his wishes to leave the girl be. But I will not have her in my house, do you hear? I shall not tolerate that filthy madwoman coming into my home and—"

Collin rose from his chair abruptly. Towering almost a foot above the woman, he looked down on Harriet Luxley's astounded face, his own fixed with a furious expression.

"Madam, might I remind you that this is *my* home now? My guests should not concern you."

The widow lifted a quivering chin. "But she's quite mad, you know."

"Is she?" Side-stepping Lady Luxley, Collin strolled to the fireplace and braced an arm on the mantle. "Mayhap she is. But I have my reasons for asking the woman to stay with us. I've been advised by—"

Collin paused short of admitting the butler had actually suggested they enlist Galilea and her psychic powers to rid the house of ghosts. Realizing how ridiculous that would sound, he cleared his throat.

"I have it on the utmost authority," he began again, then was put off once more by the sudden notion that he had no idea whether Winston was an expert on the subject or not.

Pressing his eyebrows into a deep *V*, Collin quickly decided he owed the imposing widow and her family no explanations at all for his actions.

He shoved a hand through his hair and pinned the widow with a sure, steady gaze.

"Madam, I do not wish to appear insensitive to your feelings on the matter, but insomuch as you yourself are a guest here, I would suggest you do not test my hospitality. Furthermore, I shall extend that same hospitality to anyone else of my choosing without interference from you or your family."

Widow Luxley snorted and puffed out her chest. Her mouth opened, no doubt forming some snide remark, but Collin cut her off by continuing.

"And one more thing, madam. When the library doors are closed, you shall never dare to interrupt me again. Do we understand each other?"

The widow narrowed her eyes and pressed her lips into a tight line.

"Good. Now, if you'll excuse me?" Collin

gestured toward the exit. "Oh, and I'd be ever so grateful if you'd shut the door as you leave."

Lady Harriet slammed the doors, to be precise, making Collin flinch. He returned to his chair hoping to resume his former mood, but the will to write had completely deserted him.

He closed his eyes and massaged the bridge of his nose, infuriated all over again by the widow's invasion of his privacy. She had disrupted one of the most productive sessions he had ever encountered. And now all the magnificent thoughts he'd been experiencing were lost.

Heat climbed the back of Collin's neck. He wanted revenge—compensation for the damage done. Perhaps the widow wouldn't be so quick to burst in on him if she knew there would be hell to pay.

The perfect retaliation came to him then. One corner of his mouth lifted in a sardonic smile. Tonight, just for spite, he and the lovely Galilea would join the entire Luxley family for supper in the formal dining hall.

Chapter 6

Galilea sat perched on the side of the bed, waiting, clasping and unclasping her hands in her lap. Since she owned no timepiece, she'd taken the precaution of readying herself early.

Collin MacLaine would be escorting her to dinner shortly—so the maid had abruptly told her earlier. Even if Galilea hadn't had the ability to read Fanny's mind, she could have guessed the maid's thoughts on the matter by her bewildered expression.

Poor Fanny had been mortified at the prospect of being in the same room with Galilea. Galilea had sensed the trembling of the woman's heart the very moment the maid had approached the door.

When Galilea had answered the knock, Fanny had not only remained in the hall, but had backed a good four feet away as well. Obviously anxious to be gone, the maid had briefly repeated Collin's invitation to dine with him, telling Galilea the master would call for her promptly at seven o'clock. Then

Fanny had shoved a dress at her, turned, and swiftly disappeared down the hall.

Galilea smoothed the crisply starched linen skirt, admiring the feel of it beneath her fingertips. 'Twas a simple-cut, white morning gown—out of date and lacking adornment. Yet, Galilea had never possessed so fine a garment, and she had found the dress beyond charming. To complement her attire, she had also braided her hair into a thick plait that hung down her back.

Reaching up, she toyed with one of the wispy curls that framed her face and suddenly realized she had gone to such trouble for the sole purpose of impressing Collin MacLaine.

Galilea's hand stilled, a coil of hair wrapped around her finger.

She couldn't explain her intense desire to please the master of the manor. True, he was indeed comely in appearance. And there was that glowing warmth that she absorbed whenever he was near. Also, she found it rather intriguing that his mind could not be easily probed. He cloaked his thoughts quite admirably, in fact. That alone made him extremely interesting.

Galilea might have traveled further down the list of the master of Luxley Manor's attributes had a tapping sound not drawn her attention to the window.

Magus sat upon the sill, apparently perturbed because he'd been shut out. The huge black bird cocked his head and peered pointedly at Galilea, then pecked the glass impatiently again.

Galilea rose from her chair, went to the window and opened it, then seated herself on the ledge.

"Magus, my friend, how glad I am to see you," she said, stretching a hand toward the crow. He hopped aboard and walked up her arm to her shoulder. Galilea giggled when the bird nuzzled her ear. "I knew you would be back. I have the most marvelous news."

Magus fluttered from her shoulder, flew a few feet out the window, then hovered in the air and looked expectantly at Galilea.

"No, I can't go with you just now," she said. "That's the news, you see. I've been asked to stay on at the manor for the time being. Can you imagine? *Me* . . . living in Luxley Manor. Isn't it just wonderful, Magus?"

The crow landed on the window sill and flapped his black wings.

Galilea tucked her chin. "Why, Magus, you're jealous, aren't you? Don't deny it. You wouldn't be so fussy if it were *you* who'd been asked to reside in such a fine house, now would you?"

The black bird turned his back and toddled to the far side of the window.

"Really, Magus. I'd be happy for *you,* I would." Galilea lowered her gaze and plucked at the modest neckline of her gown. "You might have commented on how nice I look. But no, you're too busy pouting, aren't you?" She shrugged her shoulders. "Well, I suppose since you are in such a sour mood, I shan't bother telling you the rest of it."

Magus half-turned and discreetly glanced in her direction. Once the bird caught Galilea's eye, however, he started to preen his feathers, acting completely disinterested.

"You see, I *was* going to tell you that the master of the manor himself is coming to take me downstairs to dinner this evening."

Magus paused in the midst of his sprucing and squawked at Galilea.

" 'Tis God's truth. He's coming for me any minute." Galilea leaned her head back against the frame of the window. Gazing to one side, she took a deep breath, taking in the sweet scent of flowers sprinkled amongst the weeds in the garden below. "He's rather handsome, don't you think?"

Magus cawed loudly upon that note, then he flew from the window sill in a huff.

Galilea shook her head as he sailed away. She was about to call out to the bird when a sharp rap pelted her door.

Tidying her dress and hair, she hurried across the room and opened the door.

Master Collin stood very tall and straight in the hall, hands clasped behind his back. Clean-shaven with his long black hair gathered neatly at the nape of his neck, he looked every bit the country gentleman.

His clear, silver-blue gaze drifted slowly over Galilea, stalling on her bare toes peeking from beneath the hem of the gown. An endearing smile curled his mouth as he brought his eyes back to hers.

His smile wavered somewhat when meeting the slight curve of her own lips, and for a long quiet moment, the two simply stared at each other.

"Shall we go down?" he asked, breaking the silence.

Galilea glanced at the arm he offered. After a short stretch of hesitation, she folded her hand lightly around his elbow. The rough texture of his suit jacket grazed her fingertips, and the feel of strong sturdy muscles beneath the fabric sent an intense heat flowing over her entire body.

"Ready?" he asked with a smile that went straight to her heart.

Galilea could merely nod in answer.

As he towed her along the hall, however, her awe over her surroundings swayed her attention from the man at her side. A keen familiarity overwhelmed her. She saw things she recognized—the vase at the end of the corridor . . . the painting of children playing ring-around-the-rosy hanging on the wall at the top of the stairway. She *knew* what each room they passed looked like inside, even though the doors were shut. She had seen it all before—perhaps in a dream?

Galilea gripped Collin's arm tighter as they descended the stairs. With each step they took, a growing sense that someone followed them assailed her. Yet each time she looked over her shoulder, the space behind them proved vacant.

At the base of the stairs, Collin peered sideways at the beauty clinging to his arm. Edginess seeped from her fingertips through his coat sleeve. She seemed so fragile . . . so untainted by the world and cynics such as he. She viewed everything in great detail, her eyes lit with wonder—like a child in a toy shop for the very first time.

Up to this point, Collin had thought of nothing but thwarting the obnoxious Lady Luxley by bringing his new houseguest down to dinner.

Now, with a sickening heaviness settling in the pit of his stomach, he suddenly felt like a butcher leading a lamb to slaughter.

His conscience came too late, however. By the time he realized how vicious and direct the Widow Luxley might be toward the little fairy-queen, he and Galilea were at the threshold of the dining hall.

The Luxleys were engaged in a rather heated discussion at the table. From what Collin could gather, Elenore wanted to add another bookshelf to the sitting room of the family's London townhouse now being renovated.

Her husband, Roland blandly argued that they simply did not have the funds.

Lady Luxley murmured unintelligible comments beneath her breath, whilst the lad, Phillip, ignored them all and shoved food into his mouth.

Conversation ceased abruptly when Collin and his dinner guest appeared in the doorway. The Luxleys's collective gazes froze on Galilea. Even young Phillip put down his fork and stared, food dribbling from his gaping mouth.

Collin felt the woman at his side tremble, yet when he checked her expression, he found her cordially bestowing a serene, well-composed smile on the family.

Collin's heart shifted slightly upward in his chest. A mischievous smile of his own creased the corners of his eyes as he looked pointedly at Harriet Luxley.

"I do hope you won't mind if we join you this evening," he said, in a challenging tone. "May I present Mistress Galilea—"

Collin paused and leaned to the fairy-queen's ear. "Your surname," he whispered out of the side of his mouth. "What is it?"

"Jones," she answered softly, turning a twinkling gaze upon him.

Collin was lost for a long moment in the depth of her cool green eyes—the same rich color of a field of barley covered with a morning frost.

Realizing the embarrassing length of silence that hung between his sentences, Collin dragged his attention back to the Luxleys, then cleared his throat.

"May I present Mistress Galilea Jones. Mistress Jones, Elenore and Roland Cameron, and their son, Phillip," he said, gesturing to each in turn.

Deliberately introducing Lady Luxley last instead of first, as was protocol, Collin made a grand sweep of his arm in the frowning widow's direction. "And my dear Mistress Jones, *this,* of course, is Lady Luxley—but I'm certain she would want you to call her Harriet."

"Now you see here, young man—" the widow began, her chin quivering with indignation.

Elenore reached out and laid a hand on her mother's arm, silencing the older woman immediately. Mother and daughter exchanged a brief, unspoken confrontation of sorts.

After which, Harriet pressed her mouth into a tight line.

Elenore then rose gracefully and presented Galilea with a Mona Lisa smile.

"Welcome, Mistress Jones," she said, coming forward to grasp both of Galilea's hands in her own. "Please do come and sit beside me."

The fairy-queen glanced warily at Collin before Elenore led her away to a chair.

Collin took his place at the end of the oblong table, directly across from a glaring Widow Luxley. To his right, halfway down the table, Roland Cameron's lusty gaze was moving over Galilea in an all-too-obvious manner. Chubby little Phillip was again preoccupied with gobbling his supper.

Elenore sat to Collin's left, across from her

husband. Collin thought it a bit odd that she had seated Galilea on the other side of her, between herself and her mother—especially when Lady Luxley did nothing to hide her vexation over the placement. Indeed, the older woman literally choked.

Elenore promptly called for Fanny and ordered two more plates be brought in, and the maid swiftly complied.

As the meal was placed in front of Galilea, Widow Luxley, apparently unable to curb her tongue any longer, leaned forward in her chair and pinned the fairy-queen with a hateful sneer.

"*You may not* address me as Harriet, as Mr. MacLaine has suggested." The widow spoke each word with distinction, baring clenched teeth.

"Of course not, Lady Luxley," Galilea replied in a gentle fashion. "I wouldn't think of—"

"And don't you dare try to steal anything. I shall be watching you, you little—"

"Mother!" Elenore interceded.

"I'll handle this, Elenore," Collin cut in, the volume of his voice ringing dominant from the end of the table. He slid a practiced, steady gaze to Widow Luxley.

"Madam, it is by my good graces that I have consented to allow you to remain in this house. You should understand I will not tolerate your rudeness toward any other guest I choose to entertain. Do I make myself clear?"

"Quite." The widow rose from her chair

and flung her napkin down on the table. Speaking to Elenore as if no one else in the room existed, she added, "Do have Fanny bring my plate to my chambers. I've suddenly developed a most dreadful headache."

Without the extended courtesy of excusing herself, Lady Luxley quit the dining hall.

Collin couldn't say he was sorry to see her go. Once her overbearing presence was removed, the mood in the room lightened considerably.

Throughout the meal Collin noted Galilea paid careful attention to her table manners, watching and waiting for the others to pick up the proper fork before she did so herself. Oddly, she seemed unusually calm during the whole affair. Indeed, she evidently immensely enjoyed her attempts at following the quaint procedure, and for all appearances, acted as if she were playing some new parlor game.

In the days to come, Collin would look back upon this tranquil picture of the so-called madwoman of the meadow and realize 'twas in this very moment that her endearing charm first cracked the hard shell of his heart. He did not take part in the idle conversation Elenore and Roland drew Galilea into. Quite content to observe, he eased back into his chair, letting the sweet lyrical sound of the fairy-queen's voice sooth his senses.

After young Phillip was excused from the table, Roland nonchalantly steered the discussion from the pleasant weather and sailed straight into a cleverly disguised interrogation of Galilea.

While Elenore did not participate in the questioning, neither did she stop it. In fact, her scrutiny of Galilea's one-word answers assured Collin that she was just as curious as her husband.

Galilea responded vaguely to the first few inquiries, then refusing to reply at all, she peered down the length of the table at Collin, clearly leaving him to explain her presence at Luxley Manor.

Collin tapped a finger against his upper lip, his gaze moving back and forth between Elenore and Roland. They both believed in the ghost. They had as much as said so when he had initially asked them about the disturbances in the library. Collin himself was certain that, in the end, rather than proving a rampaging spirit was indeed responsible for the incidents, a more logical explanation would arise. But he could think of no earthly reason for not disclosing the purpose of Galilea's stay.

"Mistress Jones has come to our aid at my urging," he said with a shrug.

Collin could tell by the blank expressions turned his way that this brief explanation was not working. "She—" he waved a hand in the air, searching for the precise phrase he wanted to use. "She's kindly offered her services to rid the house of—" Collin furrowed his brow. That didn't sound quite right, either. He simply could not bring himself around to forming the word *ghost*—especially when such a thing did not exist.

In that instant, Galilea stepped in to rescue him.

"What Master MacLaine is saying, I believe, is that he's been troubled by a spirit running amok in the house. He's asked me to do what I can, and I've promised to help." Galilea smiled at Collin, hoping he'd be pleased with her rendition of the situation. "Isn't that it, Master MacLaine?"

Collin frowned all the more. "Actually, I am quite convinced, Mistress Jones, that we shall find some other, *rational* cause for the odd occurrences here. I do not, by any means, acknowledge the notion that a *spirit* is at the heart of the matter."

His skepticism struck a sudden, seldom-felt note of ire in Galilea. "I beg to differ with your opinion, sir. I do indeed sense a presence in the manor," she stated bluntly, then slid her gaze back to Elenore. "I've a gift of knowing, you see."

"Really? You read minds then?" Elenore's voice took on a tinge of excitement. "Can you read *my* thoughts? Right now, I mean. Can you truly tell what I'm thinking this very moment?"

Galilea sensed a great deal of fear and despair inside the woman but didn't wish to say so. Looking down the table at her handsome host again, she saw Collin grimace and glance heavenward.

"Nay, Mistress Cameron," Galilea continued, avoiding answering Elenore's question directly. "You see, it doesn't work that way. Actually, I have little control over it at all. Sometimes the visions or feelings come when I want them to. At other times, they don't."

"How perfectly fascinating," Elenore murmured. Propping her elbows on the table, she cupped her chin in her hands. "Isn't that fascinating, dear?" she asked her husband.

"Oh, indeed it is." Roland's reply was low and throaty. He met Galilea's gaze evenly, lowering his lids, and the seductive gleam in his eyes made *his* thoughts blatantly readable.

Galilea quickly looked away from him, returning her attention to his wife.

"I've misplaced my favorite broach," Elenore was saying. "The one Roland gave me on our wedding day. I wonder . . . could you possibly help me find it? I'd be ever so grateful, if you could."

Galilea's gaze wandered to the far end of the table again. Collin MacLaine appeared totally bored. His attitude bothered Galilea terribly for some reason. Never before had she cared whether anyone deemed her a fraud. Why she had the urge to prove herself to him, she did not know.

Elenore laid a hand on Galilea's arm, tugging her thoughts from the master of the manor.

"Please, Mistress Jones, would you try to find my broach?"

Elenore's large brown eyes reminded Galilea of a fawn she'd once seen in White Fern Forest. She could not refuse the woman's plea any more than she'd been able to resist petting the pretty fawn.

"I shall try," Galilea told her. Straightening her spine in the chair, she closed her eyes and cleared her mind.

Within seconds, she got a picture of a round-cut ruby circled with white pearls. "I see the broach . . . 'tis . . . under a blue rug, I think."

"Why, I've a blue rug in front of my bureau where I keep my jewelry box," Elenore chanted.

Galilea opened her eyes and immediately noticed that Collin had slipped quietly from his chair and vacated the room. Apparently, her effort to impress him had been in vain.

"You simply must excuse me," Elenore said as she came to her feet. "I cannot wait to see if the broach is indeed there." She looked across the table at her husband. "Are you coming, Roland?"

"You go ahead, dear," he answered, his gaze never leaving Galilea. "I'll be up shortly."

Galilea barely heard Elenore's parting farewell. She was too busy wondering if the woman was aware her husband was a philanderer. She had a sneaking suspicion that Elenore did know but rather chose to ignore the fact.

Left alone in the dining hall with Roland, the hair on the nape of Galilea's neck stood on end. She rose and bid the man a good night, not liking the intimacy of feelings flowing from him.

Within her first few steps toward the door though, Roland had jumped from his chair, rounded the table, and stood in her path.

"Tell me, Mistress Jones, can you guess what *I'm* thinking?" he asked in a purringly smooth tone, a wicked grin creasing his lips.

His intent was written all over his face. One needn't be a mind reader to see it. The man liked playing this game of cat and mouse—had done so many times before, Galilea perceived, with defenseless young serving girls.

"Good night, Mr. Cameron," Galilea repeated. She peered bravely into his dark eyes, clearly transmitting her disinterest in the game. When she attempted to side-step him, he moved in the same direction, blocking her escape.

A small chuckle gurgled in Roland's throat. His eyes glistened, and he started forward.

Galilea backed away until she felt her hip bump the edge of the table.

Roland stretched out his arms as he approached her, but before he could touch her, a deep, rumbling voice came from the doorway.

"Leave her be, Cameron."

Roland spun toward the command, his startled expression forming fast into a frown.

Collin leaned casually against the doorjamb, balancing a stemware of brandy between two fingers.

"Come, Mistress Jones," he said, "I do believe it's time I escorted you back to your chambers."

Galilea hastened to do as he bid, most grateful he had shown up when he did.

"Good evening, Roland," Collin said with a curt smile, then took Galilea's elbow. In the midst of turning to leave, he paused and looked over his shoulder.

"Oh, and Roland? If you should ever attempt to harass young innocents beneath my roof again, I shall have no choice but to thrash you within an inch of your life."

Collin lifted one eyebrow, taking a moment to drive his point home. Then, leaving Roland Cameron in the dining hall to weigh his parting words, he gallantly ushered Galilea toward the stairs.

Galilea could not take her eyes from him as they climbed the steps—for, by saving her from Roland, he had just become her champion. From then on, she no longer merely admired his good looks, she was completely enamored by his noble virtue.

Galilea lay awake for quite some time after Collin had left her at her chamber door that night.

The tree outside her window rustled in the slight breeze. A moonbeam shone through the leaves, casting a play of light and shadows into the room. Galilea gazed at the dancing pattern on the wall, her head filled with silly romantic notions featuring the master of the manner.

In her mind's eye, she visualized herself and Collin taking long walks through the fields together . . . perhaps holding hands . . . stealing shy, loving glances at each other.

'Twas truly a wonderful sight, although Galilea knew in her heart she merely imagined the scene. While no harm could come from dreaming, this particular dream could never come true. A match between a penniless vagrant and the master of such a fine estate simply "wasn't done" in the realm of the real world.

Galilea's faint smile did not falter on that thought. She was quite content with the magnificent glow warming her chest. She was fairly used to finding comfort in dreams rather than in reality.

Rolling onto her side, she nestled her cheek against the soft down pillow. Rather than facing the prospect of what might become of her after her undertaking at the manor was finished, she dwelled on the clean, fresh scent of sunshine rising from the recently washed linens.

Her eyes slid closed, and she drifted off to sleep, promising herself she'd not take for granted this special time spent at Luxley Manor.

Instead, she would cherish every moment.

Two doors down the hall, Collin reclined wide awake on his massive bed. With his hands locked behind his head, he watched a similar fluttering pattern of moonlight play against his own wall.

He could not stop thinking about the bizarre and beautiful fairy-queen. For all her odd and unconventional ways—or perhaps, *because* of them, Galilea completely intrigued him.

As if her physical beauty weren't enchanting enough, there was something much more complex about her. She seemed to have a depth to her that he had never encountered in any other human being.

Collin's curiosity walked back and forth over the peculiar actions of the lovely Galilea—until it came to him that it was probably rather useless to try to analyze the motives of a madwoman.

Is she mad? a small voice inside him asked, then answered *no, not mad . . . simply peculiar.*

Collin closed his eyes upon that note, too weary to contemplate the matter any further.

But when he fell into a deep, peaceful slumber, he had the strangest dream. He and Galilea walked through a field of wildflowers . . . holding hands . . .

Chapter 7

There was no sign of ghostly activity for the next few days. Even so, Galilea felt the spirit's presence quite strongly.

Given permission to roam the manor freely, she spent most of her daylight hours in search of Wee Lizzie.

One afternoon, Galilea ventured up to the third floor of the house and discovered a whole wing of unused rooms. When she stepped into the upper corridor, a wave of cold air rushed through her. She moved instinctively past several closed doors, walking straight toward the chamber at the end of the hall.

Stopping at the door, Galilea's sixth sense tingled with the knowledge that someone stood just inside. With slow measured moves, she reached for the brass knob, then gave it a quick twist.

The doorknob caught against the lock, refusing Galilea entrance. After a couple of more unsuccessful tries, she gave up and turned to leave.

Halfway down the corridor, the distinct

sound of a door latch being lifted echoed loudly in the silence.

Galilea edged back around to find the formerly locked door wide open. Retracing her steps, she walked cautiously into the room, and paused just beyond the threshold when a chill came over her.

Dust motes floated in the scant ray of sunshine pouring through the dirty, curtainless window. Cobwebs covered everything. The chamber had most definitely belonged to a child, Galilea deemed, but had been used as a storeroom as well over the years.

Among the old trunks and wooden crates scattered about, rows of dolls and toys were placed neatly on shelves and along the top of the dresser.

Galilea experienced a sudden burst of loneliness . . . an intense, heart-wrenching pain that made her want to run downstairs as fast as her feet would take her.

Yet, something held her where she was . . . *forced* her to move deeper into the room.

She wove through the clutter, trying to gain some insight on what Elizabeth Luxley might have been like. Trailing her fingers over items she believed belonged to Lizzie, she came across a battered, stuffed bear with black button eyes. As she picked up the plaything and held it in her hands, she absorbed an endearing affection seeping from the little bear into her palms.

Just then, Galilea caught a movement out of the corner of her eye—*a flash of white? A streak of smoke? Something* that was there one moment and gone the next.

It might have been a bird flying by the window, casting a shadow that reflected off the window pane.

But Galilea didn't really think so and was prompted to examine the area where the phantom motion had occurred. As she approached the spot, she nearly stumbled on a fairly large, gold-framed painting lying facedown on the floor.

Dusting off the cobwebs, Galilea turned the picture over. 'Twas a portrait of a gentleman—a much younger version of the silver-haired Lord Luxley. Although Galilea had only seen him from a distance, she was certain of the identity. Upon his knee sat a chubby toddler with a cap of golden curls—a sweet vision of a cherub minus the wings.

Galilea tipped the painting upright and swiveled it toward the pale sunlight for a better look. Lord Luxley wore a fatherly expression of pride and love for the happy, laughing baby in his lap.

Galilea felt an odd connection to the pretty infant in the portrait—an attachment so strong, it nearly made her weep. She touched the likeness of the child and knew at once that the little girl was indeed Elizabeth Luxley—or Wee Lizzie, as she'd been so affectionately called.

Another movement distracted Galilea, this time in the corridor.

And this time, Galilea distinctly caught a

glimpse of a young girl with long blond curls dashing across the doorway.

"Lizzie?" Galilea called out, moving quickly toward the door.

When she reached the corridor, however, the hall was completely empty.

"Lizzie?" Galilea repeated softly, then stood quietly, listening for any response.

She scanned the length of the hall, and could tell the spirit of Elizabeth Luxley hovered nearby. After a few more minutes, during which nothing at all happened, Galilea came to the conclusion that *if* Lizzie decided to make further contact, the girl would do so on her own terms.

Quite disappointed that she hadn't been able to communicate with the lonely little ghost, Galilea reluctantly walked toward the stairs.

As she laid a hand on the banister, preparing to start down the steps, she had a powerful urge to glance back toward the chambers she'd just visited. When she looked over her shoulder, she froze in place.

In the doorway stood the transparent figure of a young girl in a white dress, long blond ringlets cascading over her shoulder. The child's haunting gaze pierced Galilea's.

Galilea smiled, transmitting friendly thoughts in the spirit's direction.

In return, the corners of Wee Lizzie's mouth tipped upward ever so slightly—but then, she vanished into thin air.

* * *

Galilea was drained after meeting the ghost of Elizabeth Luxley face to face. She went directly to her room and flopped upon the bed, her mind racing with thoughts of Wee Lizzie.

Staring at the ceiling, she struggled for a way to put into perspective the impressions she'd had in the room on the third floor.

She had been both exhilarated and somewhat startled by the event. Never in her life had she reached such a grand level of awareness. 'Twas as if, when she'd stood in the middle of the dead child's chambers, Elizabeth Luxley's emotions had merged with her very own . . . almost as if, for that brief period, the two had been one in the same person.

Galilea couldn't explain the sampling of kinship she had experienced toward Wee Lizzie. To be quite honest, the explanation was not important. Regardless of the reason, Galilea was now bound to help the poor restless soul find peace.

Her need to delve deeper into Lizzie's troubled spirit intensified. From what Winston had told her, Elizabeth Luxley had died twelve years ago at the tender age of seven. Had Lizzie lived on, she and Galilea would have been the same age. Perhaps that fact had some bearing on why Galilea felt so close to the deceased child. Whether it did or not, Galilea was certain the two had been brought together for a specific purpose.

Upon coming to these conclusions, Galilea's eyelids grew heavy. Her mind wandered, and soon, with her body sinking deep into the soft mattress, she fell fast asleep.

She slept through supper, well into the evening hours. Her chamber was quite dark when she was awakened by an insistent rapping at her door.

Stumbling from the bed, Galilea crossed the room, still slightly drugged with the aftereffects of slumber. When she opened the door, the brightness of a single candle held high nearly blinded her. She squinted, adjusting her eyes to the light.

Collin peered around the candle, his face fixed with an impatient frown.

"What on earth took you so long?" he asked. "I've been knocking for a full five minutes."

Galilea opened her mouth to reply, but before she could utter a word, Collin took her by the arm and ushered her down the hall as if the house were afire.

"It's happening again," he muttered, without missing a step down the stairway.

"Happening again?"

"In the library," Collin replied briskly. "Things are flying about."

"Wee Lizzie is there *now*, you mean?" Galilea inquired as she hurried along beside him. She almost tripped at the base of the stairs, and Collin paused briefly to steady her.

He looked briefly into her eyes, his skepticism wavering for once. Then he furrowed his brow. "Damn it all. Just come with me and I'll show you."

Collin picked up his hasty pace again, dragging Galilea with him. The poor man was clearly flustered, and Galilea felt a twinge of sympathy for him. Her concern for Collin was forgotten, however, when they approached the open doorway of the study.

"See? What did I tell you?" Collin gestured toward his desk. "Have you ever in your life seen such ridiculous nonsense?"

"Something very similar, actually," Galilea answered, taking in the sight of Collin's journal hovering above the desk—while his ink pen danced in midair busily scribbling on the page.

"Well?" Collin jutted his chin toward the commotion. "Are you just going to stand there and watch?"

Galilea glanced at him and the dancing pen, then lifted an eyebrow. "What would you suggest I do?"

"I don't know. *Something.*" Collin grimaced and waved a hand in the air. "Use some of those magical powers or whatever it is Winston claims you're gifted with. Simply make it stop," he said, then slanted a challenging gaze Galilea's way. "That is, if you can."

Viewing the floating pen and journal with a critical eye, Galilea sighed and squared her shoulders. "I shall do what I can, but I shan't make any promises, you understand."

She gave Collin a pointed look before she walked toward the desk. Pausing beside the desk chair, she held out her hand, palm up.

"Lizzie," she said in a smooth, though quite

stern voice, "you are behaving rather badly. Now give me the ink pen."

The pen immediately stalled against the page of the journal, yet both objects continued to float motionless a good four feet above the desk.

"Come, Lizzie," Galilea prompted. "Give over."

The ink pen quivered in hesitation for a moment or two, then it moved to Galilea's open palm.

"That's a good girl," Galilea said with a smile. "Now the journal."

Collin's journal dropped onto the desk.

"Very good." Galilea scanned the room, trying to pinpoint the child's spirit. "Now, run along, if you please. Master Collin must have his quiet time to work. Do be a dear, and you and I shall have a nice visit later."

A rush of wind passed through Galilea, making her close her eyes and hold her breath. The sensation lasted no more than a few seconds.

When Galilea reopened her eyes, the chill had left the room—and so had Wee Lizzie.

Galilea blinked, and her gaze automatically dropped to the journal lying open on the desk. In a childish scrawl, two words had been written over and over again upon the page: *help me . . . help me . . . help me . . .*

Tightness gripped Galilea's throat. Agony and pity for the poor spirit converged upon her to a point of making her tremble.

Galilea flinched at the touch of the hand closing over her shoulder.

"I'm afraid I owe you an apology, Mistress Jones." Collin stood so close behind her, she could feel the heat of his body seeping into hers. Reaching around her to set the candle on the desk, he turned her to face him.

"You did it." His expression was a mixture of amazement and amusement. The smile creasing his lips put a bright gleam in his pale gray eyes. "By damn, I don't know how. But, you did it."

Galilea stared up at him, feeling the warmth of his hands band her upper arms. She could not speak for the weight in her chest.

He was so logical-minded, yet he chose to ignore the evidence he had just witnessed. His ardent disbelief in the spirit world, his moodiness, in fact, *everything* about the man baffled Galilea, and she had to wonder if Lizzie was merely tormenting him to prove her existence.

Still in all, Collin MacLaine was every young girl's fantasy—the knight in shining armor of a lass's dreams. He was tall, and handsome, and noble, and wise.

And far above someone like herself, Galilea swiftly rationalized. 'Twould be folly to fall in love with someone like him.

"Will you stay with me tonight?" he asked in an impetuous manner.

Collin's question was jarring. Galilea searched his silver eyes, but once again his thoughts were unreadable.

"Stay with you?" she asked, unsure of his precise meaning.

"Just for a short while." Collin motioned to the chair beside the fireplace. "Simply sit with me until I'm finished working. I won't be long, I promise."

Collin gave her a charming smile that would have surely coaxed her into agreeing to anything he might have suggested.

"Of course," she murmured softly, then edged around him to take the seat he had indicated.

Collin settled in his desk chair, flashed her one last smile, then went to work.

As the night wore on, Galilea curled her feet beneath her and viewed Collin without reservation. He was so absorbed in his writing, he wouldn't have noticed her watching, anyway.

So she openly admired the way his long fingers gripped the pen . . . the way his hand moved in a graceful, rhythmic motion. With a lock of hair falling across his forehead, Galilea could imagine him as a boy bowed over his studies. She loved how he fixed his mouth in a straight diligent line whenever he paused to re-read what he'd written.

Somewhere in the very back of her brain, Galilea was aware of what she was doing . . . *aware* that placing sentimental significance on every little thing Collin did was not in her own best interest. The two of them were much too different. They held contrasting views. Indeed, if she hurled her heart down this dangerous course, there could be nothing but pain at the end of the path.

Yet, at present, rather than dwell on the inevitable pain that waited ahead, Galilea immersed herself in the glowing pleasure she gained from simply being so near him and observing his every move.

The warmth of Galilea's gaze radiated across the room and wrapped itself securely around Collin.

He knew she stared at him, but oddly, her scrutiny did not distract him in the least. On the contrary, her watchfulness brought him a great deal of comfort. Instead of viewing her as an intruder, he considered her more of . . . well, a *guardian angel* of sorts, he supposed.

In fact, Galilea's presence inspired him. As he breathed in her sweet scent filling the room, his thoughts flowed freely, and his pen glided easily across the paper. He filled page after page with brilliant prose of a romantic piece he called "The Fairy-Queen."

Collin did not notice when the candle burned out, and the pale gray shades of daybreak crept across his desk. About the time his vision began to blur, the crow of a faraway rooster penetrated his thoughts.

When he looked up from his work, he found the little fairy-queen curled up and asleep in the chair by the fireplace. Closing his journal, he rose from his seat and stretched, then walked to Galilea's side.

He stood for a moment gazing down at the sleeping beauty. Tousled blond curls framed her lovely face. Her breast rose and fell with deep, peaceful breaths.

Collin gave in to the temptation to touch her cheek. Her skin was indeed as smooth as it appeared—softer than the finest silk from the Orient. The feel of her sweet flesh beneath his fingertips suddenly made his temperature rise.

Curling his fingers into a fist, he promptly withdrew his hand, though his gaze remained on Galilea, and a smile lingered on his lips.

"Come on, my little angel," he whispered, scooping the fairy-queen into his arms. "Off to bed with you."

When he picked her up, Galilea stirred slightly and snuggled against his chest, but she did not open her eyes. On impulse, Collin dropped a light, chaste kiss upon her forehead as he carried her from the library.

Galilea awoke the next day fully dressed in her bed. She sat up and squinted at the bright sunshine pouring through her window and assessed that it must have been nearly noon. Shoving a hand through her hair, she remembered dozing off in the library. Aye, she remembered indulging in silly, romantic notions while she had watched Collin work. Those notions seemed very foolish indeed in the light of this day.

Yes, she clearly remembered falling asleep in the chair beside the fireplace in the study. She did *not*, however, recall climbing the stairs to her chamber in the middle of the night.

But she had made progress in forming some sort of rapport with Elizabeth Luxley. *That* much she had certainly not forgotten.

Suddenly too excited over the encounter with the ghost to give any further thought to mooning over Collin, Galilea climbed from bed and hurriedly changed her dress.

The pale blue garment she chose was a simple, well-worn gown made for service—another hand-me-down from Fanny, for which Galilea had not yet properly thanked the maid. As she hastily braided her hair, she made a mental note to show her appreciation for Fanny's kindness as soon as possible. At present, though, she had another important mission in mind.

She planned on visiting the family cemetery she had seen from Collin's bedroom window. Forfeiting breakfast, she moved swiftly down the stairs and out the door. Perhaps if she stood at Elizabeth Luxley's graveside, she might gather more insight on how to help the little soul find rest.

The walk to the Luxley family plot wasn't a long one, although some may have disagreed. Galilea enjoyed the nice stretch of her legs.

A rectangular, gridiron fence surrounded the cemetery. Pushing the creaking gate open, Galilea shoved the overwhelming perception of dead souls aside and centered her senses on Lizzie.

She strode steadily yet reverently past the

elaborate tombstones shrouded with weeds. Making her way directly to the far side of the enclosed yard, she knew instinctively that the large angel statue she approached would mark the grave of Elizabeth Luxley.

Galilea stopped in the shadow of the heavenly guardian's outspread wings. Her heart constricted as she stood silently reading the inscription at the base of granite angel.

ELIZABETH ANN LUXLEY
BELOVED DAUGHTER OF
SIR CHARLES AMOS LUXLEY
BORN OCTOBER 19, 1857 - DIED JUNE 8, 1864

'Twas the very last line cut into the marble monument that moved tears past the brim of Galilea's eyes.

REST IN PEACE, SWEET LIZZIE

Emotionally pulled toward the grave, Galilea went down on one knee and placed a hand upon the small grassy mound. She had never felt as close to anyone as she did here and now to this long dead child. Not even Ollie, though she'd loved him dearly. There was no rhyme or reason for her to experience such grief over someone she'd never known—a child who had died twelve years ago, when Galilea herself was only seven.

Yet the pain was there, and it was very real, very intense.

"What happened, Lizzie?" Galilea whispered. "What keeps your spirit earthbound? You were a good girl, I know. What could have possibly occurred in your young life that could keep you from seeking your heavenly reward?"

The breeze picked up, fluttering the stray curls at Galilea's temples. But no answers came with the gust of wind. Not that Galilea had truly expected any simple solution to the puzzle she'd been given.

"You must find a way to tell me, Lizzie," she said, while busying her hands with the task of plucking weeds from the grave. "I must know what has happened if I'm ever to help you find peace."

A squawk followed by a human cry interrupted Galilea's thoughts. She came to her feet abruptly to see Magus tormenting the boy, Phillip, a few tombstones away.

The crow wasn't truly harming the lad. Magus merely flew in circles around Phillip's head, flapping his large black wings. Still, by the sound of all the shrieking, the boy was clearly terrified, swinging his pudgy limbs furiously in a windmill fashion.

"Magus, stop that nonsense this instant," Galilea commanded. Walking forth, she held out an arm. "Come here, now."

Magus obeyed immediately, roosting so fast upon Galilea's wrist that she wondered if the bird was misbehaving simply to gain her attention. One look at Phillip's guilty expression though, made her suspect otherwise.

Magus paced back and forth along her forearm, fussily chirping.

Galilea glanced at the lad who seemed to have regained some of his bravado and now stood boldly beside a gravestone, frowning and shaking a chubby, doubled fist at the bird.

"What is it, Magus?" Galilea asked.

The crow stopped pacing, cocked his head, then gestured with his beak toward Phillip.

"Spying, you say?" Galilea lifted a brow, then slid her gaze to Phillip. "Is it true, lad, what Magus tells me? That you were spying upon me?"

"I wasn't spying," he said, dropping his fists to his sides and puffing out his chest. "I was just listening to you talk to dead people, that's all."

"Oh." Galilea gave him a small smile, then set Magus upon her shoulder. Strolling forward casually, she clasped her hands in front of her. "And did no one ever teach you, 'tis terribly bad manners to eavesdrop on a private conversation?"

The boy squared his shoulders as Galilea came to a halt before him. "I have impeccable manners, I'll have you know," he stated with a lift of his chin. "And you couldn't exactly call it eavesdroping, considering it wasn't truly a conversation. After all, I heard no one but *you* speaking. Dead people can't talk, you know, and they certainly couldn't have heard you, either. They're . . . *dead.*"

Galilea nodded thoughtfully. "Tell me, Phillip, what makes you so sure the deceased cannot hear us when we speak to them?"

"They simply can't, silly." Phillip rolled his eyes, then assessed Galilea curiously. "Of course, I suppose *you* wouldn't know that—being a madwoman, and all."

Magus squawked loudly and ruffled his feathers, appearing about to pounce upon the child again.

"Hush, Magus," Galilea told the crow. "He's entitled to his opinion." Fastening her attention on the boy once more, she widened her eyes. "So you think me mad, do you?"

" 'Tis what my father says." Phillip squinted one eye, peering up at her. "But . . . you do seem somewhat sane right now. Perhaps . . . well perhaps, you aren't quite so mad— perhaps, you're a witch."

Galilea placed a hand at the base of her throat and feigned astonishment. "A witch? Really? And how, pray tell, might you have come to that conclusion?"

"Well, my grandmother did recently mention something of the kind," the boy answered in a tone of arrogant honesty. "Actually, *I* figured you were a witch of sorts from the very start."

He draped an arm over the tombstone, and Galilea noted his eyes glimmered as he displayed a nasty little smile. "And now I have proof, you see. I distinctly heard you talking to Wee Lizzie's grave. Only a witch would go round cavorting with dead people and . . . *crows.*"

Phillip pinned Magus with a narrowed gaze and added, "I hate that bird. I should like to have Fanny cook him for supper."

Galilea had missed the boy's last remark—though by the way Magus had tensed his claws against her collarbone, she could fairly guess it was some insult directed toward the bird.

Quite frankly, Phillip had lost her interest past his mention of Wee Lizzie. Her mind had stalled on his familiar usage of the little spirit's pet name.

"Phillip, what do you know of Wee Lizzie?" she could not stop herself from asking.

Phillip shrugged. "Only that she was a silly, foolish girl who fell in a hole and died before I was even born. She doesn't bother me at all." He flicked an ant from the top of the marble headstone. "She frightens Mother and Grandmother sometimes, though."

Before Galilea could question him further, someone called out Phillip's name from the near distance.

Both she and Phillip looked around to find Roland trekking toward the cemetery.

Magus squawked at the approaching intruder, then hopped from Galilea's shoulder and flew away.

Phillip sauntered toward the exit wearing an angry frown, and Galilea trailed behind him. The two of them met Roland at the gate.

"Phillip, whatever are you doing out here?" Roland scolded as he swung the rusty gate wide. "You know you're not to play in the cemetery."

"I wasn't playing. I was talking to—" Phillip pointed a thumb over his shoulder at Galilea "—to *her*."

It wasn't what Phillip had said, but rather the obviously rude way in which he had presented it that struck both adults.

Roland snatched the boy by the ear, hauling him outside the graveyard. "Phillip, you shall not speak of Mistress Jones in such a manner. Now, you'll apologize, this instant."

"Why should I?" Although grimacing from the tug on his ear, the boy's chin went up defiantly. "You said yourself she was as mad as—"

Roland slapped a hand over his son's mouth. Giving Galilea a brief empathetic smile, he reeled the lad in closer, then stooped to meet Phillip eye to eye.

"Your mother is looking for you," he said between his teeth. "Now run along."

Roland promptly spun the boy in the direction of the manor and applied a good whack to the child's backside, sending him on his way.

Galilea turned to close the cemetery gate. When she swiveled back around, Roland had assumed a dignified pose.

"I must apologize for my son's behavior, Mistress Jones. I fear his mother spoils him overly."

Galilea noticed the same cocky gleam in his eyes that she had witnessed in Phillip's earlier.

" 'Tis quite all right," she replied. "Phillip

is but a boy, and children do have a tendency to speak their minds." Galilea tried to end her comment with a smile, but found her mouth somewhat unwilling to cooperate. She could not forget her encounter with Elenore's husband in the dining hall.

"Now, if you'll excuse me," she said as kindly as she could manage, then walked around him, heading toward the manor.

Roland fell in step beside her. "Mind if I join you?"he asked in an cheerful tone.

Yes, actually she did mind, but she held her tongue. Ollie had taught her at a very young age that if you cannot say anything nice, you shouldn't say anything a'tall.

Her lack of response, however, seemed to encourage Roland instead of putting him off.

"Would you care to take a stroll through the gardens, Mistress Jones? I know of a quaint, little secluded spot where we could—"

He paused, and although Galilea looked straight ahead, she could feel the heat of his gaze traveling up and down her body.

"Well, it's a place where we could get to know each other better," he finished in a low, sultry voice.

Galilea's footsteps faltered slightly. Anger was not something she experienced frequently. Still, she had learned to handle the unfavorable emotion by shoving it down as soon as it arose. Yet, Roland's assumption that she would even consider wandering off into the bushes with him made the process of curbing her temper extremely difficult.

"Thank you just the same, Mr. Cameron, but no. I've already taken my stroll for the day."

"Do call me Roland," he said, completely ignoring the fact that she'd declined his invitation.

Galilea's patience reached its limit. Halting briefly, she turned her head and met the man's gaze levelly. "Under the circumstances, I do believe 'Mr. Cameron' is more appropriate," she said, placing emphasis on every word. "Now, good day, sir."

Without waiting for his reaction, she resumed a brisk pace, swiftly moving within range of the manor.

Several yards from the house, Roland caught up with her and snagged her wrist from behind.

"A word of advice, Mistress Jones," he said, whirling her around to face him. "Take care who you trust at Luxley Manor. Dreadful accidents have been known to happen in this household."

Galilea searched his eyes and found nothing but malicious intent behind the threat. His words were meant to frighten her, no more than that. Regardless, an involuntary shiver ran up her spine.

Wrenching her arm free of his grasp, Galilea backed away from him, then turned and hastened toward the house.

Chapter 8

As Galilea approached the servants' entrance, fighting off the fury she felt, her gaze landed on a scattering of wildflowers in the weeds at the base of the stoop.

A certain philosophy of Ollie's instantly crossed her mind. The wise old tinker had claimed the magic solution to almost any problem was not so very hard to figure out. "Aye, Lassie, if you'll just go out and do something nice for another," Ollie must have told Galilea more than a hundred times—and he had always winked before following that line with, "Do that, dear child, and your own worries will soon be wilting away."

'Twas only one of Ollie's many sayings Galilea kept close to her heart. The thought of her beloved Ollie and his well-remembered quotes brought a smile to her lips.

She walked straight to the patch of flowers growing beside the stoop and bent to pick a nice nosegay. Then hiding the bouquet behind her back, she strode up the steps in search of Fanny.

She found the maid hard at work in the

kitchen, busily scrubbing pots and pans. Upon catching sight of Galilea, Fanny stilled in the midst of her chore.

Galilea could sense the woman's apprehension, could see the wariness in her eyes. Striving to calm Fanny's fears, Galilea smiled in a friendly fashion and moved forward with easy steps. When she neared the maid, she stretched the bouquet toward her.

"These are for you," she said, presenting Fanny with her humble gift. "For all the kindness you've shown me since I've been here."

Fanny's mouth dropped open as she focused on the small bunch of flowers. Hesitantly, she set the pot she'd been cleaning on the long table in front of her, then she hastily wiped her hands on her apron.

"Wots this? Flowers? For me?" she asked, wrapping her fingers gingerly around the stems of the pretty bouquet. Fanny closed her eyes as she lifted the fragrant wildflowers to her nose and sniffed several times. "Aaah. Wild roses is one of me favorites, it 'tis, and I'm quite fond of the 'oney-suckle, as well, I am." Upon reopening her eyes, a smile lit Fanny's gaze. "Thank ye, miss. Nobody's ever bothered givin' me flowers afore."

When the smile in the maid's eyes reached her lips, Galilea realized the woman wasn't near as old as she had initially appeared—possibly only in her early thirties.

Galilea felt Fanny gradually warming toward her. Yet, she could also tell that the maid still held *some* reservations.

Glancing about the messy kitchen, Galilea took in the pots and pans stacked high upon the table, waiting to be washed.

"Might I help you with your work?" she asked Fanny.

The maid tucked her chin. " 'Tain't really necessary, miss. Since 'is lordship passed on, and the widow pared down the 'ousehold help, I've gotten rather used to doing it all myself, I 'ave."

"I'd consider it a kindness, Fanny, if you'd allow me to earn the dresses you've given me." Galilea settled on one of the tall wooden stools beside the table and rolled up her sleeves. "If you'll simply tell me what you want done, I'll be happy to oblige."

Fanny assessed her with sidelong gaze. "Well . . . I suppose you *could* wash and slice the potatoes for tonight's supper, if you've a mind to."

Galilea gladly accepted the task. She and Fanny labored side by side in companionable silence for quite some time—Fanny polishing her pots till they shined, Galilea dicing vegetables for mutton stew.

Fanny slid her gaze over Galilea now and then.

Galilea, in turn, watched Fanny from the corner of her eye. Fanny's nervous condition appeared to have eased considerably within the passing hour. Still, Galilea could feel a strong mixture of anxiety and confusion lingering inside the maid. A various range of questions and misconstrued opinions rampaged through the woman's thoughts.

Galilea soon grew tired of holding her tongue. She simply could not sit there any longer allowing the debate that was going on in Fanny's mind. The woman couldn't quite decide what kind of creature Galilea was and kept circling around to three separate conclusions. According to Fanny, Galilea most certainly had to be a *witch . . . no, no, a fairy . . . oh, dear heaven, or a madwoman . . . nay a witch, was what she was . . .*

"Fanny, you've no cause to be afraid of me," Galilea stated abruptly, without looking up from her task. "Go ahead and ask me whatever you wish."

Fanny pressed her mouth into a tight line for a matter of moments. Then, keeping her attention fastened on her work, the maid expelled a long sigh.

"Well . . . 'tis true, I 'ave been wonderin' a thing or two, I 'ave." Turning a large soup pot upside down, Fanny scrubbed frantically at the blackened bottom. "I wouldn't want to go crossin' no boundaries 'ere, ye understand. And if there's some code you'd 'ave to break in the tellin', then by all means, spare me the curse and don't dare be utterin' a word."

Fanny paused briefly in her attack on the scorched pot, looked pointedly at Galilea, then resumed her chore vigorously.

"Go ahead and ask," Galilea said softly, assuring the maid there'd be no curse to contend with.

Fanny's hands stilled on the soup pot. She kept her eyelashes lowered, viewing her reflection in the shiny spot on the bottom she had cleaned.

"All right then, miss. 'Tis just one thing I'd like t' know." Fanny swallowed hard, then took a deep, slow breath before continuing. "Be ye a—" The maid's mouth hung open for a heartbeat or two, then her gaze skipped to Galilea's. "Well, wot I mean t' say is . . . might you be from a coven of—" Fanny's mouth fell motionless once more.

"Nay, I am *not* a witch." Galilea smiled timidly and lifted her brow. "Truly, I'm not."

Fanny narrowed her eyes, unaware that she projected her next line of thought quite clearly.

Galilea bit her upper lip to hold down her amusement."And rest assured, I've nothing a'tall to do with Merlin's black magic."

Fanny flinched, startled, no doubt, by the spoken reply to a question she had not yet put into words. Staring wide-eyed at Galilea, she shifted uncomfortably on her stool.

"God's truth, Fanny." Galilea leaned forward, and the maid edged back. "I'm no more than what you see. A commoner, the same as you."

Fanny jumped off her stool, and clutching the edge of the table, moved around to the other side. With a slow shake of her head, she squinted one eye at Galilea. "Nay, you're not like the rest of us."

"Oh, but I am," Galilea responded most sincerely.

Fanny straightened her posture and folded her arms over her chest. "Would you mind explainin' then, 'ow it is you knew exactly wot it was I was about to say just a bit ago? Tell me that much, lass. You were answerin' m' questions afore I'd finished askin' 'em."

"Just because I have a knowing of things sometimes before they are said or done, that does not mean I'm a witch." Mustering a little dignity of her own, Galilea stiffened her spine, as well. "Nor am I a fairy. And neither do I consider myself a madwoman . . . *really*."

Galilea picked up her knife and started chopping an onion in the rythmn of agitation. "Actually, I'm not all that different from you or anyone else." The onion fumes floated upward, making her eyes water, and she sniffled. "Indeed, my heart beats the same as anybody else's, and—ouch!"

Nicked by the knife, Galilea grimaced, and stuck the tip of her injured finger in her mouth.

Fanny hurried back around the table. " 'Ere now, let me see wot you've done t' yerself," she ordered, stretching out her palm. "Come on, stop yer weepin', and let me see. Could be it might need a stitchin', and I'm right 'andy with a needle, I am."

Touched by the maid's concern, Galilea slipped the finger from her mouth, and held it up for inspection. It suddenly struck her as enormously funny that Fanny had taken one look at her red-rimmed eyes, and assumed she'd actually shed tears over the tiny slit in her finger.

"Fanny, I wasn't crying. 'Twas the onion, you see, that made my eyes water."

"The onion, you say?" The maid tucked her chin, then a chuckle burst from her tightly drawn lips. "Lud," she said with a shake of her head.

Catching Galilea's wrist, Fanny pulled her hand closer, and peered thoughtfully down her nose at the small cut.

"Well now, 'tisn't so very bad after all," the maid commented, "I've some salve that should make it right again. You just sit right 'ere, and I'll fetch it."

Galilea watched Fanny go to a nearby shelf and, standing on her toes, drag down a battered, old hatbox. Bringing the box to the table she set it down and opened the lid. Inside were a variety of items; balls of yarn, a jar of buttons, bits of cloth and embroidery thread, all sorts of ointments and homemade remedies.

"Ah, 'ere's wot I'm lookin' for." Fanny picked up a small tin of salve then reached to the bottom of the box and pulled out a handful of clean, white linen strips—most likely the remains of an old, worn sheet.

Fanny administered to Galilea's injured fingertip with the utmost of care, frowning in concentration while she tenderly applied the salve.

"You see?" Galilea couldn't keep from saying. "I even bleed like everyone else—now, don't I?"

The maid chose to ignore the somewhat gloating statement. Reserving any comment, she diligently bandaged the non-fatal kitchen wound.

When she had finished, Fanny turned Galilea's hand this way and that, examining her handiwork. "There now," she said. "That should do nice— Wait a minute . . . wots this?"

The maid referred to small clover-shaped discoloration on the inside of Galilea's wrist.

" 'Tis a birthmark, I believe," Galilea replied with a shrug. "Ollie told me it has always been there."

"Ollie?" Fanny wrinkled her brow. " 'Oo's this Ollie? Your brother?"

"Nay, Ollie was . . ." Galilea fell prey to a bittersweet streak of melancholy. "He was a wise and kindhearted tinker who raised me. I looked upon him as my father."

"He didn't truly sire you then?"

Galilea noted Fanny was still gripping her wrist and paying a great deal of attention to her responses.

"No," Galilea answered. "Actually, someone simply gave me to him when I was newly born."

"Who?"

Galilea searched the woman's inquisitive expression. Her own curiosity suddenly arose over Fanny's sudden interest. "Ollie never knew her name—'twas a young woman who stopped him on the road hereabouts."

"Somewhere round *'ere,* you say?" Fanny's eyes glazed over and drifted off to one side.

"Aye." Galilea watched the maid closely now. "That's all Ollie ever told me—except that the young woman said the oddest thing when she shoved me into his arms."

Fanny met Galilea's gaze evenly. "Lud. Wot was that?"

The maid cocked an ear, waiting for a reply.

"She told Ollie that I'd be killed if he did not take me away."

Fanny turned white. Glancing at the clover-shaped birthmark again, she let go of Galilea's wrist as if she had held a hot, iron fireplace stoker.

"I 'aven't time for all this prattle," she stated abruptly, then rushed to one of the shelves, grabbed a basket, and headed for the back door. "I need some herbs from the garden for me stew. You just finish wot you're doin', and run along. I'll never get me work done sittin' and chattin' all day."

Galilea looked from the empty doorway to her bandaged finger and back again. Fanny was gone before Galilea had a chance to sort through the woman's scrambled thoughts.

She had a feeling the maid was purposely avoiding her. Fanny hadn't wanted her to probe her mind. It was rather obvious that the maid had been disturbed by something she'd said. And there *was* one distinct impression that had sifted through Fanny's troubled thoughts before she had ducked out the kitchen door.

The woman had most definitely seen Galilea's birthmark *somewhere* before.

Galilea came to the library that evening without being summoned. She made no sound as she entered, yet Collin knew she was there even before he turned his head and saw her standing in the doorway.

He rose from his desk in a gentlemanly gesture, and without a word she ventured further into the room, her hands clasped tightly at her slim waist.

A smile tugged the corners of Collin's normally grim mouth at the sight of the fairy-queen. He was glad she had come—and had an urge to tell her so. Stepping toward her, he very nearly took her hand and kissed it. In the midst of reaching forward, he remembered himself though and stopped just short of touching her hand.

Lacing his fingers behind him, he rocked back on one heel. "Good evening, Mistress Jones," was all he could manage to say.

She gave him a small, shy smile. "I am aware you did not call me here, sir. You see, I sensed I might be needed." She paused, fixing her beautiful, heart-shaped face with a most serious expression. "I have an inkling Wee Lizzie might leave you be as long as I am with you."

While she had spoken, Collin's attention had stalled on the thickness of her incredibly long lashes. A space lingered after her last statement, for it took a few moments for Collin's brain to calculate what she had just told him—'twas something about her coming to ward off Wee Lizzie, he believed.

"Oh . . . certainly, most certainly. Do come in," he blurted out, hoping his reply might be reasonable enough to sustain whatever it was she'd actually said. For good measure, he motioned toward the comfortable chair beside the fireplace. "Please, sit down."

Collin watched her take her seat, admiring the way she nearly glided across the room. He stood motionless, staring at her for almost a full minute after she sat down—then he realized what he was doing and made a move toward his desk.

Collin's backside had barely met the seat of his chair when he stood up again and lifted an eyebrow in the fairy-queen's direction. "Um, do you need anything? Tea? Would you like some tea? I could ask Fanny to—"

"No, thank you," she said, cutting him off in a gracious manner. She peered pointedly at the journal lying open on his desktop. "Shouldn't you be working?"

Collin's gaze followed hers.

"Yes, I *should* be working," he replied and settled determinedly in his chair. He picked up his pen, dipped it in the ink well, and poised it above the page.

Instead of writing though, he ended up tapping the pen-point against the top of his paper, creating tiny black ink spots in lieu of wordy lines of inspiration.

Looking up from the messy blotches he had made on the page, he found Galilea watching him intently.

"Do you read?" he asked on impulse.

"Is this question relevant to your work?" she asked in return.

Collin's gaze wandered over his desk and landed on the poem he had entitled "The Fairy-Queen," lying in plain sight.

He slid his hand over the hastily scrawled title, smiled at Galilea, and answered, "No. It is not relevant to my work. I was simply going to suggest you might want to select a book from Lord Luxley's impressive library." He waved a hand toward the well-stocked bookshelves at either end of the room.

"Oh, I see." Galilea lowered her gorgeous eyelashes, and Collin frowned at the distraction. "My watching you work bothers you."

"Quite frankly, it does," Collin answered, then shoved a hand through his hair. What had he been thinking—*offering her tea*? Good God. Perhaps he was the one going mad.

"Very well, then," Galilea commented, barging into his thoughts once more. "I shall read."

Collin tried to concentrate on the notes he had made the night before, but his eyes trailed after the fairy-queen as she walked to the shelf, promptly selected a book, then returned to her chair.

It was quite some time before he did more

than merely pretend to focus on the unfinished poem in front of him.

By and by, though, Galilea's presence worked its magic once again. Collin drifted into the peaceful state he had experienced the previous night when she had sat with him.

He sank into a deep meditative mood, and within the next stroke of the grandfather clock in the foyer, he had gone from doodling in his journal, straight into writing line after line of prose that could have only come from some heavenly source.

Galilea peered discreetly at Collin above the book she was supposed to be reading. She had gone through the motion of flipping each page at proper interments. She had even read a phrase or two, here and there. The poetical works of Lord Byron simply didn't hold her interest the same way the handsome master of Luxley Manor did.

And so the evening passed, with Galilea nestled contentedly in the warm glow Collin provided while she secretly observed him. As the candles in the room burned low, he became lost in his writing, and in the process, Galilea was assured he had quite forgotten she was still there.

Which was why she was a bit surprised when, some several hours later, he stretched his arms high above his head and suddenly met her gaze.

He blinked a few times, appearing to have just awakened from a deep sleep.

"Dear lord," he said, rising from his chair.

"I apologize for keeping you up so late. Time tends to get away from me when I work."

" 'Tis quite all right." Galilea smiled, thinking how charming he looked in his weariness—with his hair disheveled from periodically raking his fingers through it, and his eyelids stationed at a lazy level. "I'm not at all tired," she said earnestly.

He smiled then and slid a hand over the dark shadow of whiskers shading his jaw. "In that case, perhaps I can persuade you to join me in a glass of sherry."

"I should love a bit of sherry."

A glance of uncertainty passed between them, before Collin moved to the fireplace, took the decanter from the mantle, and poured the drinks.

He raised his brow as he offered her the filled crystal glass. "What should we drink to?" he asked.

Galilea cast her eyes toward the ceiling. "How about . . . toasting Wee Lizzie?"

"Wee Lizzie?" Collin frowned, considering the suggestion. "Why should we toast Wee Lizzie, pray tell?"

Galilea couldn't very well say, "If it weren't for Wee Lizzie, we might never have met," so she opted for an alternative motive. "Well . . ." She let her gaze wander around the room, making up a reason as she went along, "Lizzie was extremely well-behaved tonight, was she not?"

"Aye, well, I suppose we should be thankful there were no disturbances to speak of this evening." Collin answered with caution, his dark, slanted eyebrows dipping even deeper. "Do you not agree, we should pay her some tribute for that?"

Collin grinned broadly. He lifted his sherry in salute. "If you wish, Mistress Jones." Then he clinked his glass against Galilea's and spoke into the air.

"To Wee Lizzie, whoever, whatever, wherever, you are."

Galilea took a small sip, while Collin tossed down half his glass.

Hooking an arm on the mantle, he cocked his head, acknowledging Galilea's sudden sober mood.

"Why, Mistress Jones, you do not seem at all appreciative of this poet's humble tribute to the infamous Wee Lizzie. Was it not to your liking?"

Galilea held her glass at mouth level, breathing in the intoxicating aroma of the sweet sherry. She lowered her gaze from Collin's and peered down into the amber liquid.

"You should not mock her, you know."

Collin's smile faltered but did not completely disappear.

"You're right, of course," he said, then stared off into the distance. "Now, let me see . . . ah, here's one you might like better. How about this?" Clearing his throat, he raised his glass again. "To the lovely Wee Lizzie, the ghost of Luxley Manor . . . respectively."

He looked to Galilea for her approval, and

she could not keep from being amused by his foolishness.

"Better?" he asked with a feigned, hopeful expression.

"Somewhat," Galilea answered, trying to temper her smile.

Collin viewed her for a long quiet moment with a slight twinkle lighting his eyes. Then he settled down on the rug on the floor in front of the fireplace. Setting his sherry and the decanter on the hearth, he reached out, took the poker from the stand, and stirred the dying embers. A few blue flames licked upward between the logs, casting a pale lavender light into the room.

Collin replaced the fireside tool, then bracing his forearm on one bent knee, he watched the low blaze rise and turn to gold. A soft, yellow illumination outlined his profile.

"I saw her, you know." Galilea's voice blended gently with the popping and crackling of the fire.

Collin swiveled his head toward her. Yet, instead of the cynicism she had expected to see on his face, his expression displayed—well, if not quite acceptance, at least an openness, if you will—an *eagerness* to understand.

"Our resident ghost, you mean?"

"Aye, in a room on the third floor."

He absorbed that information with shades of his original skepticism reappearing on his features. The corners of his mouth tipped upward in a cocky fashion, making it quite clear that he wasn't sold on the idea just yet.

"And of course, you thoroughly explained to the little pest, I hope, that she is not, under any circumstances, to play any further games in the library. Did you not?"

Despite his effort to make light of the matter, Galilea maintained an air of seriousness. "Actually, there wasn't time to discuss either *you* or the library. Lizzie was there one moment, and gone the next, you see."

By the narrowing of Collin's eyes, Galilea could tell, he was truly striving to grasp the possibility that Lizzie was more than a figment of the household's imagination. He simply hadn't reached any absolute conclusion yet.

Galilea smiled indulgently. She set her book and glass of sherry on the table beside her, then straightened in her chair and clasped her hands in her lap. "You still cannot believe in such things as spirits who might have gotten lost in this world on their way to the hereafter, can you?"

Collin grimaced.

"No," he said, then grabbed the poker once more and piddled with the fire. "I cannot believe in such things. Books—" he circled a hand above his head"—do not simply up and fly about all by themselves. Yet, since coming to Luxley Manor, I've seen it happen with my very own eyes. Even so, I've no doubt whatsoever that a *ghost* is not responsible."

Collin tossed the poker on the hearth, finished off his sherry, then pinned Galilea with a perplexed look tinged with agitation. "There must be some logical explanation for the disturbances going on in this house. But I have thoroughly examined every possible theory I can think of—and nothing, *nothing* I have come up with to date, can even come close to explaining the bizarre incidents I have witnessed here."

Galilea pondered on the enormous amount of frustration radiating from Collin. She sensed his almost painful dilemma, over whether or not souls could linger on earth, stemmed from a much deeper anxiety—perhaps developed long ago.

"May I ask what made you so dreadfully close-minded?" she inquired upon impulse.

At first, Collin had no answer.

"I don't honestly know," he began, then without much further thought he added, "My father, I suppose."

Collin poured himself another drink and held the glass up, peering through the amber liquid at the fire. "He was ... *a Scot,* you know. Very ..." He paused and licked his lips, seemingly searching for just the right words to describe the man. "Very strong-willed, I guess you could say," he remarked at last, then shrugged and took a swallow from the glass. "*Bullheaded,* to put it bluntly."

Collin wrinkled his brow, appearing to tolerate the memory of his father, rather than cherish it.

"Did the two of you get on well together?" Galilea prompted.

A small bitter smile creased Collin's lips.

"Not at all. As I recall, we never had a discussion, actually. He always dictated, and I always held my tongue. My father was a professor at Oxford, you understand. He was obligated to see that I was well-educated. Any other facet of my life was of very little importance to him."

An ache pricked Galilea's heart. She knew she was prying, possibly steering Collin through some remembrances he might just as soon want to forget. Yet, an uncontrollable need to know everything about him drove her onward.

"What of your mother?" she asked. "Winston mentioned . . . well, he may have been teasing me, of course—but with Winston one never knows." Dropping her gaze, Galilea laced and unlaced her fingers together in her lap. "He said you told him your mother was a Cheyenne Indian. Is that true, or were you merely jesting?"

Galilea peered up at Collin to see his cocky little smile was back.

"It's true," he replied, after stretching the suspense for a matter of seconds. "My father met and married my mother during an expedition of the American West. Does that startle you?"

"No. I find it fascinating, really."

"Do you?"

"Yes."

"Why so?" Collin followed the question by taking a long, slow drink of his sherry, staring all the while at Galilea above the brim.

He was playing a tantalizing little game with her, she realized, his eyes steadily gleaming and riveted to hers.

He was conveying interest in her with his low-lidded gaze, yet Galilea had to wonder if he might merely be trying to divert her from the subject of his mother.

"I've never met an Indian before," she stated, doing her best to appear calm while her heart raced at a breathless pace inside her breast. "What . . . what was she like, your mother?"

Collin seemed a bit offended that she had remained unaffected by his attempt to seduce her with his eyes. Leaning back and bracing himself upon an elbow, he set down his empty glass, then stretched his long legs out in from of him, and crossed his ankles.

"If you must know, I really wasn't very well-acquainted with my mother. Not that she neglected my primary needs, mind you." He focused his attention on dusting ashes from his shirt sleeve as he went on. "It's just that she kept to herself and was so quiet and reserved that one could have easily forgotten that she was in the house."

Collin tilted his head toward Galilea once more and arched an eyebrow. "And just in case you're thinking of asking, I have no brothers and sisters. I am an only child. Now, is there anything else you wish to know, Mistress Jones?"

Chapter 9

Galilea could think of no words to say that could soothe the burning hurt in Collin's eyes. She had barged into his life uninvited this evening and had opened old wounds from his past.

Collin was making a valiant attempt to act as if he didn't care, but Galilea was sure that behind the wall of nonchalance lived a boy who'd grown up in a home without affection. She pitied that child inside the man.

Not for Luxley Manor and all of Collin's worldly goods would Galilea have traded Ollie's love and her days of happiness traveling in the peddler's wagon.

She closed her eyes feeling quite ashamed for coaxing Collin into revealing more and more about himself. 'Twas her own selfish, secret yearning to possess a small part of him that had pressed her to do it.

"I should apologize, Master MacLaine," Galilea said softly, squeezing her eyes a little tighter shut. "I seemed to have forgotten my place here. It was very improper of me to be prying into your affairs. Be assured, sir, it shall not happen again."

The room fell silent except for the hissing and popping of the fire. When several endless seconds passed without Collin uttering a word, Galilea opened one eye and peered at him.

He was grinning from ear to ear. "You apologize very prettily, Mistress Jones."

Becoming a bit tiffed that he hadn't taken her seriously, Galilea frowned. "I truly meant it most sincerely."

"Oh, I'm sure you did." Collin stretched lazily toward the decanter of sherry and poured himself another drink. "But, what is it they say?" He furrowed his brow, raising a pointer finger above the brim of his glass. "Isn't there some rule or something pertaining to turnabout being fair play?" He paused and squinted thoughtfully. "There *is*, if my recollection is correct.

"Cheers, Mistress Jones," he said, tossed his drink down his throat, then wrist-wiped his mouth and smiled brightly. "I believe it's my turn to ask you questions now."

Galilea glanced at the sherry she had barely touched sitting on the table beside her. Picking up the glass, she took a sizable sip then set it aside once more.

"Very well," she replied, looking straight into Collin's playfully glinting eyes. "Ask away."

"Hmmm." Collin tipped his head and examined the ceiling. "What extremely personal question might I ask you? Let me think . . ."

Galilea squirmed in her chair. She would have enjoyed this game much better, if the inner-workings of Collin's brain were clearer. As it was, she could only scan the surface of what he was thinking. Whether 'twas by conscious effort or not, he secured his deepest thoughts behind some impenetrable, locked door.

"Ah, I've got it." Collin narrowed his eyes on her. "Are you ready for my question, Mistress Jones?"

Galilea made a small unsure movement of her head.

"Very well, then," Collin said, apparently taking her hesitant gesture as an affirmative sign. "You must tell me your deepest secret."

"My . . . *secret*?" Galilea's cheeks stung with heat. Could it be, she had not been quite as clever as she had assumed about keeping her fascination of him hidden? In trying too hard to conceal the fact, had she gone too far in the opposite direction—making herself even more conspicuous?

"How *do* you do it, Mistress Jones?"

Collin's voice broke boldly into her worrisome thoughts. Galilea widened her eyes. "Do what?" she asked, in the dire hope that his original inquiry had merely been misleading.

"Read minds and all, of course. What else would you think I was talking about?"

"Oh, nothing," she said much too quickly, then fussily smoothed her skirt.

Eying her suspiciously, one side of Collin's face lifted with a grin.

"It is your turn to tell all, Mistress Jones." He took a swig of his drink, and his mildly amused expression moved gradually into a contemplative one. "Is there some scientific method you use, I mean? Or, is it done by sheer willpower? I really am curious to hear your own personal views on the matter."

As Galilea considered his questions, she looked past Collin at the dancing flames in the fireplace. "I've never really given much thought to precisely how it works, actually. Perchance, I shall never know," she remarked, then guided her gaze back to his. "I simply see pictures . . . hear voices in my head. Truthfully, I have very little control over it a'tall. The visions come and go as they please."

Digesting her words, Collin's features took on the most serious of his appearances so far. He shifted from his lounged position, sitting upright.

"Can you read *my* thoughts *now*?" he asked as he lowered his lids a fraction, his eyes fairly piercing hers.

Galilea's pulse pumped hard in her throat. The way he looked at her made her cheeks flame.

"I cannot read your mind at all," she answered honestly. She glanced at her hands, nervously at play upon her lap. "You block your innermost thoughts. Not just from me, from everyone, I'm thinking. You hold others at bay—keep them away."

"I do?"

"Yes," Galilea replied quietly.

"Hmmm, that's odd," he commented pensively. He stared at her for a short spell longer, then rolled onto his side and propped his head up with a hand. "I didn't know I did that." After a few more moments of pondering, he shrugged, adding, "I wonder why I would do such a thing since I've nothing at all to hide in my somewhat boring past."

Perhaps because you've been hurt somewhere along the way, Galilea wanted to say, though she refrained from doing so. She had no wish to drudge up any more memories that might upset him.

"Well now, 'tis awfully late, I fear." Stifling a yawn, Collin pushed up off the floor, then dusted his britches. "This has been quite an interesting evening, wouldn't you say, Mistress Jones? Or should I call you Galilea, after everything we've shared about each other this evening? Yes, I believe I should. And you shall call me Collin—no more *Master MacLaine*—sounds much too stuffy, don't you agree?" He gave her that charming little smile of his as he stretched out a hand to help from her chair. "Come, sweet Galilea. I shall escort you to your chambers at once."

Without any hesitation at all, Galilea wrapped her fingers firmly around his. It felt so right, his hand in hers, the warmth of it seeping inside her. Before she realized she did so, she lifted an unguarded expression, and looked directly into his pale gray eyes.

Collin's smile faded. He gave her hand a gentle squeeze and tugged her to her feet.

He stood much taller than she did, and as she rose she tilted her chin to keep his face in view. His gaze darkened to a smoky silver, then dipped and held steady on her mouth.

The room suddenly seemed to lose all its air. Galilea labored for each breath. Her heart beat hard, jarring her breast, and the floor beneath her moved like a wave on the ocean.

"Galilea?" Collin's deep voice sounded as if it came from the far end of a tunnel.

A soft sigh was all she could manage upon trying to answer him.

"Are you quite all right?" Collin asked, furrowing his brow. "You look a bit green around the edges. I think we should get you up to your room immediately."

Total humiliation flooded over Galilea.

Muttering that he hoped she wasn't coming down with a cold or something, Collin led her from the library.

Little did he know, what she had *caught*, she highly suspected, was a fatal case of lovesickness.

Collin bid Galilea a brief good night after being assured she was quite all right and simply weary. He had examined her with great concern as he had guided her up the stairs. By the time he left her at her chamber door, he had offered at least three separate apologies for keeping her up till such an ungodly hour.

Galilea paused just inside the room, waiting, listening for Collin to continue on down the hall to his own chambers.

For several seconds, she heard nothing, as if he stood on the other side of the door.

When next his footsteps fell, he moved in the opposite direction toward the stairs.

Galilea wondered if he might be returning to the library to resume his work without her. Although she knew she had no right to have such feelings, the thought of his doing so *hurt*.

'Twas well past midnight, somewhere in the wee hours of the morning, Galilea would guess. The room was dark, but she did not bother lighting the candle to change into her nightclothes.

Disappointment weighed her down as she climbed into her bed. She might have sank deeper into her disturbing notions concerning Collin, had she not dozed off a moment after her head touched the pillow.

She could not have been asleep for long, for the room was still veiled in darkness when her eyes suddenly opened wide.

The shutters of her window flapped open with a strong gust of wind, blowing an icy chill into her chambers.

Galilea tried to sit up, but she found her body would not perform the function. In her paralyzing state, she could do no more than watch while the cold, eerie current of air billowed the curtains.

Then she heard it—the whispering again.

Sounding faraway and tinny, the voice rushed in through the window with the wind and swirled about in fragments from one corner to the next in the fashion of a hurricane.

The pieces of phrases gathered eventually, centering at the end of the bed.

A strange calm came over Galilea as she lay there unable to move. Her gaze riveted on the footrail.

There, before her very eyes, a small pillar of what appeared to be white smoke formed. The figure took shape gradually, evolving into the image of the young girl that Galilea had glimpsed on the third floor of the manor.

Lizzie. Galilea tried to speak, but could not. She could only watch and listen as the ghost of Elizabeth Luxley's lips moved out of sync around the whispering.

Lizzie struggled, obviously striving for a frequency Galilea could understand. When, at last, the warbled words matched the movement of the little spirit's mouth, the whispering became clearer . . . more distinct.

"Don't go, don't go," Lizzie pleaded, her long blond curls dancing in the wind. *"Don't let them make you go away. I need you. I need you . . ."*

The child's voice echoed with a soft agony.

Galilea's heart went out to the little girl. She strained against the invisible bonds imprisoning her body in the bed. She yearned to reach out to Lizzie, comfort the poor child in some way. Just the same, even if she could have broken free of the force that held her, Galilea instinctively knew that her hand would have passed right through the transparent figure.

"Don't go," Lizzie repeated in a hauntingly pitiful tone. *"She knows. She knows. But she won't tell."*

She? Who? Galilea tried in vain to transmit the numerous questions racing through her mind, for her larynx still would not work. *Who, Lizzie? Who won't tell? And what is the secret they keep?*

While Lizzie's mouth continued moving, the whispering faded into the sound of the rushing wind. The filmy form of Elizabeth Luxley grew dimmer and dimmer until it vanished completely.

The wind calmed to a breeze, and the room's temperature warmed considerably. An instant tingling drained into Galilea's limbs. Flexing her numb fingers, she sat up on the side of the bed.

As the deep purple shadows of dawn crept into the room, Galilea attempted to decipher Elizabeth Luxley's desperate message from the grave.

The ghostly phrases played over and over in her head. Lizzie had used the pronoun, *"she." "She knew." "She* wouldn't tell."

What woman, or girl—for that matter, could Lizzie have been speaking of? Elenore? Widow Luxley, perhaps? Who? *Who* knew *what* about Elizabeth Luxley and refused to tell?

Galilea sighed and ran a hand over her face.

On the edge of exhaustion, she was no closer than before to solving the mysterious reason Wee Lizzie had been doomed after death to roam the halls of Luxley Manor.

She stood and arched her back, releasing the tension that had settled in her spine. Then she crossed the room to close the window. As she leaned out to catch hold of the shutters though, something in the middle of the garden below caught her eye.

Collin sat in an oversized wicker chair, his long legs stretched out in front of him. Bathed in the lavender shadows of the coming daybreak, he stared off into the far horizon.

Galilea propped her elbow on the window sill and braced her chin on her hand. He looked so solemn, so lonely. Yet, Collin was a man of many faces, she deduced. It was altogether possible even the one he wore now, sitting alone in the garden, might be a mask.

Galilea knew she had not imagined the sensuality in his eyes earlier in the library. She had responded to the look—indeed, she had overreacted, to be more precise.

She could not believe he had not felt something in those endless moments that their gazes had held steady. He *had*. Of that much, she could be certain. Yet instantly after the incident, he had elected to act as if the attraction that had passed between them had never happened.

And he was wise to do so, Galilea had to agree, at this point.

There were numerous reasons why the two

of them should not become involved. For her own good, in fact, she should follow his example from this day forward. She should avoid standing so close to him in the future. And no more gazing directly into those alluring, pale gray eyes.

Galilea pushed away from the window sill. For a matter of minutes, she stood in the shadows, watching the first rays of sunlight burst above the dark horizon . . . and cast a soft golden glow over Collin MacLaine.

Then, she closed the shutters.

For the last couple of mornings, Collin had taken up the habit of watching the sun rise. He found a certain amount of peacefulness in the ritual. In the quiet time just before daybreak, with the sweet solitude of the garden surrounding him, he collected his thoughts.

In the midst of this dawning day, as on the previous mornings, his reflections had come full circle and centered once more on Galilea.

He had experienced an intense desire for her earlier in the library. With every gesture and expression of her innocent sensuality, she had enticed him. He had come so close to taking her into his arms . . . so close to sampling her tempting lips.

Collin furrowed his brow, his passion at war once again with his logic and practicality.

He had considered the notion of marrying, someday. He had expected to eventually come across a suitable young lady who might share his household and bear him children.

On the brink of thirty-four, he was after all, most assuredly of a marriageable age.

He had anticipated experiencing a normal amount of physical attraction toward the woman he would choose to live his life with. Then again, from a logical standpoint, he had always known the crowning selection of his mate would be based upon common interests and beliefs. In a word, *compatibility* would be the determining factor when his time to enter into a nuptial agreement came at last.

Somewhere in the distance a rooster crowed. Collin squinted as the bright orange brim of the sun crested the skyline. He flexed his fingers on the arms of the wicker chair.

He had never dwelled long or often on the subject of matrimony. Why he did so now—and in conjunction with meandering thoughts of Galilea, he'd no idea. The fairy-queen, as lovely as she was, was nowhere close to the woman he had envisioned as his future bride.

Yet, Galilea provoked unexplainable feelings inside him. Genuine heart-stirring feelings—and not merely of a carnal nature.

Aye, her clear green eyes affected him. He would be lying if he denied it. Her pink, luscious lips tormented him as well, at each and every encounter.

But there was so much more to the fairy-queen than simple surface beauty.

Collin respected her extraordinary mind . . . her views . . . her unearthly wisdom. All the other eligible maidens he had looked at prospectively, while charming and sufficiently skilled in the art of domestication, had been, quite frankly, *boring* when it came to conversation.

Granted, he and Galilea were worlds apart in their theories concerning almost any subject in general. Still, the idea of spending eternity engaged in an intelligent lifelong debate was suddenly rather appealing.

The fire that Galilea ignited in his breast was, of course, an added bonus. Whether 'twas true and endearing affection he harbored for the woman known locally as the madwoman of the meadow, he could not say. He had once thought himself above such sentimental nonsense.

Actually, he had always considered "love" to be an over-rated fantasy of sorts. The few wedded couples with whom he had been acquainted, including his own parents, had most definitely not seemed to be all that madly in love. Therefore, in Collin's opinion, *love,* while sounding wondrous in the form of prose and poetry, was essentially unnecessary in marriage.

The morning sun climbed in the sky, spreading a golden warmth over Collin's face. Meanwhile, as he mulled over the aspects of love and matrimony, his thoughts wandered back through the evening's discussion with Galilea.

She had said he was a private person—and most generally, he was. Yet, he had spoken to *her* without reservation about his miserable youth. 'Twas a matter he had refrained from telling anyone before.

Oddly, he presently felt somehow cleansed—as if years of a bottled-up resentment over his parents had been uncorked and set free.

Collin had never contemplated how his father's willfulness and his mother's apathy might have affected him later in his life.

He did so now.

His family had never been close. They had not been affectionate. Spontaneous hugs or pats on the back had never been cheerfully bestowed upon him as a boy. Collin had been expected to excel at his studies. When he had done so, he'd not been rewarded by any means. On the other hand, upon the few occasions when his marks had been less than perfect, there had most assuredly been hell to pay.

Looking at his youth in retrospect, Collin could plainly see why, as his publisher had so bluntly put it, his work "lacked feeling."

He, himself, he realized with a grim twist of his mouth, *lacked feeling*.

All the same, during the hours he had spent writing with sweet Galilea sitting nearby, he'd obviously gone through some sort of emotional metamorphosis. For, without a shade or shadow—true, heart-wrenching, unmistakable emotion had glided from his pen onto every single page.

* * *

'Twas noon the next day when Galilea awakened. She was rousted from her bed by a knock at her chamber door.

Upon Galilea's beckon to enter, Fanny poked her head in.

The maid's eyes widened at the sight of Galilea's ragged sleep-induced appearance.

"Oh dear, 'tis truly sorry I am to be disturbin' your rest, miss. Thought you'd be up and about by now. I'll just come back a bit later, I will."

"No, no, Fanny. 'Tis quite all right," Galilea insisted as she sat up on the edge of the bed and shoved a tangled mass of hair from her face. "Please—" she paused in the midst of the sentence to stifle a yawn "—do come in."

The maid scurried into the room toting a tray of tea and biscuits. "Thought you might be 'ungry since you didn't come down for breakfast."

Galilea sensed an immediate conflict going on inside the woman.

Setting the tray on the bedside table, Fanny glanced awkwardly at Galilea, then began fussing in a nervous fashion with the napkin and silverware.

The maid was easily readable. Not even a trace of fear was detectable in Fanny, yet she was definitely in a hurry to do her job and leave the room before Galilea noticed her nervous state.

As Galilea eyed her intensely, an onslaught of mixed emotions flowed from Fanny. 'Twas a blend of confusion and great anxiety that told Galilea the maid was terribly worried over some grave indecision.

"Fanny is there something amiss with you?" Galilea inquired with concern. "Perhaps, I could help, if you'd care to talk—"

"Oh no, miss." Fanny straightened and focused a glazed stare on Galilea.

Galilea had a strong impression the maid wanted to impart something of dire importance . . . something that actually involved Galilea herself.

Fanny opened her mouth, but on the very verge of revealing her dilemma, she pressed her lips together, sealing them tightly closed.

"I cannot, miss," she sputtered with a glistening of tears shining in her eyes. "I simply can't."

"Fanny, wait," Galilea called as the maid hurried toward the exit. "Please, if there's something you wish to tell me—"

Fanny stopped in the doorway. She turned slowly,wringing her hands together at her waist. " 'Ave mercy, miss. Don't ask no more o' me. I've no place else to go, if I was t' lose my position 'ere."

With one last pleading look in Galilea's direction, Fanny whirled and was gone.

Galilea furrowed her brow, completely perplexed by the maid's parting actions. What on earth could Fanny have possibly said that might endanger her long-standing position in the Luxley household?

With a shake of her head, Galilea rose from the bed. She chose a light muslin day dress from the wardrobe and slipped it on. As she brushed out her hair her thoughts shifted back and forth between the maid's curious behavior and poor Wee Lizzie's unfortunate plight.

Taking a first-things-first approach, Galilea finally decided to concentrate her efforts for the moment on solving the mystery surrounding Elizabeth Luxley. Later on, she might visit Fanny, and once again offer her services as a friend.

She left the room in search of Winston. The butler seemed to be the only one in residence at Luxley Manor eager to discuss Lizzie's life and death. Everyone else had avoided even the most innocent of questions concerning the little ghost.

Chapter 10

After finding Winston nowhere in the manor, Galilea spied him at last outside in the vegetable garden.

She made her way through the neatly planted rows of greenery to where the old butler stooped beside a cluster of potato plants.

Absorbed in his task of pulling weeds, he took no notice when Galilea stopped beside him. Locking her hands behind her back, she smiled down upon the bald spot on the crown of his head. "Hello, Winston," she said.

The butler looked up, a bit startled by the intrusion.As he shaded his eyes against the bright sunlight with a hand, his perturbed frown swiftly changed into a stiff, formal smile.

"Why, Mistress Jones," he said, straightening and dusting the dirt from his hands. "What a pleasant surprise. Is there something I can do for you, miss?"

"Yes, actually there is." Galilea reached out and caught a leaf of one of the potato vines between a forefinger and her thumb. "I was wondering if I might persuade you to tell me more about Elizabeth Luxley."

Winston's smile faded and he narrowed his eyes. "So you've seen our little Lizzie, have you?"

"Aye, we've met." Galilea took great interest in brushing mealy bugs from the leaf she fingered. "Lizzie spoke to me, Winston," she said, then glanced sideways at the butler.

Winston curled his lower lip thoughtfully. "Did she, now?"

"She did indeed." Dragging her gaze from the potato plant, Galilea focused her attention on the old butler. "Which, in truth, is why I've come to you. I'd like to help the poor wee spirit find rest, you see. But in order to do so, I need to know more about her."

"Lizzie was a most precious child," Winston commented, letting his gaze drift to one side. "I was highly fond of her."

After a short pause, the butler's tired old eyes met Galilea's once more. "And I should very much like to assist you, but in all honesty, I'm not certain I can. I believe I've already told you all there is to tell."

Galilea, nibbling the inside of her lip, was silent and pensive a moment. "Perhaps, if we simply talked about her, you might recall something you may have forgotten about Lizzie."

"Perhaps." Winston furrowed his bushy silver eyebrows, then shrugged. "I suppose we could have a go at it. Would you mind terribly if I continued my work while we talked?"

"Not at all."

Shoving his rolled-up sleeves higher, Winston resumed his haunched position. " 'Tis an unending chore, this weeding," he muttered.

Galilea seated herself on the ground beside him. "I wasn't aware tending the garden was part of your duties," she said as she gripped a sprig of stray grass and pulled it up by the roots.

"It isn't part of my duties, actually. After the gardner left, I merely took it upon myself to tidy the garden now and then, though I'm not very apt at it as you can well see. It simply breaks my heart to have the old place go to ruins."

Winston kept his head down, digging diligently in the dirt as he spoke. Galilea imagined that, had he lifted his face, a certain sadness would have surely shown upon it.

"Now, what is it precisely, that you want to find out about our Lizzie?" he asked, promptly changing the subject.

Galilea considered what inquiries she might start with. "Well, her mother, for instance. You said she was an actress. Did you know the woman? What did she look like?"

Winston peered from beneath his brow at Galilea and her rapidly fired questions. "I never saw the young woman myself. To my knowledge, she was attended by none other than the midwife."

"Do you happen to recall the actress's name, by any chance?"

Winston shook his head. "I'm not all that

certain that his lordship even knew her by anything but her stage name. If he did, 'twas a secret he took with him to the grave."

Galilea pressed her lips into a tight line. Remaining silent for the next few minutes, she worked along the row of potatoes with the same tenacity as the butler at her side.

She wasn't exactly sure what she'd been fishing for by pursuing answers concerning Elizabeth Luxley's mother. She simply assumed if she began at the point of Lizzie's birth and moved upward through the years, some tidbit of importance might surface.

"What about the midwife?" she asked impulsively. "Do you think she would speak to me if I paid her a visit?"

Winston stopped pawing in the dirt, and turned a blank stare Galilea's way. "The midwife who delivered Elizabeth died some years ago, Mistress Jones."

Galilea's disappointment must have been evident, for he laid a hand upon her shoulder and added, "I'm afraid I'm not being much help, am I?"

Giving him a small smile, she patted his wrinkled hand. "I do not wish to seem ungrateful, Winston. It's just that I had so hoped to gain more insight on Lizzie. I must learn what it is that keeps her here and find some resolution so the child's soul can journey on to its rightful place."

Winston nodded as if he hadn't the proper words for reply. He did not speak until he was well into his gardening again.

"If I do remember something, I shall be sure to tell you," he said quietly, without looking up. "It would do my heart good to have our Wee Lizzie at peace."

Galilea's lips curved slightly upward as she observed him. Behind the stiff staunch facade he presented to the world, he was a good and kind man.

Following his example, she too returned to scratching in the rich brown earth and tugging weeds. The task was soothing, yet it sent her thoughts traipsing off along still another path of unanswered questions.

"Winston," she said against a background of chirping birds, "would you have any idea what might be troubling Fanny?"

"Fanny?" Winston shifted, moving to the next potato plant, his forehead wrinkled in consternation. "No, I can't say I do. But come to think of it, she has been acting a bit odd, lately." His eyes brightened then, and he set his gaze on Galilea's. "Oh dear. Perhaps, I do, after all."

Galilea waited for him to go on.

After a moment's more consideration, however, he simply shook his head, and went back to work tilling the ground of the garden.

Galilea sat back on her heels and frowned at him. "Winston," she said, her voice an octive higher than normal. "You cannot just say, 'oh yes, perhaps I do,' and not continue. 'Tis awfully rude, you know."

The butler's hands stilled in the dirt. "'Twould it not be even worse of me, mistress, to contribute to the spread of vicious rumors?"

"Rumors? What rumors?"

Winston sighed, and tilted his head to one side. "I refuse to repeat such untruths, Mistress Jones. Now, if you will please just stop—"

Galilea placed a hand upon his arm. " 'Twill go no further, I swear it. Nor am I a gossiper, Winston. It's just that I wish to help Fanny if she's in some sort of trouble."

Winston sighed again, heavily, this time. "Fanny is in no peril, mistress—at least not to my knowledge. I fear she's merely upset over what she may have heard recently."

"And what might that be?" The butler stalled, and Galilea tucked her chin. "Come, Winston, give over."

Winston turned and searched her face. "You must promise not to tell Master Collin. Scot, that he is, I've come to admire him . . . for *some* strange reason. I shouldn't want to see him damaged by all these silly lies."

Galilea crossed her heart. "On my honor, I shall not breathe a single word you say to another living soul."

"Very well, then." Winston pinched his mouth tightly before going on. "As if Luxley Manor didn't have a dark enough past—concerning the circumstances of Lizzie's death and all—now the villagers are talking about Master MacLaine."

"And they are saying?" Galilea prompted,

giving his arm a small shake. "What? *What* are they saying, Winston?"

The butler shrugged. " 'Tis all such nonsense, but somehow they've gotten it into their rather lame brains, that Master Collin is . . . well, that he's . . ."

"Just say it, for the love of Saint Peter," Galilea blurted out. "They think he's . . . *what*?"

"Well, they believe he's . . . a creature of the night of sorts." Winston rushed through the sentence then closed his eyes, seemingly humiliated he'd been forced to speak the words. "The people in the village, you understand, are a superstitious lot," he went on, prying one eye open on Galilea. "And it's somehow gotten out that Master Collin stays up all night and sleeps throughout the day. 'Tis all a bunch of hogwash, but it doesn't help matters that he brought *you* to the manor—" The butler's face blanched white. "Er, I mean—"

"You're referring to the notion that I'm supposedly mad, of course." Galilea smiled indulgently. "Yes, I know it's what they say. Do go on."

Winston sniffed and held his aging shoulders erect. "Why, you've more sense than all of those gossipmongers put together," he declared with a lift of his chin.

"Thank you, Winston."

" 'Tis nothing but the truth, mistress." The butler looked past her, narrowing his gaze on the manor. "She's the worst of them, you know," he said, gesturing toward the house.

Galilea glanced over her shoulder. "She?"

"Aye, the widow. 'Tis more than likely all *her* doing, these ridiculous stories going round about Master MacLaine."

After spending the better part of the afternoon in the garden with Winston, Galilea went to the kitchen to wash the dirt from beneath her nails.

Fanny, who was busily preparing supper, eyed her briefly when she entered the room, then the maid turned her back, focusing her utmost attention on her chores.

Galilea scrubbed her hands in silence, wondering if the maid might be lured into conversation. A great deal of anxiety filled the air in the kitchen, and the source of the tension came from Fanny.

"May I help you with supper?" Galilea asked as she dried her hands on a clean towel.

"Nay. 'Tis all but done," the maid answered without so much as a glance in her direction.

"Might we have a spot of tea and chat when you're finished then?"

Fanny whirled around and faced her. She could not hold her brown eyes steady on Galilea's though. "I'm much too busy for tea or chattin'. Beggin' your pardon, miss, but if you'd just leave me to m' work, I'd be ever so grateful."

Galilea sensed a tremendous amount of turbulence in the woman.

Stretching a hand toward the maid, she

took a few steps forward. "Fanny, there is no truth to the rumors circulating about Collin MacLaine, if that's what has you worrying."

Fanny shuffled sideways, ducking Galilea's touch. Wrinkling her nose, she dipped her gaze to Galilea's extended hand. "Rumors? I've 'eard no such rumors. Nor do I wish to."

Galilea furrowed her brow. "But . . . well, you're obviously upset about *something,* and Winston said—"

"Aye, Winston," the maid muttered under her breath. "I might've known 'e'd be at the bottom of this. Now, there's the one you'll be wantin' to chat with."

Pursing her lips, Fanny untied her apron and tossed it on the table. "Go and tell *Winston* your gossip, Mistress Jones. I'll not be listenin' to none of it, I won't."

Fanny strode out the back door upon that note, leaving Galilea standing in the kitchen alone.

Completely baffled over the maid's sudden burst of anger, she leaned a hip against the table and picked up a raw carrot, nibbling it thoughtfully.

If indeed Fanny had not heard the villager's false speculations about Collin, then the maid could not possibly have been upset by the news—as Winston had suggested. Yet Fanny most certainly had her dander up on some account.

And it seemed 'twas Galilea herself who tended to set her off.

Galilea crunched the carrot, pondering the

notion that she had lost the maid's trust almost as soon as she had gained her friendship. She could think of nothing that had happened that might have warranted Fanny's sudden change of attitude toward her. At one point, she and the maid had been civilly chatting and making mutton stew together. The next thing Galilea knew, Fanny was chasing her from the kitchen.

Galilea's thoughts on the matter were interrupted when Elenore swept into the room looking for the maid.

Elenore stopped just inside the kitchen, apparently abit taken aback to find Galilea there.

"Mistress Jones," she said in greeting, gaining her composure rather quickly, and giving Galilea a brief smile. "Have you seen Fanny?"

Galilea slipped the carrot behind her and, shoving away from the edge of the table, straightened her posture. "She just stepped out a moment ago. I'm sure she'll be back straight away."

Elenore looked at the door Fanny had just exited and batted her lashes a couple of times.

"Oh," she said. "Well, would you mind telling her she needn't set a place for Mother tonight. Mother's . . . feeling a bit under the weather, shall we say." Elenore flashed Galilea another subtle but curt smile. "I shall take a tray up to her myself."

Galilea nodded, feeling an odd assortment of emotions stirring within Lord Luxley's eldest daughter. "I shall be certain to tell Fanny as soon as she comes in."

"Very good, then." Elenore started to leave the kitchen at a brisk pace, but stopped at the doorway to the dining hall and slowly pivoted toward Galilea once more.

She frowned and glanced about the room before speaking.

"Mistress Jones, I should apologize," she said in a timid fashion. She clasped her hands tightly against her waistband. "I should not expect you to convey messages on my behalf. You are not a servant here, and 'twas very ill-thought-out on my part to treat you as such just now. Can you ever forgive me?"

Elenore's large brown eyes were quite appealing, and Galilea had a hunch she used them for effect fairly often.

"Of course," Galilea answered. "I was not at all offended."

Relief moved over Elenore's features. Her lips curved upward in what appeared to be a genuine smile this time.

"You are too kind, Mistress Jones. Would you join us for supper this evening? I know you generally like to take your meals in your room, but . . . well, since Mother won't be there—" Elenore's pleasant expression faltered sightly upon saying the word "mother". "I mean, 'twould be splendid to have another female at the table to converse with for a change. Please . . . you will come, won't you?"

Elenore's invitation was most sincere. All the same, Galilea got the strange impression she might be masking other motives behind this friendly approach.

In the end, Galilea agreed to take supper in the dining hall that evening, out of curiosity more than anything else.

"Tell me, Roland," Collin remarked as he struggled to cut the tough venison on his plate, "approximately how many head of sheep are kept on this property?"

"Why, I've no idea," Roland replied, turning his head toward the opposite end of the table.

Collin followed the man's gaze unwillingly to where Elenore and Galilea sat, engaged in their own conversation.

Frowning down at his plate, Collin shoved the less than tender meat aside and tried once more to solicit answers from Roland. "I was going over the accounts this afternoon," he said, "and can see no reason why this estate is not making a profit."

"Really?" Roland commented, completely disinterested in Collin's findings. He lifted his glass and sipped his wine, seemingly much more entertained by the two ladies.

"Have you any more news about the townhouse?" Collin asked.

"Hmmm?" Roland's attention drifted briefly back to Collin. "The townhouse?"

"The townhouse in London. The one you are renovating, remember?"

"Mmm, 'tis still mostly in the planning stages, I fear." Roland answered, his mind focusing again on the ladies.

Collin did not like the man, nor his obvious

ogling of Galilea. Collin himself had done his best to forget the women were present. Yet, admittedly, he too, was guilty of allowing his eyes to stray to the fairy-queen at the far end of the dining table.

He had not expected Galilea to grace them with her presence at supper. She had walked into the hall like a breath of fresh air shortly after the clock had struck seven.

By habit, both men had risen to their feet when she'd entered but before either of them could move to seat her, Elenore had rushed forth and ushered Galilea into the chair next to hers—as far away from the men as possible.

Collin tipped his wine glass, taking the sweet nectar into his mouth slowly and observing Galilea above the brim. He noted she had no trouble choosing the proper fork this time, having gone through this procedure only once before. She had greeted the men politely when she'd taken her place at the table, but she had not spoken directly to either of them since. Elenore had monopolized her attention, drawn her into conversation, and Galilea appeared quite comfortable with the situation as it was.

Collin's purpose in attending this cozy little family gathering this evening had been to corner Roland and Widow Luxley. After examining the account ledger, he had certain questions to ask them. So far, none had been answered. The widow had conveniently taken ill, and Roland was completely preoccupied with viewing the lovely Galilea.

Not that Collin could blame him, really. The fairy-queen did tend to distract one. All through supper, he had glanced her way almost as often as Roland had, albeit much more discreetly.

Each time he'd caught her eye, however, Galilea's gaze had skipped away from his. He found it strange that she was apparently avoiding looking at him for some odd reason.

Suddenly growing tired of Roland's insolent company and being ignored by the ladies, Galilea in particular, Collin drained his glass, then rose from his chair.

"If you'll excuse me," he said. "I believe I shall retire to the library now."

When Galilea started to leave the table as well, he lifted a hand to stop her. "Please, Mistress Jones, finish your supper at your leisure. I've some revisions to make on last night's work. I'm sure I can manage on my own for a while."

Tension settled between Galilea's shoulder blades as she watched Collin leave the dining hall. Having him seated at the same table had somehow fortified her.

Alone with Elenore and Roland, an edginess crept upon her. She stared at the half-eaten portions on her plate and no longer felt hungry, but rather a bit queasy.

"Phillip tells me the two of you had a nice little chat the other day."

Elenore's statement trickled into Galilea's

silent brooding over Collin. She looked up at her hostess with a blank expression, trying to absorb what the woman was saying.

"My son, Phillip," Elenore repeated, apparently aware Galilea's thoughts had been elsewhere. "He tells me you spoke with him . . . in the cemetery. Roland forbids him to go there, don't you, dear?" She looked down the length of the table, addressing her husband.

"Indeed, I do," Roland replied. " 'Tis no place for the boy to be playing."

Taking his involvement in the discussion as an invitation to join the ladies, Roland picked up his plate and moved to the empty place on the other side of Galilea.

A burst of fire flickered in Elenore's eyes as her husband sat down. Although Galilea sensed a strong streak of jealously in the woman, Elenore swiftly masked the green monster behind a sickly sweet smile.

"I, on the other hand, do not discourage Phillip's interest in the cemetery," she went on. "I feel that death is part of life and should not be totally discounted even at Phillip's tender age."

Elenore had kept her gaze fixed upon Roland's face as she voiced her opinion, all but daring him to disagree. When he did not rise to the challenge, she shifted her attention to Galilea once more.

"Phillip said you visited Elizabeth's grave."

The comment was presented in the manner of a question, and left Galilea no choice but to answer.

"Yes, I did." Galilea twisted the napkin in her lap. She felt hemmed in by the couple, and once again she experienced a wave of uneasiness.

" 'Twas such a terrible tragedy losing my only sister," Elenore said, her voice quivering slightly. "I truly hope you will succeed in helping her find rest."

"Well, of course you do, my dear," Roland put in. His lips twitched at the corners as he viewed his wife, and his eyes glistened with the effect of the wine. Of a sudden he slid his gaze to Galilea. "Elenore is simply terrified of the ghostly little twit, did she mention that?"

Seeing Elenore's eyes glaze with tears, Galilea reached out and covered the woman's hand with her own. "I shall do everything I possibly can, Elenore, to bring Lizzie to her peace. This, I promise."

Great compassion moved over Elenore's features as she looked at Galilea. "Thank you," she whispered sincerely.

Once assured Elenore had calmed, Galilea took the next available opportunity to excuse herself and made straight for the library.

When she knocked at the study door and received no response, she entered the room uninvited to find Lizzie up to her marvelous mischief again.

Head bowed and cradled in his hands, Collin sat at the desk, evidently trying not to acknowledge the book flapping open and closed in midair some three feet in front of him.

"Lizzie, shame on you," Galilea said in a stern tone from the doorway. "Haven't I told you not to bother Master Collin while he's working?"

Collin peered over his shoulder at the sound of Galilea's voice. "So nice of you to join us, Mistress Jones," he said with an ill-humored smile. "Do come in. Your so-called ghost doesn't seem to want to listen to me."

Galilea walked forward and, rounding the desk, snatched the floating book out of the air and snapped it closed. "Did you ask her nicely?" she inquired with a lift of an eyebrow. "Or did you yell at her?"

Collin leaned back in his chair and folded his arms across his chest. "I did not *yell,* I merely shouted."

"Well then, there's the problem, you see," Galilea remarked as she moved to the bookshelf and replaced the book. "You only antagonize Wee Lizzie when you raise your voice."

"Are you suggesting I be cordial to a phantom who has done nothing but pester me from the very first day I walked into this room? By God, this is my library now—*my* home. I shall not put up with any more of these childish pranks, do you hear? And I shan't be kind in telling . . . *whoever's* . . . or *whatever's* at fault so."

Frowning profusely, Collin straightened his posture. "Why, may I ask, are you smiling at me like that?"

Galilea sucked in her lips, but could do nothing about the mirth lingering in her eyes.

Crossing the room, she sat down in the chair beside the fireplace and clasped her hands in her lap. "You're beginning to believe in Lizzie, aren't you?"

It wasn't a question. It was an accusation. And from the look on Collin's face, he was not at all pleased by Galilea's observation.

He merely grimaced in answer to the question.

Galilea lifted her brow. "Doesn't it feel good to free yourself from such skepticism?"

Collin lowered *his* brow. Picking up his pen he poised it above his open journal. "I do not wish to discuss the matter any further, if you don't mind. I've work to do."

For the remainder of the evening, Collin kept his head down and his gaze fastened on his writings. He refused to glance even once in Galilea's direction.

Yet a vision of her eyes, so full of childlike innocence, kept blurring across the page and blocking out his thoughts. After several hours of scribbling the same line over and over, he gave it up and decided to quit work early.

Lifting his head, he caught Galilea watching him. She quickly lowered her gaze to the open book she'd started reading the night before.

"I believe we should have our sherry now," he said with a smile. He closed his journal, rose from his chair, and stretched.

"None for me this evening, thank you," Galilea replied, coming to her feet. "If you're finished, I should like to go up to my room."

Collin's lazy smile faded. "Well, of course, if you wish—" He cocked his head, noticing she seemed a bit nervous. "Have I . . . done something to offend you, Galilea?"

"No," she said, without meeting his gaze. "Nothing."

"Are you sure?"

"Quite. Good night, sir." Moving at a brisk pace, she skirted around him and hurried out the door.

Collin stared after her for a long moment, then walked to the mantle and poured himself a sherry. Settling into the chair beside the fireplace, he nursed his drink, and brooded over her hasty departure.

In the past, he had cherished his solitude. He had never minded being alone. Tonight, however, a great surge of loneliness filled him.

He had looked forward to Galilea's company this evening—just the two of them, sharing a quiet moment by the fire, engaged in conversation.

Collin stirred uncomfortably in his chair. Somewhere deep inside, he realized he had hoped for something a bit more intimate than conversation to progress between them tonight.

He had wanted to take Galilea in his arms . . . *needed* to hold her . . . *needed* to feel the length of her sweet body pressing against his own.

Collin closed his eyes and tilted his head back, completely baffled by the complex emotions gushing inside him. He had been alone too long, he feared. For now, when after all these years, his heart was on the verge of reaching out to another—he was at odds as to how he should proceed to win Galilea's favor.

Chapter 11

Galilea practically ran all the way up the stairs. She realized, as she did so, that she was running more from herself than from Collin.

She had tried so hard not to look up from her book this evening, but her eyes had had a will of their own. Once her gaze had latched on to Collin, she'd been lost. She'd given in without a fight to the fantasy of running her hands through his long silky hair. Even worse, she had been imagining how his lips might feel against hers, when he'd raised his head and met her gaze.

A small amount of her humiliation ebbed once Galilea reached her chambers and closed the door behind her. The room seemed a safe place to hide her heart.

Moving woodenly to the wardrobe, she slipped out of her dress and changed into her nightclothes. She wanted nothing more than to crawl into bed and let blessed slumber drown her. Yet with so many disturbing thoughts rushing in circles in her head, she knew 'twould be forever before she fell asleep.

Hoping to soothe her tattered nerves, she walked to the bureau and picked up the brush. She stared unseeingly into the looking glass above the bureau and began combing out her hair with methodical strokes.

Logic told her 'twas best to battle with all her might against these highly improper yearnings she was having for Collin MacLaine. For in truth, as soon as Wee Lizzie's spirit left the house, Galilea herself would be put out of the manor, as well. Facing the world alone again would be hard enough without the added load of a broken heart.

Still, somewhere deep inside, another, more gentle voice would not be silenced and warned that love such as this might never pass her way again. Though much softer in volume, the gentle voice advised Galilea to revel in these wondrous feelings whilst she had the chance—and promised a lifetime of cherished memories she could carry away with her when she left.

Galilea closed her eyes and dragged the brush slowly through her hair, trying desperately to decide which voice she should heed.

Of a sudden, a strange tingling came over her, stalling the brush halfway through her hair. Opening her eyes, Galilea looked into the mirror and saw the filmy form of Elizabeth Luxley standing behind her.

When Galilea whirled around to face the

ghost, Lizzie no longer stood in the same position but was clear across the room by the door.

"She knows. She knows," Lizzie warbled, her pale, lovely features etched with pain.

"Who, Lizzie? Who knows?" Galilea took a step toward the transparent figure, spreading her hands wide in appeal. "Who knows about you, Lizzie? You *must* tell me."

Lizzie turned and glided through the closed door as if it wasn't there, disappearing into the corridor.

Galilea snatched her robe from the bedpost and, shoving her arms into the sleeves, dashed after the little ghost.

Upon opening the door, Lizzie was nowhere in sight.

When Galilea stepped into the hall, however, she spied Lizzie at the top of the stairs, beckoning to her.

Lizzie moved as if running in slow motion, yet her feet never quite touched the ground. Galilea followed her down the stairs and through the dining hall.

The ghost of the little girl led her into the kitchen, stopping at the mouth of a narrow hallway that housed the servant's quarters.

"She knows," Lizzie repeated and pointed down the corridor toward Fanny's room. *"She knows,"* the spirit of Elizabeth Luxley echoed over and over again.

The child's haunting voice began to fade out. The outline of her see-through form dimmed, and then she was gone.

Galilea braced her legs against the floor to keep her knees from buckling. For the longest time, she stood wide-eyed and dazed in the middle of the kitchen, staring down the servant's hall at Fanny's closed door.

She had to talk herself out of simply barging into the maid's quarters and waking the woman at this ungodly hour. In the end, Galilea's rational side convinced her 'twould be best to wait until morning to confront Fanny, after she herself had taken time to think this new revelation through.

Galilea was up and dressed the next day before the rooster in the distance had finished crowing. Though she'd hardly slept a wink, she could not wait another minute to talk to Fanny.

'Twas much too early for anyone else to be up and about, and the hall was as quiet as a tomb. The grandfather clock in the foyer ticked loudly in the stillness. Galilea crept down the stairs, flinching each time her foot fell upon a creaky step.

She heard someone stirring in the kitchen as she approached the doorway, and glimpsed Fanny padding back and forth as she prepared breakfast.

"Good morning, Fanny," Galilea said upon entering.

The maid jumped and whirled around at the sound of her voice. Then frowning, she pressed a hand to the base of her throat. "Lud. You like to've scared me outta m' wits.

What on earth are ye doin' sneakin' about at this hour?"

Galilea stopped at the end of the work table and traced a knothole in the wood with a fingertip. "Did you sleep well?" she asked, gazing intently into the other woman's eyes.

"And why wouldn't I?" Fanny sniffed, turned her back, and continued rolling out her biscuit dough.

Galilea edged around the table and seated herself on one of the high stools directly across from Fanny.

"We both had a visitor during the night, you and I," she commented, watching the maid's face closely.

"Hah! Not I, missy," Fanny remarked without looking up. She moved her rolling pin to and fro with a vengeance. "Nary a soul was in *my* 'umble room, save me, last eve—"

"Lizzie came to visit us both."

Fanny froze upon that note and lifted a startled gaze to Galilea's. "W-wee Lizzie . . . w-w-was in my chambers?"

"Well, not *in* your room exactly, but at your door." Galilea tilted her head to one side and straightened on the stool. "She claims you know a secret, Fanny."

The maid frowned and puffed out her cheeks, then took to rolling out the dough again. "Well, she's mistaken, Lizzie is. Truth to tell, there ain't many secrets 'round 'ere anymore. Seems everybody knows everybody else's bloody business these days. Lud, gossip travels 'ere-abouts faster'n—"

"Lizzie led me to your room last night, Fanny," Galilea broke in, ducking her head to meet the woman's gaze. "She specifically pointed to your door and told me you know something. Obviously, Lizzie wanted me to ask you about this certain secret."

Fanny's eyes widened on Galilea's, and her rolling pin rocked to a stop.

"I'm sure Lizzie would want you to reveal whatever it is you're keeping from me," Galilea went on. "And you know how upset Lizzie can be when she doesn't get her way."

The maid's face flattened. She stumbled backward from the work table, hugging her ribs.

Galilea hastened around the table. Catching Fanny's elbows, she steadied the woman and guided her into a nearby chair.

"What is it, Fanny?" she asked. Stooping beside the maid, she peered up into her frightened features. "What is it you're hiding? Tell me."

Tears gathered in Fanny's eyes, and a wretched sob broke from her throat. "She . . . she's your . . . s-sister."

Galilea felt the floor shift beneath her. Fanny had whimpered the words. Surely, Galilea had misunderstood her. Yet, when she settled her roving gaze again on Fanny, the maid nodded.

" 'Tis true, I swear it. I was there when the two o' you were birthed."

Galilea came to her full height. Opening

and closing her fists at her sides, she eyed the maid suspiciously.

"I was there, I tell you," Fanny insisted. "See here, and I can prove it." Reaching out, she grabbed Galilea's hand and swiveled it palm up. "See this mark?" Fanny pointed to the small clover-leaf shaped discoloring on the inside of her wrist. "Aye, 'tis a birthmark, all right. You were born with it, I'm telling you. Lizzie had the same marking—only 'twas on the other arm."

Galilea stared at the birthmark in disbelief. It took her a moment to digest Fanny's statements. What the maid claimed seemed impossible.

Twisting her wrist from Fanny's grasp, she strode a few feet away, then turned, cradling her marked arm.

"Twins?" Galilea heard herself ask, though her own voice sounded foreign and faraway. "Are you saying . . . Lizzie and I . . . we're not just sisters, but . . . *twins*?"

"Aye. And I should've told you, I know that now. I'd no right t' keep it from ye, but—" Fanny's lower lip puckered, and she broke down once more. Covering her face, she wept into her hands.

Galilea closed her eyes, striving to maintain her balance. If indeed Elizabeth Luxley was her sister, that could only mean . . . that old Lord Luxley was her natural father. 'Twas a concept a bit too large to swallow.

Yet . . . it all made sense somehow—the powerful attachment she felt to Wee Lizzie . . .

the unseen lure that had drawn her to the meadow on Luxley land.

Grasping the possibility of the idea, Galilea opened her eyes on Fanny.

The maid rocked back and forth, her boney shoulders quivering with her sobs.

Galilea went to Fanny, and kneeling on the floor before her, tugged the woman's hands from her face and held them tightly in her own.

"Please, tell me all of it," she said pleadingly. *"All of it."*

Fanny sniffled, then nodded. "Aye, 'tis time." She took a deep shuddering breath before going on. "I was just a lass myself at the time—no more'n twelve. But I used t' help m' Auntie May bring babies into the world 'ereabouts, I did.

"I remember, 'twas a cold October night. Bitter cold. Your mother, she 'ad a 'ard time of it, she did. Auntie May saw it comin' and sent for me." Fanny's red-rimmed eyes glazed over. "Auntie May believed in the old ways, you understand."

Galilea furrowed her brow. "The old ways?"

"Aye." Fanny met her gaze briefly. " 'Tis said two wee ones sharin' the same womb, also share the same soul. 'Twas the old way t' do away with one child, so that neither would walk the earth with only 'alf a soul."

Wrenching her hands from Galilea's, Fanny clasped them tightly in her lap. "After the birthin' . . . Auntie May placed your small fragile body int' my arms. She told me I was t' take you to the river, put you in a toad sack filled with rocks . . . and toss you far out int' the water."

Picturing such a scene, Galilea's stomach knotted. "You were to drown me?"

"Aye. But I could not. I went to the river's edge, I did. But I 'adn't the heart t' do away with such a precious little thing. That's when I 'eard the wheels of a wagon rollin' down the road. And I ran t' catch up with it, I did. 'Twas a tinker, I could tell by the pots and pans rattlin' on the side of the wagon. 'E had a kind face, so I bid him take you, so's you shouldn't be kilt."

"Ollie," Galilea whispered, her own eyes brimming with tears now.

"Aye, 'twas 'im, I s'pose," Fanny said. "I never knew his name."

"His name was Oliver Jones," Galilea felt compelled to remark. "And yes, he was indeed a dear, kind man."

The silence of the morning seeped into the kitchen, along with a soft golden ray of sunshine coming through the window. There was nothing more to be said.

Rising to her feet, Galilea squeezed the maid's shoulder lightly then turned and left the room.

Galilea walked up the stairs automatically, her feet touching the steps without thought. She hadn't any idea of where she might be going, she only knew she had to keep moving. 'Twas the only way to ward off the notion that she was dreaming.

Lizzie . . . Elizabeth Luxley was her sister—the very part of Galilea that had always been missing—the reason she had always felt so separated . . . so different.

Ollie had put it kindly by calling her *special.* He had reassured her often that *the knowing* was a blessed gift, not a curse, like some were prone to believe.

Yet, even with all the love and confidence Ollie had given her, she had still felt as if she'd walked about the world lacking something all the rest of mankind possessed—a normal mind, free of voices and visions.

Now, she had an inkling the hollow, empty space inside her . . . belonged to Lizzie. That certain something she had been lacking had been her twin sister—or perhaps, at least the knowledge that a sister did indeed exist.

The conception that she, too, was Lord Luxley's daughter washed over Galilea, consuming her to the point that she strode right past her chambers without noticing.

Without conscious effort, she scaled the third-floor stairway, not knowing she had done so until she stood before the door to Lizzie's room.

The door opened all by itself.

Accepting the gesture as a formal invitation, Galilea entered the chambers.

The scent of blooming tea roses swirled around Galilea in a light wind that sifted through her hair. A child's bubbling laughter immediately drew her attention to a shadowed corner.

Lizzie, her small form clearer and more distinct than ever before, sat atop a large wooden crate, stockinged legs swinging to and fro. In her arms, she cradled the battered stuffed bear, stroking his shaggy fur ever so tenderly.

Galilea glimpsed her as she had once been—so full of life, so long ago.

But here and now she was only the empty shell of a child.

"Lizzie," Galilea whispered, moving closer to the figure and stretching out her arm.

In a delayed response, Lizzie continued petting the toy bear. As if gradually becoming aware of Galilea's presence, she lifted her head slowly.

When Lizzie's gaze met hers, Galilea's heart doubled in size. 'Twas as if she were looking into an angel's eyes.

In small measures, Lizzie's hand moved forward and merged with Galilea's. Though no solid form touched Galilea, a warm, glowing force radiated through the tips of her fingers.

There was no need for words between them. They both knew their origin now. They knew who they were and where they had come from. And for this single fleeting moment, they were together just once more.

Galilea wished to hold onto her sister forever. Now that she had found Lizzie, she did not want to let her go.

Nevertheless, the voice of reason told Galilea that she must set her sister's spirit free. Lizzie no longer belonged on earth. 'Twas a faraway place awaiting Elizabeth Luxley in the realms of heaven.

A heavy pressure settled in Galilea's chest as she curled her hand into a fist, breaking contact with her twin's fingertips.

"You can go now, Lizzie," she said around the swelling at the base of her throat. "You've stayed here all these years . . . waiting for me to come. You have fulfilled your destiny by telling me who I am. Go now, and find the peace you seek . . . the blessed rest you deserve."

Galilea backed away from her sister's form, prepared to watch Lizzie disappear for all time.

The only thing that vanished though was Lizzie's smile. Tucking her feet beneath her, the child curled into a ball atop the wooden crate.

"No-o-o, not yet . . . not yet," Lizzie wailed pitifully. *"It is not finished. I cannot leave. Not yet . . . not yet."*

Books, toys, and various other objects took flight in the room, as if suddenly caught up in a small hurricane.

Covering her head with her arms, Galilea dashed from Lizzie's chambers to keep from being bashed by the articles flying about at random. The door slammed open and shut behind her as she ran down the hall. Leaving the third floor, she half-slid, half-stumbled down the stairs and did not stop until she reached the quiet confines of her own quarters.

Once inside her room, she fell across her bed, closing her ears to the sound of the continuing racket on the floor above.

Yet Lizzie's words played over and over in her mind, and would not be silenced. *It is not finished . . . I cannot leave . . . not yet . . . not yet . . .*

Collin walked cautiously into the library, as he generally did these days. He had most recently begun to pause in the doorway and scan the room for signs of ghostly activity.

Since nothing at all was flying about, he assumed 'twas safe to enter. He moved with bold steps to his desk and sat down in his chair.

Collin pulled out his notes and attempted to go over them, but his mind continually strayed from work. He kept glancing up from the pages from time to time, expecting some sort of nonsense. The evening's ritual disturbance was long past due, and the uncommon tardiness set him on edge. He feared that if the ghost of Elizabeth Luxley *was* the culprit, she might be planning some truly special prank this evening. And, quite frankly, he detested surprises.

Tonight, however, the library appeared almost too quiet for comfort.

Collin laid down his pen, tilted his chair back, and peered at the ceiling. As odd as it seemed, he was going to miss the alleged spirit of Wee Lizzie when she was gone. She did at least liven up the manor.

Collin smiled, disbelieving he had actually approached the possibility of ghosts. But—how was it Galilea had put it?—it honestly *did* feel good to get rid of some of his stuffy old skepticism. Made him feel years younger. In fact, he was feeling so chipper, perhaps he wouldn't write at all tonight. Perhaps, he would simply spend the evening engaged in charming conversation with Galilea.

Returning his chair to an upright position, Collin glanced at the door. He took out his pocket watch, checked the time, then looked at the door again. Galilea had never been this late before. He couldn't imagine what could be keeping her.

After waiting close to half an hour more, Collin worried something might be amiss and decided he should look in on Galilea. Just as he rose from his chair, the library door opened.

"I'm sorry, sir," Galilea said quietly, moving into the room with her head bowed. "I fell asleep and—"

"Galilea, look at me." Collin was aware of her distress even before she lifted her face. For reasons beyond him, he knew her eyes would be swollen.

"Have you been crying?" he asked, crossing the room to where she stood.

Galilea tried to turn away, but Collin caught her by the shoulders.

Her bright tear-glazed eyes met his for a brief second. Then she ducked her head again.

"Yes," she answered, not bothering to deny it. "I have been crying. But 'tis nothing to concern yourself with, sir. I'm here now, and you can go on with your work. I'll just—"

"Galilea." Collin caressed her soft, smooth cheek, then hooking a finger beneath her chin, lifted her face. "Would it be presumptuous of me to ask why? I mean, I would hope that you could consider me your friend."

Curving his lips upward slightly, he added, "And not that I'm bragging, mind you, but the majority of my comrades would testify that I am, if nothing else, an extremely good listener."

Galilea cracked a smile at his clever remark. "Aye," she said, wiping the corner of her eye. "I suppose I should tell you all I've learned, considering you brought me here to do just that."

"Of course, you should." Collin guided her to the chair by the fireplace then dragged his desk chair next to hers.

Settling into his seat, he tugged a clean handkerchief from his breast pocket and handed it to her. "Now, do tell me, Galilea. What is it that's caused all this weeping?"

"Well," Galilea began, " 'Tis Lizzie. She—"

"Wait." Collin lifted a finger. "Just one moment, please." Giving Galilea a lop-sided smile, he stood, grabbed the decanter and two glasses from the mantle, then sat back down. "If this has to do with Lizzie, I'd best have a sherry first," he said, pouring himself a drink. "Would you care for one?"

She shook her head.

"No? Then do go on." Taking a generous sip of the liquor, he gave her his full attention. "I'm ready now."

Collin adored the way she fidgeted. In fact, he suddenly realized there wasn't anything about her he didn't adore.

"Lizzie . . . is my twin sister," she blurted out.

Collin's study of the way her hair tumbled over one shoulder in a mass of blond curls came to an abrupt halt. He furrowed his brow. "What?"

"I said, Lizzie—"

"Is *your twin sister*?" Collin finished, thinking surely he'd heard her incorrectly.

"Aye," Galilea replied, proving him wrong. "You see, Fanny's aunt was the midwife who delivered us."

Collin's mouth fell wider open as she went on with the story. By the time the tale had ended his chin nearly touched his chest. Upon noticing he was gaping, of course, he adjusted his expression, attempting to recover his dignity.

"Well," he remarked, assuming he should say *something* after such incredibly shocking news. "I . . . I can certainly understand how you would have been affected . . . how learning you were born a twin and had a sister might . . . move you to tears."

Collin was rambling on like a fool, he

noted. Reaching for his drink, he finished off the remainder of the glass.

"'Twas not the knowledge I had a sister that made me cry," Galilea commented softly. "It made me very happy to learn Lizzie was my twin."

Collin searched her face. She seemed so tranquil, so at peace with herself for the moment, then a shadow passed over her serene features.

"You see, I thought, when I found out who I was—who *Lizzie* was, that perhaps she could leave this world and go on to her just reward." Galilea dropped her gaze to her lap and twisted her hands into the fabric of her skirt. "But, I was wrong. My knowing about her, her knowing about me, was not the key to freeing her soul from the manor. There's more."

"More?" Collin asked, trying hard to follow her evaluation of the bizarre situation.

"Aye. Another secret, I think." She peered at Collin, and the agony etching her beautiful eyes tore at his heart. "Lizzie told me as much this afternoon. She said she *could not* leave yet."

Collin stared into the fire, pondering Galilea's irrational statements. He didn't believe in ghosts. But he did believe in Lizzie. Was it possible to harbor both opinions at the same time? 'Twas a most confusing matter, indeed.

At present though, he was more concerned with Galilea's well-being. She looked completely miserable, sitting there fretting over what might be causing her sister's spirit to linger on earth.

Collin set his mind to work. There had to be a reason Elizabeth Luxley's soul still roamed the manor. What could a seven-year-old child want to convey so badly that she would forsake heaven's glory to do so?

Collin slid his gaze to Galilea and reaching out, laid his hand over the nervous fingers in her lap. "It is a theory of Winston's, you know, that foul play was involved in Lizzie's death. Could it be true?"

Galilea widened her eyes and fell very still and quiet for a matter of moments.

"I . . . suppose it could," she said at last. " 'Tis not uncommon for a spirit to want justice. Maybe . . . that's what Lizzie wants."

Her expression brightened suddenly, and she clasped Collin's hand tightly between both of hers. "Oh, Collin. It *must* be. I have to find out what really happened to my sister. She'll be free then, I just know it."

Moved by her excitement, Collin leaned forward. "And I shall help you. Together, we will uncover the truth. I promise."

Without thinking, he lifted her hand and pressed a kiss upon her fingertips. His eyes slid closed as his lips savored the sweetness of her skin. He yearned to spread kisses up her arm, across her shoulder, over her mouth.

Galilea sucked in her breath involuntarily. His moist lips pressed firmly against the back of her hand jolted her heart and set her cheeks ablaze.

'Twas a chaste kiss, yet the lingering length made it embarrassingly awkward, Collin realized when Galilea cleared her throat.

Opening his eyes, Collin gave her back her hand. By way of apology, he half-grimaced, half-smiled.

"'Tis getting late, sir," she said with a small bashful grin of her own. "Should you not be writing?"

Encouraged by a twinkle of mutual attraction in her eyes, Collin reached out and fingered a lock of the silky hair cascading over her shoulder. "I've decided not to work this evening, after all," he whispered.

With a quick intake of air, Galilea tugged her curl from his grasp then came to her feet. "In that case, sir—"

"Collin. You're to call me Collin, remember?"

"Very well," she said, edging around the desk toward the door. "In that case, Collin, I shall bid you good night."

Collin smiled after her. To have left the room so flustered, the fairy-queen must have been a bit affected by his charm.

Picking up the decanter, he poured himself another drink, then raised his glass to the empty doorway. "To you, my sweet Galilea. Sleep well, my love."

Chapter 12

Galilea had been both flattered and shaken by Collin's advances. In a quandary over how she should've reacted to his kiss on the hand, she had chosen the easy way out and retired to her room.

She later had second thoughts, however, and wished she hadn't been so quick to leave Collin in his obviously amorous mood. After spending a torturous night of tossing and turning and wondering what might have been had she stayed in library, 'twas nearly dawn before she'd fallen asleep.

Awaking late the next day, Galilea was not surprised upon opening her eyes to find Collin MacLaine's sensual smile still lingering in her mind. His vow to aid her in learning the truth about Lizzie echoed in Galilea's heart.

At the same time, a voice inside scolded she should be thinking about Lizzie, not Collin, and heeding such advice, Galilea climbed from bed.

Dressing hastily, she set out for the vegetable garden.

The day she had worked with Winston

pulling weeds, she had noticed a certain peacefulness had accompanied the task. Perhaps she could recapture that blissful state and, in the process, solutions to all her problems might simply come to her without effort. 'Twas her own opinion that at times, she thought too much.

After making her way down the green leafy rows of vegetables, Galilea picked up the weeding where Winston had left off. Digging in the rich brown dirt and tilling the soil around each plant did indeed calm her. The chore gave her a needed rest from her troubles.

Although, the break from worry did not last long enough.

Galilea had been in the garden less than an hour, she would guess, when an prominent shadow fell across her. Shading her eyes from the sun, she looked up to find Collin towering above her.

"Come on, Galilea," he said stretching a hand out to help her up. "You won't want to miss this."

Completely baffled, Galilea gripped his forearm, and pushed off the ground.

"Miss what?" she asked, wiping her hands on the apron she'd snagged from the kitchen.

Giving her one of his cocky smiles, Collin caught her elbow and steered her toward the manor. "Someone in this house must know what really happened to Elizabeth Luxley. You and I are going to find out precisely *who, what,* and *why.* And here's how we shall go about it."

Collin looped his arm through hers at that point, tucking her close by his side as they walked on. "As we speak, Winston is gathering the Luxley family in my library. Fanny's to be present, as well. We shall all discuss Lizzie's death openly and honestly, revealing our suspicion that she may have been murdered. Surely, one of them must remember *something* odd about the day your sister went missing. At the very least, some tidbit of information could surface that might provide us with a clue as to why the poor dead child's soul is imprisoned here."

Galilea stared at Collin in amazement, listening to him rattle on. He truly had gone through some miraculous transformation as far as his previous misgivings about ghosts were concerned. Gads, at present, he was actually putting his scholarly, diplomatic brain to work at solving the phenomenon.

Collin paused at the base of the stoop that led to the kitchen and frowned at Galilea.

"Why are you smiling at me like that?" he asked. "Haven't you heard a word I've said?"

Galilea bit the inside of her lip and, striving for a more serious expression, shrugged. "Aye, I heard you. And 'tis an absolutely brilliant idea. Now, shouldn't we hurry along to the library?" she asked in conclusion, then ran up the steps ahead of him.

* * *

Everyone else was present and waiting when Collin and Galilea reached the library.

Winston had graciously arranged the required amount of chairs in a semicircle in front of the fireplace. Elenore and her mother were seated next to each other, whispering between themselves. Fanny sat in the chair farthest from them, head bent, and fingers entwined in her lap. Roland stood beside the fireplace with one elbow hooked over the mantle, a glass of Collin's sherry already in hand.

Winston was anxiously dogging the lad, Phillip, who insisted on skipping about the library, handling objects he shouldn't have been touching.

Everyone paused in their pastimes to focus on Galilea and Collin when they walked into the room. Even Phillip, once glancing their way, stopped piddling with the paperweight on Collin's desk.

Out of all assembled in the library, Widow Luxley displayed the most displeasure at being summoned. Elenore showed concern mixed with curiosity, while her husband seemed a little perturbed and somewhat bored with the whole affair.

"Thank you all for coming on such short notice," Collin remarked, playing the perfect host. Sliding his gaze to Phillip, whose chubby little fingers were crawling toward the journal on the desk, Collin added, "You, lad, may be excused. This discussion will not require your being here."

Immediately tucking his hands behind his back, Phillip stood erect, and stuck out his lower lip. "But I don't wish to be excused. I should like to hear what's said." The boy turned his puffy, pouting face toward Elenore. "Can't I stay, please, Mother?"

"No, you cannot," Roland put in before Elenore had a chance to answer. "Now go outside and play, and do not come in until you are called. And do be quick about it. The sooner you do as you're told, the sooner we can find out what this little gathering is all about."

Roland lifted his glass in a toast to Collin. "Am I not right, *Master* MacLaine?"

"Exactly right," Collin answered, unaffected by Roland's smugness. "Do run along, lad," he said as he guided Galilea into the chair next to Fanny.

Phillip stomped a foot. "But, I don't—"

"Do as your father says, Phillip," Elenore commanded in a sharp tone, then softened her voice. "We'll not be long, dear."

After the boy had lumbered from the room, slamming the library door quite loudly behind him, Collin turned once more to his expectant guests.

Tapping a finger against his chin, he moved to stand in the center of the row of chairs. "I suppose you're all wondering why I've asked you here."

"Precisely, young man." Widow Luxley shifted forward to the edge of her seat, her eyes flashing daggers. "Just what the devil is the meaning of this? I'll have you know, I'm under doctor's orders and should be napping this time of day. I've no idea what could be so blamed important that you should—"

"Patience, madam," Collin cut in, raising a hand to shush her. "I will explain." Strolling a casual few steps to where Roland stood propped against the mantel, Collin took the decanter from the man's grasp. "Would anyone else care for a glass of sherry?" he asked.

Only Winston came forth. "Don't mind if I do, sir," he said, accepting a glass from Collin.

After pouring himself and the butler a sherry, Collin set the decanter farther down the mantel out of Roland's ready reach.

Collin took a sizable swallow of his drink, then furrowed his brow. "Now, where was I?"

"You were just about to explain why you've called us together," Elenore supplied, her manner not unkind, though a bit strained.

Widow Luxley grunted.

"Ah yes." Collin braced a boot on the hearth. "Well, you see, Mistress Jones and I have some inquiries to make concerning young Elizabeth's death. We thought if those of you living in the manor at the time she passed on could give us an accurate account of the day Lizzie went missing, we might stumble upon what really happened."

"What really happened?" Elenore echoed. "Whatever do you mean?"

Collin shifted his gaze from Elenore to the

glaring Widow Luxley and back again. "We suspect Lizzie may have been murdered."

"Murdered?" The word rippled from one member of the family to the next.

Galilea watched their reactions closely. Elenore and Harriet registered shock, while Roland merely yawned with disinterest.

"Yes," Collin remarked with a lift of an eyebrow. "We can think of no other reason the child should haunt the manor."

"And you think one of us did her in?" Roland asked, a wry grin spreading across his thin lips. "Is that what you're saying, MacLaine?"

Elenore's large brown eyes widened on her husband. Then she looked pointedly at Collin. "Is it true? Are you actually accusing someone here . . . in this room?"

"Perhaps," Collin replied, dusting a piece of lint from his sleeve. "Perhaps not. We're merely trying to get to the bottom of all of the bizarre disturbances occurring in this house."

"How dare you," Harriet Luxley muttered angrily between her teeth.

"Mother, please," Elenore injected, placing a hand on the widow's forearm. "Do let him finish."

"Oh hush, Elenore." Harriet jerked away from her daughter's touch and narrowed her gaze on Collin. "You didn't even know the wretched child. You, sir, are no kin to this family, *or* Elizabeth, for that matter. You cannot come barging in here drudging up something that happened more than ten years ago.

And you've no right whatsoever to accuse us of anything."

Collin lowered his eyelids in a lazy fashion. "You are absolutely correct, madam, in saying that I am of no relation to Lizzie, and therefore have no claim on answers concerning her."

Setting his drink on the mantel, Collin strolled around behind Galilea's chair and folded his hands over her shoulders. "However, I am speaking on behalf of Mistress Jones, who, by the way, *is* related to the deceased child."

This statement piqued even Roland's interest, albeit vaguely.

Harriet's face paled considerably.

Elenore tilted her head, observing Galilea carefully. "Galilea . . . and Lizzie related?" she whispered. "How so?"

Galilea reached up and touched the back of Collin's hand still resting upon her shoulder.

"I have just recently learned that Elizabeth was my twin sister," she announced softly.

"Preposterous!" the widow shouted, coming to her feet. "Why, I've never heard so much nonsense in a single day! Everyone knows that harlot gave birth to only one child. 'Tis common knowledge."

"Nay, madam," Fanny said quietly, her gaze bouncing between Galilea and Harriet Luxley. "Master MacLaine, 'e's tellin' the truth, all right. I 'elped me Auntie May deliver the both o' them, I did. I was t' do away with this one," she said, gesturing to Galilea.

"But when it came right down to it, I couldn't. So I gave 'er instead to a traveling tinker, thinking we'd never 'ear of 'er again."

"Lies! All of it, lies," Harriet shrieked and whirled on the maid, pointing a finger. "You made it all up, Fanny, you wicked wench."

"Nay, I didn't!" Though Fanny's lower lip quivered, she lifted her chin and looked the widow in the eye. "As God is my witness, I didn't."

"Hmph. I refuse to listen to any more filthy fibbing from the likes of you," Harriet stated, then heaved her buxom frame toward the library door.

Silence reigned supreme for several awkward moments after the widow left the room.

The stillness was broken when something between a laugh and a sob bubbled upward from Elenore's throat. Turning tear-glazed eyes on Galilea, she rose from her chair.

"I can hardly believe it," she said, moving forward to catch Galilea's hands in hers. "The resemblance is so apparent. I cannot imagine why I did not see it before. And now . . . I have another little sister to replace the one I lost."

Galilea experienced a strange sensation radiating from Elenore's cool palms—'twas an odd mesh of sentiment and distorted emotions that, for some reason, Galilea could not read.

Galilea could well imagine how the woman must feel, discovering she had another stepsister after all these years. Galilea herself had been quite disconcerted upon first learning about her own link to Lizzie and was now moved by the notion that Elenore wept as she had.

"What an utterly fascinating tale," Roland commented. "How fortunate for you, Elenore, my dear." He gulped a bit of his drink, then lifted his glass in salute to Galilea. "Oh yes, and I suppose I should welcome you to the family, shouldn't I, sweet sister?"

Galilea did not so much as glance at Roland. He was deliberately being cruel and heartless toward poor Elenore's sensibilities. And Galilea would not give the man the satisfaction of knowing she'd noticed.

" 'Tis a very special day indeed, for me as well," she said, smiling at Elenore. "I have always wanted a sister. What a blessing to now learn, I have *two*."

"Ladies, I'm certain you have much to talk about." Collin's voice came over Galilea's shoulder, his breath fluttering the wisps of hair beside her ear. "I do beg your pardon, but might I suggest you chat a bit later? I should like to get back to the discussion at hand."

Elenore nodded and took the chair next to Galilea, one hand still gripping her newfound stepsister's.

Collin eyed Roland who was eyeing the decanter again. Shifting his attention, Collin let his gaze rove over the remainder of the assembly: Fanny, Galilea, and Elenore, all seated in a row, and Winston, who stood stiffly behind them.

"Now, if you please, I would appreciate those of you who were indeed present at the time, each telling me in turn everything you can remember about the day Elizabeth disappeared. Elenore, we shall start with you."

Elenore wet her lips and squeezed Galilea's hand a little tighter. Her eyes took on a faraway glow.

"I don't recall anything out of the ordinary," she said, then frowned as if looking harder into her memory. "Lizzie often played at the old castle ruins. She liked to pretend she was a princess. She and I used to go there together sometimes and pick flowers along the hillside. But that day . . . I asked her to bring me a nice nosegay, and I stayed behind. I'd wanted to finish a tapestry I was making as a surprise for Mother."

Wrenching her hand from Galilea's grasp, Elenore covered her face and burst into tears. "How I wish I'd been there," she murmured. "If I had, perhaps . . . Lizzie might be with us still."

"There, there, now, madam." Winston stepped forth and patted Elenore on the back, then presented Collin with a pinched expression. " 'Tis hard for us all to speak of that dreadful day, sir."

Collin reached for his handkerchief, but remembering he'd lent *his* to Galilea the night before, he twisted around and snatched Roland's from his breast pocket.

"Here," he said, giving Elenore her husband's handkerchief. "Forgive me, madam, for upsetting you. Please, take all the time you need to—"

"No, no. Do not apologize," Elenore intervened with a sniffle. Accepting the hankie, she dabbed at her eyes. "I'm quite all right, really I am." She gave him a partial smile as proof. "I should like to go on, if I may. I do so want to help."

Roland sighed heavily and rolled his eyes, then shifted his weight.

"Is it necessary that *I* stay for the rest of this?" he asked with a grimace. "Elenore and I had not even been introduced when Lord Luxley's ill-gotten daughter breathed her last breath."

By the brightness of Roland's eyes and his slurred speech, everyone else in the room was quite aware he'd had more than his share of the devil's drink. In fact, as Galilea recalled, he'd been at it even before she and Collin had arrived.

Collin pivoted toward the man, and while clearly restraining himself, his expression of disgust was not so well disguised.

"Roland," he said, his voice dark and threatening, as if he'd like nothing more than to choke Elenore's husband.

Collin paused, appearing to weigh his next words carefully. In an abrupt manner, he reached out and grabbed the decanter from the mantle, strode forth, and stuffed the half-empty bottle of sherry into the drunken fool's hands.

"Do sit down, before you fall down," he said, shoving Roland into the nearest chair.

Raking a hand through his hair, Collin then turned to face the others, and put on a smile. "You may continue, Elenore, whenever you're ready."

Elenore nodded, then took a deep shuddering breath. "Lizzie . . . was missing . . . for three whole days," she stammered, crumpling the handkerchief into a ball in her lap. "'Twas simply horrid, the waiting. They . . . finally found her beneath the old fortress ruins, but she was so terribly ill when they brought her home."

"It seems she had fallen into a sink hole, sir," Winston put in, "and had been trapped in one of the cold, drafty tunnels beneath the castle. Poor child was too delirious with fever to say otherwise."

"Yes," Elenore whispered, staring off into the distance as if she were blind. "And, less than a week later . . . at the tender age of almost seven . . . my dear, sweet sister passed away."

Galilea sat motionless, feeling the blood drain from her face. The phrase, *at the tender age of almost seven,* drummed through her brain. She realized that her own scrape with death had occurred at the very same age. The horrible fever Galilea had suffered for almost a week had left her with the ability to hear things and see things in her mind—to read others' thoughts. She had to wonder, now, if the illness that took Lizzie's life had somehow been connected to the one that had given her the so-called gift of the knowing.

Collin continued his questioning throughout the afternoon. To the tune of Roland snoring in the background, similar accounts of the day Lizzie went missing were repeated by Fanny and Winston. Although told from three different points of view, each summary contained the same particulars. No one had seen or heard anything unusual.

After going over the story time and again, Collin finally took a moment of rest, closed his eyes, and massaged the bridge of his nose.

Taking advantage of the opportunity, Fanny rose and asked to be excused to tend to supper.

Collin raised his head and blinked, as if his thoughts remained elsewhere. He let his gaze drift over the weary group, frowning at the sight of Roland dozing in the chair.

"Of course, Fanny," he said, still rather preoccupied. "I've kept you much too long as is, I see. I do apologize. Please, all of you, carry on with . . . whatever it is you generally do." Leaning back against the fireplace mantle, Collin rubbed his chin pensively. "But if any of you happen to recall anything, *anything at all*, please come to Galilea or me and let us know."

Galilea didn't think Collin even noticed when everyone else filed out of the library.

He appeared to be miles away when she paused in the doorway, trying to catch his eye.

There came a time in every soul's life, she knew, that one needed to be alone to ponder upon certain things. Most likely Collin needed a bit of solitude at the moment.

In truth, so did she—and the manor suddenly felt too confining.

Striding straight out the front door, Galilea walked down the overgrown path that led to the entrance of the estate. She shoved the rusty iron gate open and took to the road in the direction of the castle ruins.

She'd not gone far when a tall shadow stretched out alongside hers on the dirt road.

"Mind if I join you?" Collin asked, falling in step beside her.

Without breaking her stride, Galilea gave him a shy smile. "Not at all," she replied softly.

In companionable silence, they journeyed on at a brisk pace for a matter of minutes.

"May I ask where we're going?" Collin inquired, his lengthy legs taking one step to every two of Galilea's.

"To the castle."

"The castle? So far?" Collin peered sideways at her, furrowing his brow. " 'Twill be dark by the time we get there, you know."

Galilea slanted her gaze to his. "Are you afraid of the dark?" she asked.

Collin shrugged. "Frankly, I am sometimes, I suppose. Aren't you?"

"No." Galilea smiled and stared into the distance. "When I was very small, Ollie convinced me 'twas no need to be afraid of the night or dark places. He taught me that we all have a light that forever shines within us—a light that may grow dim at times, but never quite goes out."

Collin appeared to consider her words. "I believe I would have thoroughly enjoyed discussing philosophy with this Ollie fellow."

"Yes," Galilea murmured, her eyes misting with memories of her old friend. "Ollie was very wise indeed."

Collin and Galilea both fell speechless once more, yet they moved in sync, their mismatched steps fitting together in perfect rhythm.

The sky had turned from shades of gray to purple when the castle came into view. The silhouetted towers stood ominously atop the hill in the twilight.

Collin followed Galilea's lead as she turned off the road and made her way up the grassy slope toward the ancient ruins. Now and then, as they climbed over the boulders jutting from the hillside, Collin would mutter a curse behind her. Upon hearing his labored breathing, she consciously traveled a bit slower.

"Galilea, please . . . promise me something," he said, as they rose above the last cliff wall.

Hiking her skirt, Galilea stepped onto the ridge, then turned and offered him a hand.

"What is it that you would have me promise?" she asked, tugging him up onto the ledge.

Collin bent forward slightly, bracing his hands upon his knees. He peered at Galilea from beneath his brow, and inhaling deeply, took a moment to catch his breath.

"Swear to me," he said in a rather raspy tone of voice, "that you'll not take a notion to go dancing along the bailey wall this evening. Cross your heart and hope to die, or so help me, I'll go no further."

Chapter 13

"Very well." One corner of Galilea's mouth lifted, and a twinkle of humor touched her eyes as she made an *X* on her chest, then raised her right hand. "I promise not to dance upon the wall. But only . . . if you shall promise to waltz with me in the courtyard."

She pivoted and, picking up her hem, raced toward the arched entrance in the bailey.

The fairy-queen moved as if gracefully gliding, her golden hair swinging from side to side across her back—and all the wild horses in England could not have stopped Collin from sprinting after her.

Galilea, he was only now beginning to realize, had cast a spell upon him—the moment he'd seen her dancing on the old castle wall. Here, amidst the ruins of an ancient keep, even while he'd thought her stark raving mad upon that very first, stormy night, he had fallen victim to her charm.

Enchanting laughter trailed behind her, bewitching him all over again. Collin pushed onward, gaining on Galilea just as she reached the center of the cobblestone courtyard. She let out a playful squeal when he caught her from behind, causing an eruption of laughter from him as well.

He turned her slowly in his arms, and she lifted her face to the moonlight. A soft, teasing smile lingered on her lips. Her eyes glimmered with mischief.

Viewing her striking features, Collin's mirth dwindled with an sudden, intense aching in his chest. 'Twas as if, in that instant, Galilea had thrust a sword into his heart.

All rational thought deserted him. Completely consumed by a great need to feel her mouth against his, he lowered his head in small measures—all the while, searching Galilea's gaze for some sign that she wanted him as much as he did her.

Collin's face was within an inch from Galilea's when something close to panic spread across her expression. Abruptly, she pressed a finger to his lips, and a nervous giggle broke from her throat.

"Wait here," she said, then stepped away from him. Peering over her shoulder, she walked off into the darkness, disappearing in the shadows of the castle walls.

Collin ran a hand through his hair, feeling like the fool he was. What on earth had he been thinking? How could he have expected Galilea to brazenly accept his kisses when he'd not gone through the proper courting procedures? He had not even expressed his affection yet, and here he'd taken her into his embrace as if they'd been promised.

"Fool," he murmured beneath his breath, and frowned, thoroughly disgusted with himself.

Galilea was an exquisite woman and should be treated as such. She was an extraordinary human being possessed of mystical qualities. Indeed, she'd worked her magic on him, had she not?

Aye, she most certainly had. Collin reached up and scratched his ear and smiled. *He,* once the king of all skeptics, would believe the fairy-queen could fly to the moon if she but told him so.

Collin shook his head, recalling a time, not so long ago, when he had doubted he *owned* a heart. Mayhap, the old ticker had been there all along—but he'd never noticed it, never *felt* it beating, until the fateful night he'd met Galilea.

A tinny sounding melody began to play, filling the ancient courtyard with a hauntingly beautiful tune. 'Twas the same music Collin remembered from his premiere journey down the road that ran alongside the hill.

The sweet melody echoed all around him. He turned, seeking the source—and found Galilea standing behind him.

"I would ask for this dance, sir," she said, "but 'tis proper, I believe, for the gentleman to do the asking."

A grin stretched across Collin's mouth. He took a step backward, then bowed gallantly from the waist. "Mistress Jones, would you do me the honor of this waltz?"

Galilea lifted her wrist and examined it. "Well, I do see my dance card is rather full . . . but I suppose, I could manage to squeeze you in."

"How kind of you," Collin remarked. With a broadening of his smile, he placed a hand lightly upon her waist, and raising his other arm, clasped her fingertips in his.

Holding her at a chaste distance, Collin waltzed her about the moonlit courtyard. Together, they moved to the tinkling rhythm of the music box as if dancing to a fine quartet of violinists in the grandest of ballrooms.

"You're very light on your feet, Mistress Jones," Collin commented conversationally. "Is there some special beau in your background who taught you to waltz so expertly?"

The outer edges of Galilea's eyes crinkled with a hint of humor.

"No beau," she answered. "Just Ollie."

"Ah, yes, Ollie—a man of many talents, I take it." Collin squinted, viewing Galilea in a more serious light. "You loved him very much, did you not?"

"Aye." Her gaze drifted to one side. "*Very* much," she whispered.

"And has no one else ever won such devotion from you, Galilea?"

Galilea peered up at him. His head was rimmed with silver moonlight and framed by a sky full of stars. Her body moved to the sweet melody of her music box, yet her heart stood still. Yes, secretly, she admired Collin. Perhaps, she did truly love him. But devotion was something altogether different than love. Devotion, in her opinion, required a lifetime commitment—and was a most improbable outcome as far as the master of Luxley Manor was concerned.

"No, no one else," she said, then dipped her gaze to the hollow at the base of his throat.

"I find that hard to believe." Arching an eyebrow, Collin swirled her around. "Someone as beautiful as you must have surely had suitors chasing behind that tinker's wagon, weeping most pitifully for your hand."

Galilea could not contain the sputtering laugh that slipped from her mouth. " 'Twas never like that. Most people thought me odd, and they kept a good distance from me."

"And you kept your distance from them, as well. Am I right?"

Galilea wrinkled her nose, considering that possibility. "Now that you mention it, I suppose I did."

"Did you have no comrades?" Collin asked, slowing his footsteps to accommodate the tune of the music box winding down.

"I had Ollie . . . and Magus, of course." Galilea felt his fingers tighten around her own.

"Magus?"

"Aye, the crow," Galilea answered absently, a trifle disturbed in that instant by the warmth of Collin's palm seeping into her hand.

"The crow?" Collin asked with a perplexed expression.

Galilea focused on the first button of his shirt, trying to veer her thoughts from the potency of his touch. "He's . . . really very wise, Magus is. You should come with me and talk to him sometime."

Collin tucked his chin. "I don't think this Magus cared for me much upon our first meeting."

"Oh, well, he was—" Galilea glanced up at Collin. "He was simply jealous, you see. I'm certain Magus would like you once he got to know you."

"Jealous? A bird . . . of me? Whatever for?"

"Because he thought you and I were—" Galilea lifted one shoulder in a shrug. "Well . . . that we were fond of each other . . . you and I, I mean."

"Well, we are . . . are we not?" Collin's voice was low and husky, and his gaze held steady as he looked into Galilea's eyes.

The music box chimed out its last note, and their dance came to an end.

Yet, neither let go of the other.

Galilea nodded in reply to his question, unable to utter a single word.

"I want you, Galilea," Collin said in a whisper, his eyelids falling to a sensuous level. "I want to kiss you . . . to love you."

Galilea's heart thumped furiously against

her breastplate. Of a sudden she could not take enough air into her lungs.

"You . . . you can't," she stammered. "I mean, no one's ever . . . you . . . you just can't want me, that's all."

Breaking free of his grasp, she turned to flee, but Collin caught her and whirled her around to face him.

"Why would you say such a thing? Tell me," he demanded, tilting her chin so that she met his frowning gaze. "You believe in ghosts. Why should it be so hard for you to accept the notion that I could want you?"

Tears gathered in Galilea's eyes, blurring her vision. "Because, I'm different. *No one* really likes me. They . . . they're all afraid of me. As soon as anyone learns I have the knowing, they think I'm—"

"Of course, you're different." Collin framed her face with his hands, rubbing his thumbs back and forth across her cheeks. "But, don't you see? That's one of the many things that makes me desire you. You are not strange, Galilea. You're unique."

Collin dropped his gaze and stared at her mouth.

Galilea's chest constricted. She could not run—did not *want* to, anymore. What she wanted was for Collin to kiss her . . . and for his kiss to chase away her fears.

She curled her hands into fists against his shoulders, and stood watching and waiting for him to lower his lips to hers.

Collin's eyes shuttered closed as his mouth

brushed as softly as a summer breeze across hers. He took a deep breath, then promptly stepped backward.

"Come on," he said, gesturing in the direction of the road. "We should be getting home. It's late, and we've both had a long, trying day."

He started toward the hill.

Galilea stood still, experiencing a great surge of disappointment. The moistness of his lips lingered upon her own and left her burning for something she could not name . . . something beyond the simple kiss.

Collin turned. "Galilea?"

"Coming," she replied, struggling to keep a frown from forming upon her face.

"I only wish we could have learned more about Lizzie today," Collin commented as she fell in step beside him. "But let us not discuss it tonight—we shall talk of it tomorrow."

Together, they trudged down the rocky slope, both silent until they reached the dark road. There, Collin paused and viewed Galilea quite intently, his strong, handsome features glowing in the pale moonlight.

"With your permission," he said, "might I hold your hand on the way back to the manor?"

During the course of the next week, Galilea returned to the castle daily.

The morning after she and Collin had walked home hand in hand, she'd gone back to the ruins in search of the sinkhole into which Lizzie had allegedly fallen.

The place had been boarded over, and she had no trouble spotting it on the grounds just north of the bailey wall.

From then on, Galilea begin picking wildflowers on her way up the hill and dropping a small bouquet between the slats covering the opening in the earth.

She'd come to the conclusion that her visits to the castle weren't solely based upon paying her respects to her sister's unmarked shrine.

Today, as she sat upon the rocky ledge overlooking the sinkhole that had swallowed poor Lizzie, Galilea realized there was more than one reason driving her from the manor day after day.

Ever since Collin had exposed Galilea as the missing twin of Elizabeth Luxley, the whole household had been set on edge. Although Lizzie's ghost had not shown herself again, nor caused any recent disturbances, her powerful presence lingered like a heavy fog throughout the manor and had affected all therein.

Words exchanged were sharp and curt. Feelings had been sorely damaged, and tempers had flared much too frequently. With such emotions running amock about the manor, Galilea had not been able to think clearly within its walls.

A soft breeze now rushed over Galilea, lifting her hair from her shoulders, and fluttering the tall grass surrounding the flat gray rocks.

In the stillness, the guiding voices in her mind were more distinct.

Unfortunately, the various utterances held conflicting priorities and pulled her in two separate directions.

Her thoughts constantly jumped between her growing affection for Collin and her duty to unlock the mystery that imprisoned Lizzie's soul.

Galilea had so tried to focus on her sister's plight. She'd gone to the third floor over and over again in the past week, seeking answers from Lizzie.

But Lizzie had completely stopped appearing and wasn't whispering anymore.

Galilea closed her eyes, attempting once again to penetrate the barriers that kept her from contacting her twin's ghost. The harder she reached for the pictures and messages that formed in her mind, however, the more distorted the sounds and images became. The visions changed in volume and shape to mirror *Collin's face . . . Collin's voice . . .*

Galilea opened her eyes on the tall stone towers of the crumbling castle keep, yet the master of the manor remained most vivid in her head.

Collin had been courting her over the past few days—'twas the only name she could give his attentiveness. Aye, and with every golden word he'd said, his eyes had shown sincerity.

She might have enjoyed his soft seducement, had she been more certain how she should receive it. As it was, she was unsure what he hoped to gain by such an endeavor. She half-expected him to ask her to stay on at the manor and serve as his mistress.

Worse yet, she feared that if Collin did indeed propose such a notion, she might actually consider the arrangement.

A screeching cry in the near distance broke Galilea's concentration and lifted her gaze to the highest turret where Magus pranced back and forth, no doubt, to gain her attention.

Smiling at the sight of her old friend, Galilea came to her feet and waved to the crow.

For almost a full minute, Magus pretended not to see her, then he casually looked her way and acted surprised.

With a wide spread of his black wings, he sailed toward her and landed atop her head.

Galilea rolled her eyes upward and grimaced. "And I suppose I deserved that, didn't I, you silly bird? I *have* been neglecting you of late." With a giggle, she cocked her arm out in front of her as a perch. "Come on, get down from there, and let me have a look at you."

Magus hopped onto her forearm and immediately gave himself a quick preening for her inspection. After smoothing a few feathers, he looked at her squarely and waited patiently for his apology.

"Oh, very well," Galilea said patronizingly. "I truly am sorry if I've hurt your feelings."

As if the regrets she'd offered weren't quite

good enough for him, Magus turned sideways and nudged his beak into the air.

The crow's unforgiving attitude, for some strange reason, pushed Galilea past a breaking point. Her lower lip began to quiver and a lump rose in her throat.

"Magus, please, don't be angry with me," she whispered, just on the brink of a sob. "Please . . . *help* me. I'm . . . I'm frightened."

Magus ran up her arm to her shoulder and, cooing, nuzzled her ear.

Reaching up, she petted his wing. "Oh, Magus. I don't know what to do. I'm so confused about Collin . . . and I cannot find a way to help Lizzie. 'Tis all spinning round and round in my head."

The crow fluttered from her shoulder onto the large gray slab where she'd been sitting. Pecking at the rock, he indicated she should take a seat and tell him her troubles.

Galilea lowered herself once again to the stone and clasped her hands between her knees.

"Magus," she said, staring solemnly into his darkly beaded eyes, "on top of everything else, I feel the tremor of something terrible about to happen. I don't want to stay at the manor anymore . . . but I must."

The bird paced to and fro for a short while, his head ducked as if he were in deep thought. Of a sudden, he cawed loudly, then took to the air.

Flying in a lazy circle, Magus spiraled

downward and lighted upon the boards covering the sinkhole.

Galilea sat motionless, watching him, wondering what he was up to.

The crow teetered across the wooden planks to the edge of the opening and began scratching in the grass that bordered the hole.

In a matter of minutes, Magus tugged something from the dirt, then flew back to Galilea dangling the object from his beak.

When Galilea opened her hand to accept the buried treasure, the black bird dropped a locket tangled in a broken chain into her palm.

Nudging the dainty silver heart with a fingertip, Galilea flipped it over, and found a tiny, dirt encrusted inscription on the other side. Two initials. *E* and *L*.

"E . . . L," Galilea murmured, letting her gaze stray to the boarded up sinkhole. "*Elizabeth Luxley.*"

"Ah, Galilea, there you are."

Galilea paused at the base of the stairs, then turned toward the sound of Collin's voice.

Collin grinned and moved forth in a wide stride with a twinkle dancing in his pale gray eyes. "Where have you been all day, my lovely?"

Galilea opened and closed her hand on the carved banister. "At the castle."

Collin's pleased expression changed to one of concern. "Galilea . . . I don't think you should go there alone anymore." He frowned and his gaze drifted to the side. "I . . . I just have this . . . this *inkling,* I suppose you could call it, that it wouldn't be too wise under the circumstances."

Collin blinked, and his frown disappeared. Focusing his attention on Galilea again, a smile returned to his lips. "In any case . . . I've been looking for you. Would you mind stepping into the library?" He waved a hand in the direction of the study. "I have something of great importance to discuss with you."

"Is it about Lizzie?" Galilea asked anxiously. "Have you learned anything more?"

Collin lowered his head and shook it sadly. "No, regretfully, what I have to say has nothing to do with Lizzie." He peered at her from under his brow, and Galilea noted another sparkle flickered in his eyes. "Actually, it has to do with—"

Collin's mouth hung open a moment, then he pressed his lips into a thin line and glanced up the stairway. "I think this should be a private discussion, Galilea. There's something I'd like to ask you."

Galilea searched his face and felt numbness creeping into her jaw. With a nod, she skirted around him and started for the library. As Collin moved along beside her, she sensed his question was of a highly personal nature.

By the time they stood behind the closed doors of the study, severe doubts had arisen in Galilea over whether or not she was entirely prepared for the man's probable suggestion. What *would* she answer, if Collin proposed they become lovers? She wasn't at all certain her conscience could agree to anything less than moral. Ollie, God rest his soul, had raised her better.

"Galilea? You look a bit pale," Collin stated, coming forward to take her hands in his. "Come, sit down."

Galilea allowed him to guide her to the chair next to the fireplace. He continued holding her hands when she seated herself.

His face was radiant as his gaze met hers. "Galilea, I realize this is ill-timed, but if I do not speak my mind soon, I shall surely lose it."

Galilea widened her eyes. Collin's fingers tightened around her own, causing her pulse to beat hard in her temples.

To her alarm, he went down on one knee before her, and raising her hands, dropped a kiss upon each of them. "Would you do me the honor of becoming my—"

Galilea squeezed her eyes shut, bracing herself for the word, *mistress*.

"Wife," Collin filled in, instead.

Galilea squinted one eye open. "Did you say . . . *wife*? Y-you want me to . . ."

"To marry me properly," Collin supplied with a soft smile. "I know this is sudden, but I do believe we would suit very well together. Don't you?"

Galilea's hands went limp in his. Her gaze drifted right through him for an instant. "Suit well together" didn't sound like a very romantic way of putting it.

As Collin's face came into focus once more, she curled her fingers and slipped them from his grasp, bracing her hands against her midriff.

"Well?" Collin dipped his head in an attempt to meet her downcast eyes. "Will you not give me your answer?"

"Collin, I . . . I'm speechless." Galilea stared at him—all the while, tossing around the idea that he might have been working too hard lately. "I . . . I'm very flattered indeed, but—"

"But you need time to think it over, is that it, my sweet?" Collin reached up and brushed a stray hair from her forehead.

"Aye, exactly," Galilea commented, feeling more and more stunned with every second that ticked by. "W-Would you mind terribly if I asked you to wait a few days for my response?"

"Take all the time you need, Galilea." Collin's expression was most sincere, yet a hint of worry creased the outer edges of his eyes. He rose slowly to his feet. "After all, I shouldn't expect you to simply jump at the offer. Marriage is . . . well, a most serious institution and, by all means, should be given a proper amount of consideration. But we are attracted to one another, I believe."

Collin turned, and strolled a few feet away, combing a hand through his hair. "And, I dwelled long and hard on the matter before coming to the conclusion to propose," he said, then cocked his head over his shoulder.

As his gaze touched Galilea's, his dark eyebrows came together. "Are you sure you are quite all right?" He asked. Pivoting, he strode to her side, pressed the back of his hand to her cheek. "You do seem a bit warm. Are you not feeling well?"

Collin's voice somehow broke through to Galilea. Noting his concern, she realized she'd been sitting as still as a marble statue for quite some time.

Sensing her inability to move must have stemmed from shock, she concentrated on Collin's face, then inhaled deeply and blew the breath out slowly.

"Galilea?"

Pressing her fingertips to her cheek, Galilea felt her skin tingle. "My head does ache," she said, squinting at Collin for effect. "I should like to retire, if you don't mind."

"Not at all." He promptly caught her elbows and helped her from the chair. "Here, let me take you to your chambers. And I'll ask Fanny to bring you some nice warm tea."

Galilea allowed him to escort her as far as the door. Placing her palms flat on his chest, she stopped him at the threshold. "Please, Collin, stay and continue on with your work. Don't trouble yourself."

A smile lifted one corner of Collin's mouth. On impulse, he cupped Galilea's face and brushed his lips across her cheek to her ear.

" 'Twould be no trouble," he whispered. " 'Twould be my pleasure."

Galilea's heart pumped hard in her breast, quivering the fabric of her bodice. Collin's breath trickled into her eardrum, rapidly heating her insides.

Her eyes slid closed of their own accord. More than anything, she yearned to slide her hands up over his shoulders . . . and pull him closer.

Resisting the urge, Galilea conjured up all the strength she owned. Pushing away from him, she backed out the library door.

Once in the hall, it took her a moment to regain her balance. To keep from teetering from one foot to the other, she entwined her fingers tightly at her waist, and commanded herself to be calm.

Her gaze melted into his. "I think 'twould be wise to go to my room alone, Collin," she said with a rush of embarrassment. "I . . . I am drawn to you, Collin, by a force I cannot fight. The temptation to blatantly wrap myself around you like a wanton harl—" Galilea closed her eyes, striving for a more appropriate way to phrase it. "I mean . . . well, under the circumstances, I cannot resist—"

"I understand completely." Collin squared his shoulders and locked his hands behind his back. "Believe me, I do," he muttered beneath his breath. His thoughts appeared to wander off for a moment or two.

Then putting on a strained smile, he cleared his throat. "Good night then, Galilea. Sleep well, and with the angels. We shall discuss this all again . . . whenever you are ready."

Collin stretched out his hand and timidly grazed her cheek.

Galilea lightly touched the back of the hand he held against the side of her face. "Sweet dreams, Collin," she said, and meant it with all her heart.

Chapter 14

Galilea practically floated up the stairway. A silly grin creased her lips, and no matter how hard she tried to curb her foolishness, the smile remained intact.

She trailed her fingers over the carved handrail, moving slowly from step to step. *'Twas no dream,* a voice inside whispered. For reasons far beyond Galilea, Collin MacLaine truly *had* asked her to be his bride.

Tomorrow, she would wonder why. Tonight, she refused to ponder upon Collin's purpose. Tonight, she would close her mind to the fact that he'd not professed his everlasting love. Tonight, as she lay in bed watching the moonlight dance across her wall, she would merely bask in the glorious magic of it all.

With such merry thoughts filling Galilea's head, she didn't notice the pale shrouded figure at the top of the stairs until she'd placed her foot upon the last step.

Her gaze had barely lit upon the indistinguishable specter, when the form rushed at her from the landing.

A flash of white caught her eye, then something solid hit her chest, knocking her backward.

In the horror of slow motion, Galilea tumbled down the stairs, her body twisting and turning at different angles as she banged from step to step. She felt her head strike the banister hard, once . . . twice . . . then, everything went black.

Galilea wandered through the deepest, darkest of tunnels. Magus cawed in the distance, and she heard the echo of Lizzie's weeping but could not see her sister.

From somewhere much farther away, Collin called her name. Galilea turned from the ghostly sobbing and soared toward the sound of his voice.

"Galilea, come back to us, my sweet."

As she pried her eyes open, Collin's face came into focus.

He looked so ill, Galilea thought. Dark circles were prominent beneath his red-rimmed eyes. A good two days' growth of whiskers shaded his jaw. His hair fell in wild array about his shoulders.

Galilea reached up and touched his prickly chin.

A rumbling laugh started in Collin's chest then broke from his throat and, in accordance with his ragged looks, made him appear quite the madman.

"Thank God," he whispered, grasping her

raised hand and raining kisses upon it. "You're going to be all right."

Galilea opened her mouth, but no sound came forth.

"Don't move, my sweet. Don't try to speak." Collin rose from the edge of the bed and moved swiftly to the open door.

"Fanny!" he called, poking his head into the hall. "Come quickly. She's awake."

A wide smile split his face as he started back across the room, making him look more like himself. Dragging a chair closer to the bedside, he sat down and brushed the hair from Galilea's forehead.

"God, I thought I'd lost you," he murmured. "You must have slipped or missed a step. I had asked Fanny to bring you some tea, and she found you lying at the bottom of the stairs. You've given us all quite a fright for the past couple of days."

A stabbing pain pierced Galilea's temple, and at the same time pricked her memory.

"Collin," she said, catching his shirtsleeve. "I did not slip . . . I was pushed." Her voice came out dry and raspy, and much lower in volume than she'd intended.

Collin furrowed his brow and leaned nearer. "You were *what*?" he asked.

"Pushed." Galilea strove to form the word more clearly. "Someone . . . *pushed* me."

Collin's features moved by small degrees into a dangerous expression. "Someone pushed you," he repeated, narrowing his gaze. "Maybe . . . just maybe, you were getting a bit too close to the truth about Lizzie."

A clanking noise in the doorway turned Collin's head.

Fanny stood white-faced just inside the room, the teacup on the tray she held rattling against the saucer. She moved forward shakily, glancing between Collin and Galilea. "Lud, sir. I 'ad me a 'unch it weren't no accident, I did. And I was right, I was."

"Fanny," Collin began, "I'd appreciate it, if you kept this quiet until I have a chance to—"

"Kept what quiet?" Elenore asked, entering the chambers.

"Lud, Mistress Elenore, somebody went and shoved our lit'le Galilea down them stairs, they did." The words tumbled from Fanny's mouth in an excited fashion. "Can you believe it? 'Tis terrible, but true. I 'eard Master MacLaine 'imself say so when—"

"Fanny." Collin spoke her name in a tone of voice that immediately silenced the maid. "I believe you've brought Galilea some hot tea, have you not?"

"Oh . . . aye, sir, that I did." Fanny rushed to set the silver tray on the bedside table. " 'Ere now, miss," she said to Galilea. "Let's 'elp you sit up."

Galilea grimaced with the intense pain shooting through her head when Collin lifted and supported her upper body long enough for Fanny to fluff the pillows against the headboard.

Once propped in an upright position, Galilea felt a bit more human. When she wrapped her hands around the warm tea cup and took a sip, the hot liquid eased the aching of her joints and soothed her throat.

"What happened, Galilea?" Elenore asked. Moving to the end of the bed, she gripped the footrail. "Can you tell us?"

Galilea closed her eyes, seeing the white veiled figure charge her. "Someone . . . was waiting for me at the top of the stairs."

"Who?" Collin asked, placing a hand upon her shoulder.

Galilea opened her eyes and met his steady gaze.

"I . . . don't know," she said. "They were completely covered by . . . some pale-colored cloth."

Fanny sucked in her breath, making a small squeaking sound.

"Can you recall anything else? Think, Galilea," Collin said. "Anything at all?"

Galilea reached up and rubbed the sore spot on the side of her head.

"Nothing," she replied after a moment's thought.

Elenore and Collin exchanged worried glances.

"Galilea, you don't think—" Elenore twisted her hands around the bed rail and frowned. "I mean, well . . . Lizzie's been obnoxious before, but she's never done anything so dreadful. You don't suppose 'twas her doing . . . do you?"

"It wasn't Lizzie." Galilea raised her chin

with confidence. "My own sister would never do such a thing." Galilea shifted her gaze from Elenore to Fanny, then fastened it on Collin. All of them viewed her with expectancy.

"It was *not* Lizzie," she assured Collin. " 'Twas done by human hands. I *know* it wasn't Lizzie."

"Are you certain you'll be all right out here by yourself, Galilea? I could easily move you closer to the house, if you wish."

Galilea smiled up at Collin from her seat in the wicker chair.

"I love this part of the garden," she said, then shooed him away with a wave of her hand. "You go tend to your business—see your man about the shearing of the sheep. I'll be fine."

"Very well then, if you're sure." Collin stooped, tugged the shawl more securely about her shoulders, then kissed her lightly on the forehead. "I shouldn't be too long, my sweet. I promise I'll be back as soon as I've—"

"Go." Galilea set her jaw and pointed toward the manor. "Go on. 'Twas awful being cooped up in the house for the past week with you and Fanny spoiling me. To be quite frank, I would cherish a moment alone."

Galilea fought to keep her expression stern, but the glimmer of humor in Collin's eyes infected her.

The corners of her mouth twitched upward and she lowered her lashes. "Collin, please.

'Tis extremely unnerving to have you look at me like that."

"Like what?"

Galilea glanced at him and made an awkward gesture toward his handsome face. "Like . . . *that*," she said, unable to find suitable words to describe the sensuous gandering he'd taken up lately.

Collin's smile broadened. Bending forward at the waist, he clasped the arms of the chair and smiled rakishly into her eyes. "It bothers you, does it?"

"Yes," Galilea admitted with a shrug. She shifted her weight slightly, set on edge all over again by the mere nearness of him. "Yes, it bothers me terribly, if you want to know the truth of the matter."

"Good." Collin straightened, shoved his hands in to his pockets, and rocked back on his heels. " 'Tis a reassuring sign, I hope. Perhaps, I'm beginning to affect you, after all, and you'll soon say yes to my proposal. I'd hate to think all this charm of mine has already gone to pasture, and in these my very best years."

Galilea rolled her eyes at him but smiled all the same.

Appearing rather pleased with his small conquest, Collin winked, then rounded her chair. "I'll have Fanny or Winston come out and check on you directly," he said as he started toward the manor.

Galilea peered over her shoulder, watching him stride off.

Catching one corner of her mouth between her teeth, she fixed her gaze on his hips. The swagger of his walk intrigued her . . . indeed, 'twas totally mesmerizing—the way his finely shaped bum swayed ever so slightly from side to side.

Upon reaching the doorway, Collin turned and waved at her.

Galilea was a bit surprised to feel herself blush. At this distance, Collin could not have possibly noted where her eyes had been.

Raising her hand, she wiggled her fingers at him and returned his smile.

Collin blew her a kiss, then he disappeared into the house.

The smile lingered on Galilea's lips as she swiveled forward again. With her heart full and her mind at peace, she observed Winston's latest efforts in the gardens.

The weeds were thinning in the flowerbeds, and the roses had recently been pruned. Although the untidy grounds had been drastically amended, 'twas still a considerable amount of work to be done.

Galilea made a mental survey of a few other improvements she might take to task as soon as she was better. Her bumps and bruises were healing steadily. And at the rate the soreness was leaving her body, she'd be able to assist the old butler with his gardening in a few days.

Galilea watched a yellow butterfly flutter about from one rose bush to the next. She was thinking what a lovely day it had turned out to be, when her contentment suddenly wavered. She felt as if a dark cloud had moved over her.

Gradually, she realized 'twas no cloud shading her from the sunlight, but rather it was the shadow of a man. Her skin prickled with the knowledge that someone stood just behind her chair.

"Are you recovering from your nasty little fall?"

Recognizing the smooth, sarcastic voice, Galilea closed her eyes and prayed for patience. "How kind of you to ask, Roland," she said without a backward glance.

Elenore's husband rounded her chair and planted himself directly in front of her—much too close for comfort.

"Cursed luck, wasn't it?" Rubbing his chin, he gave Galilea a feigned look of concern. "You might have broken your pretty little neck tumbling down the stairs that way." A sly smile curved Roland's lips, and he made a production out of lifting an eyebrow.

Galilea gripped the arms of the wicker chair and searched Roland's face. She attempted to read the meaning behind his words, but the signals she received in her mind blurred and scattered.

Since the fall, her sixth sense had somehow been damaged. Try as she would, she could not decipher whether or not Roland had anything to do with the accident. All she could discern for certain was that she did not care for the man in the least.

"Would you like me to keep you company awhile?" Roland asked, maintaining his smirk. "You seemed a bit spooked when I came along."

Stepping forward, he started to grasp Galilea's hand, but she promptly withdrew it from his reach.

"Thank you all the same, Roland," she replied, striving for some measure of courtesy. "I'd prefer to be alone though, if you don't mind."

"Really Galilea, don't you think this game of cat and mouse is getting tiresome?"

Galilea's patience and her quest for courtesy dissolved as she observed the cocky gleam in Roland's eyes. It took no wizardry at all to see what was on his mind.

"What I think," she remarked, dispensing with any form of politeness, "is that you, sir, should go and attend to your wife's affection."

Roland snickered and shifted his weight to one hip. "I take care of my wife well enough. Just ask her."

Galilea simply looked at him, in lieu of being baited into a verbal duel.

Obviously aggravated by her lack of response, Roland stooped in an abrupt motion and gripped the latticed back of the chair on either side of her head, hemming her in.

"Come, Galilea, you are as attracted to me as I am to you," he whispered, then posed his face a mere inch away from hers. "You may as well admit it."

Galilea sat very still, unflinchingly staring into Roland's eyes—yet, all the while, silently cursing the man with her gaze.

"Father?" A high-pitched voice called out, turning both Roland's and Galilea's head toward a nearby row of shrubbery.

Young Phillip stepped from behind one of the bushes. Frowning, he shifted his gaze back and forth between the two adults. "Mother sent me to fetch you, Father," he said. "She wishes to see you."

Roland straightened from his bent position over Galilea, stiffening his spine as he stood upright.

"Very well, son," he replied, without so much as a glance in the boy's direction. "Run and tell her I shall be along shortly."

Roland made no move to leave, however, and Phillip likewise stood his ground.

"Mother said to come right away," the boy insisted.

Roland exhaled a long sigh, cast a brief glare at his son, then gave Galilea a sardonic smile.

"We shall resume our chat later, dear sister. Soon, in fact," he commented, dragging a hand over her shoulder when he passed her chair. "Do remember where we left off."

Galilea let her breath out slowly as he walked toward the manor.

Not to be ignored, Phillip raked a stick along a section of the garden wall, making a clacking sound.

Galilea gave the boy her requested attention, assuming he had lingered behind for some specific purpose.

Phillip stopped a few feet away, slapping the stick against his palm. He merely stared at her for a long moment, his chubby cheeks puffed out like a bullfrog.

"You shouldn't dally with my father, you know," he stated, narrowing his eyes into slits. "Mother wouldn't like it."

"Phillip, I wasn't—"

The boy flung the stick, barely missing the side of Galilea's chair, then dashed off in the wake of his father.

Highly unsettled by her encounter with both Roland *and* his son, Galilea closed her weary eyes and tilted her head back. She tried to regain the tranquillity she'd been experiencing before Roland's intrusion, but the fresh outdoors had lost its appeal, leaving her to dwell once more on her horrible fall down the stairs.

She had attempted to forget the incident, and she had steered from making accusations. Galilea would have preferred to believe her attacker had been a startled thief stealing about the manor that night. Yet there had been no forced entry.

Galilea chewed her lower lip thoughtfully, wondering if the shrouded figure at the top of the stairs had actually meant to harm her . . . or merely frighten her into stopping her investigation of Lizzie's death.

She supposed more than one of the inhabitants of the manor might be glad to be rid of her, and for more than one reason. Roland's mannerism toward her seemed to run hot and cold. Obviously, he was not pleased with her continued rebuttals of his advances. Widow Luxley had a motive or two, as well. It was quite apparent that Lord Luxley's wife had despised Elizabeth and was not fond of Galilea. Fanny still tended to become a bit nervous in Galilea's presence. Even Elenore, while mild and mannerly for the most, appeared somewhat resentful at times.

"Hullo, mistress," Winston called out, making Galilea jump. Cocking her head over her shoulder, she smiled at the old butler in spite of her dour mood.

Winston trudged forth with two steaming cups rattling on a tray. "Thought you might care for a spot of tea about now," he said, stopping beside her chair.

"Thank you, Winston." Galilea took the cup he offered her.

Winston settled on the lowest part of the garden wall, set the tray beside him, and took his own teacup in hand. " 'Tis beginning to shape up a bit out here, don't you think?" He indicated the grounds with a nod of his head.

"Quite nicely," Galilea agreed, although she could tell by his wilting expression that her enthusiasm was nowhere near what Winston had hoped for. "The roses are looking remarkably well-tended," she added belatedly.

Apparently noticing she was distracted,

Winston furrowed his brow. "Is all well with you, miss?"

"I'm fine. Truly, I am." Galilea brightened her smile for his sake. "Would you do me a small favor if I asked?"

"Why, of course, miss." Winston tucked his chin. "Anything."

"If the need for peace and quiet strikes me again tomorrow, remind me to simply stay inside and lock my chamber door." Without giving Winston a chance to question such an odd statement, Galilea launched right into telling him about her ideas for the garden.

Galilea did indeed stay in her room the next day. 'Twas pouring rain, dark and dreary. Lightning flashed. Thunder crashed. Rivulets of water ran steadily down the window pane.

Galilea rather enjoyed the pitter-patter of rain on the roof. She reveled in the sweet solitude of her chambers. All cozy in her chair beside the window, her bare feet curled beneath her, she was quite determined to finish the novel she'd supposedly read while sitting with Collin in the library.

Therefore, she wasn't at all pleased to hear the knock at her door. Unfolding her legs, she rose from the chair and laid her book aside.

"Yes? Who is it?" she asked, before striding across the room. She paused and cocked her ear, refraining from opening the door too quickly.

" 'Tis I, Collin. Might I speak with you a moment?"

Galilea's heart sailed high upon hearing his voice. A smile automatically creased her lips as she swung the door wide.

Collin's spreading grin indicated that he, too, was affected by the sight of her.

They stood on opposite sides of the threshold for a matter of heartbeats, each absorbed in viewing the other—each seeing something new they hadn't noticed before.

Collin focused on the tiny flecks of gold blending with the green of her eyes.

Galilea observed a small hairline scar on the right side of his chin, and was prone to ask how he'd gotten marked with it. When she opened her mouth to do so, she suddenly realized she'd been standing there gawking.

"Ah . . . would you care to come in?" she asked and stepped aside to allow him entrance.

Collin blinked. "Oh . . . yes. Yes, I would, thank you."

He strolled to the window and looked out, then traced the pattern of raindrops rolling down the pane. "Dreadful day, wouldn't you say?"

"Oh, I don't know, I sort of like rainy days," Galilea replied with a shrug, then settled on the edge of the bed.

As Collin turned from the window, a burst of lightning flashed behind him, outlining his tall, sturdy form.

Galilea clasped her hands tightly in her lap and swiftly averted her gaze to avoid the temptation of staring at him again.

"There . . . there was something you wished to discuss with me?" she asked, saying the first sensible thing that came to mind.

"Aye." Collin propped a shoulder against the window frame and folded his arms over his chest. His sober expression made Galilea wonder if he was about to press her for an answer to his proposal, and she was not yet ready to give him one. She'd begun to worry of late that their varied opinions might interfere with a happy relationship.

"I made some inquiries about the Luxley family yesterday," he stated.

Galilea let her breath out slowly, grateful the conversation was not leaning toward the subject of matrimony. "Did you?" she asked with a great deal of interest.

"After my meeting, I went to the inn and bought a round of drinks for some of the locals. You might be surprised how quickly a few tankards of ale loosen tongues."

Galilea bent forward at the waist, all ears now. "Collin, did you learn something we didn't know?"

"Nothing we didn't already suspect, I suppose. 'Twas rather intriguing though, to find most people hereabout also believe Elizabeth Luxley was murdered."

Galilea was silent a moment, allowing that notion to sink in.

Collin crossed the short distance to the bed and sat down on the mattress next to her, leaving a decent space between them.

"While I have a hunch one or two of the

stories I've heard may hold some bearing," he said, "I must also bring to light the fact that almost every village from here to London generally has a certain family about whom they tend to gossip. Lord Luxley, I'm told, had his share of adulterous affairs. And the manor has a dark, mysterious reputation, I'm afraid. I know for a fact someone here was evil enough to shove you down those stairs, and I will not rest until I find out who it was."

Galilea peered deeply into Collin's eyes. She laid her hand on the bed between them, hoping he would take the hint and clasp it in his. Bracing herself for his reply, she asked the question she could not stop from asking.

"Did . . . did anyone claim to know who might have wanted Lizzie dead?"

Collin slid his hand across the coverlet and folded his fingers over hers. "No. I wish I could say otherwise. In truth, most of the tales told involved other worldly creatures rather than human beings. Nevertheless, I do believe there must be some significance attached to the whole town's insistence that your sister was deliberately done-away-with."

Collin closed his eyes and hung his head. "There has to be something we're missing, Galilea. Lizzie wouldn't stir up such accusations, then simply disappear without leaving behind some clue . . . or surely, *something* that might lead us in the right direction." Collin turned his head, viewing Galilea pensively. "Would she?"

"No, she wouldn't." Galilea twisted toward him, shifting her weight on the bed. "Oh Collin, you're right, of course. Lizzie must be guiding us in some way. We're overlooking something, I just know it."

Collin squeezed her hand. "Think, Galilea. Have you witnessed anything, anything at all, in the past few days that might be construed as a message from your twin sister?"

Galilea's gaze drifted to one side. She was in the midst of shaking her head no, when she recalled Magus giving her the locket he'd found beside the sinkhole Lizzie had fallen into.

"Wait," she said, hopping up from the bed. "There *was* something that happened that seemed a bit odd. Magus found an old piece of jewelry and brought it to me. It belonged to Lizzie, I think."

Placing her hands on her hips, Galilea glanced about the room and frowned. "Now, where did I put it?"

She went straight to her treasured tin music box atop the bureau and opened the lid.

"This is where I meant to keep it," she commented, then looked back at Collin and grimaced. "I must have left it in my pocket."

Galilea strode to the wardrobe and flung open the double doors. A putrid odor wafted from amongst her clothes, nearly gagging her.

In the next instant, a flash of lightning illuminated the inside of the closet as thunder cracked overhead.

A scream broke from Galilea's throat at the sight of some small furry creature, eyes shining like black glass beads, dangling from a string directly in front of her.

Chapter 15

Collin rushed forth and moved Galilea's rigid, motionless form aside.

Flattening herself against the open closet door, Galilea covered her face with her hands.

"Good God," Collin murmured as he reached inside the wardrobe. "What the hell—?"

He jerked the string attached to the closet ceiling loose, and pulled out the small lump of fur dangling on the end.

"Oooh, what . . . what is it?" Galilea asked in a strained, off-key voice, then peeked between her fingers.

"A dead rat," Collin announced without flair.

Galilea dragged her hands down her face and, resting them at the base of her throat, stepped forward. "A dead—?"

"Rat," Collin said again. Holding the rodent up by its tail, he inspected the small noose circling the creature's neck. " 'Twas strangled by hanging, evidently."

Galilea reached out and stroked the rat's

smooth pelt with a fingertip. "The poor little thing. Who could be so cruel, Collin?"

"I haven't the slightest idea." Collin tucked his chin and wrinkled his nose. "Egad, the smell is atrocious."

Tugging a handkerchief from his breast pocket, he wrapped the stiff rodent in it, then walked to the window and laid the small shrouded body on the sill.

Collin braced his palms on either side of the dead animal, peered out at the storm for a instant, then looked over his shoulder at Galilea. "Actually, I'm more concerned with the notion that whoever killed the rat had access to your chambers—and had they been a bit more inventive, they might have done more than frighten you."

Galilea met his gaze evenly, noting how extremely upset he was over the incident. His worry elevated hers.

"'Twas no rat in that closet when I went to dress this morning, Collin. And I've been in my room all day."

"Have you had no visitors?" he asked, furrowing his brow.

"None, save you. Fanny did bring me scones and tea at noon, but she went nowhere near the wardrobe."

"And you did not leave your chambers at all? Not even for a moment?"

Galilea nibbled her lower lip. "Aye . . . but for no longer than it took to retrieve my book from the study. 'Twas at an extremely early hour, though, and I was gone for such a short time, really."

"Long enough for someone to sneak into your chambers and leave their nasty gift."

Collin twisted from the window just as another flash of lightning lit the sky. He held out a hand to Galilea.

When she stepped forward and wrapped her fingers around his, he led her to the bed, then sat down beside her.

"I do not like this, Galilea," he said, keeping his eyes downcast and focused on their joined hands. "First the fall on the stairway, now this malicious act, both fully intended to terrorize you."

Collin skimmed his thumb over Galilea's knuckles, then shifted his gaze to hers. "And why?" He lifted one eyebrow. "Perhaps because someone doesn't want us to find out what honestly happened the day Lizzie disappeared. And just perhaps, they assume you are getting too close to discovering the truth."

Galilea tightened her hold on his fingers and shook her head slightly. "I can't believe anyone in this house would actually set out to purposely harm me," she said softly. "Surely, they only wish to frighten me."

"Think what you will, my sweet." Collin reached up and caressed her cheek. "Personally, I suspect these wee disasters may continue. They could even grow nastier. In any case, I don't intend to allow anything to happen to you." Collin's mouth lifted with a smile. "After all, I haven't yet received a proper response to my proposal, have I?"

Galilea closed her eyes and nuzzled the side of her face against his warm palm. *Yes . . . yes I shall be your beloved wife,* every fiber of her being urged her to pronounce here and now.

Yet a small niggling in the back of her brain bid her hold her tongue. *Why would he marry you? Has he pledged his love?* the nagging voice taunted. *Why you then? Why a ragged little vagabond like you, Galilea?*

Galilea's eyes stung behind her closed lids. She squeezed them tighter shut and felt a teardrop trickle down her cheek.

"Here now, what's all this?" Collin's words came deep and smooth. He whisked the tear away with a swipe of his thumb.

When Galilea raised her lashes and looked into his pale, silver eyes, her heart contracted and commenced aching.

Collin ran a hand through her hair to embrace the back of her neck. "I would cherish hearing you accept in my favor, but I will give you the time you've asked for. Pray, do not make me wait much longer."

On impulse, Galilea caught his face between her hands, and in one swift motion she crushed her mouth to his. In less than three good beats of her heart, she pulled back a bit and searched his face.

Collin's jaw was slack and his eyes at half-mast, like a man drugged by too much wine. Yet moving with all the agility of a man quite in control, he promptly resumed the kiss.

Taking her in his arms, he claimed her mouth powerfully, with the utmost of passion, until her lips were forced apart from the pressure. Something warm and wonderful stirred inside Galilea. Gliding her hands up over his shoulders, she clung to him, molding herself against the hard wall of his chest.

Collin eased his tongue into the sweetness of her mouth, and his heart shuddered as her breasts pressed harder against him. All common sense deserted him. He could not think. He could only *feel*. Nothing existed beyond the softness of her lips . . . the intoxicating scent of her skin . . . the silkiness of her hair . . .

He urged her backward with his body until they both reclined upon the bed. As he rained kisses along her throat, his hand roved up her arm, across her shoulder, and came to rest upon the swelling of her breast. Through the light fabric of her muslin gown, the bud in the center of the soft mound rose into his palm. A fire ignited down low in Collin's abdomen.

'Twas a hell of a time for his honor to awaken, yet his conscience reared its head at that precise moment.

He fell motionless, suspended between heaven and hell. At the same time, he was yet unwilling to give up this closeness with the woman he held.

No matter how badly he wanted Galilea, he could go no further. Moral obligation bade him wait until they had exchanged vows before God and man. Galilea was too special . . . too precious to desecrate. He somehow knew that to make love to her would be to touch her soul.

She stirred in his still embrace, as if she too had come round to her senses.

Collin edged off the bed and, rising to his feet, tugged Galilea to a sitting position.

She sat for a long moment simply staring wide-eyed at him. Then a blush flushed her cheeks, and she hopped up off the bed.

"Galilea, I—" Collin began.

"Nay." Galilea raised a hand. "Say nothing, please."

She took a deep breath, skirted around Collin, walked to the window sill, and scooped up the tiny body wrapped in the handkerchief. Cradling the dead rodent against her waist, she started toward the door.

"Galilea?"

She turned to Collin wearing a blank, unreadable expression. "Hmm?"

"May I ask where you're going?" Collin inquired, becoming increasingly alarmed by her odd behavior.

Galilea blinked, then glanced at the small bundle in her hands. "To bury the rat, of course."

"Bury the—? Galilea, 'tis raining cats and dogs out there."

"I know that, Collin, but the poor wee thing is still one of God's creatures and is deserving of a decent grave."

Collin gazed at her, charmed, for some bizarre reason by yet another uncommon facet of her personality.

"Very well then," he said, moving forth to open the door for her. "I shall go with you."

Taking her elbow, he guided her into the hall. "Afterwards though, I believe we should organize another household gathering. Whoever shoved you down the stairs no doubt delivered this damnable rat as well, and they will be held accountable, by God."

As Collin rubbed the towel briskly over his wet hair, he caught a glimpse of his reflection in the looking glass.

Turning more fully toward the mirror, he hooked the towel around his neck and stepped closer for a better examination.

It struck him as he did so that he could not remember smiling at his own image before. Always in the past, 'twas more of a scowl that stared back at him.

It suddenly occurred him that he had normally worn a poker face . . . hidden his honest feelings behind a mask. 'Twas a well-learned trait, no doubt inherited from his mother and father.

Collin ran a hand over his chin, then slid it down his throat to his bare chest and covered his heart. His pulse beat warm and solid against his palm.

He grinned even broader.

Galilea had changed him. His brooding face had been transformed into something not so far from a pleasant-looking fellow.

For reasons he could not name, he had formerly, *unknowingly,* hoarded his affection. He'd taken great caution, in fact, not to give too much of himself.

Quite the opposite, Galilea, for all her special sight and wisdom, had been more than willing to share herself with the world. Although she could have sat across a card table and counted the aces in her opponent's hand, she had not used her gift for ill-gained means. She spoke her mind . . . *showed* her emotions, without asking for anything in return.

The fairy-queen was an amazing woman—a true wonder, and he would forever treasure her, if she would but give him the word.

Collin peered into the looking glass at his mooncalf eyes, and with a chuckle he shook his head.

Gads. Galilea *must* have hexed him, to be sure. First, she had barged into his life and shattered his narrow-minded beliefs about ghosts and hobgoblins. Now, she had him burying rats in the rain. He had come a far cry from the man who had arrived at Luxley Manor, cursing all superstitions surrounding fairies and the like.

Collin reached for his clean, dry shirt, and shoved his arms into the sleeves. As he fastened the buttons of the garment, it came to him that he should probably tell Galilea these things, reveal these . . . *feelings* he held in his heart.

And so he would, he decided.

Slipping on his jacket, he smoothed his

damp hair back, then furrowed his brow at his reflection. Of course, he would wait until she gave her answer to his offer of marriage before he went and poured out his soul.

Catching hold of his lapels, Collin turned sideways and eyed his profile for any further alterations to his appearance. The smile came easily upon his features once again.

Aye, he had changed, all right—yet not so much that he would be willing to wage his pride against Galilea's rejection.

Collin's smile faltered. He stared hard at his mirror image, knowing if Galilea rejected his proposal, all the things he longed to tell her would be forever locked inside him.

Early that evening, Galilea paused before the doorway of the library. In the midst of the continuing storm, once again, the family and servants of the house had been assembled in the study.

Collin was the only one yet absent, Galilea noted. Placing a hand against her midriff, she took a long deep breath, and surveyed the occupants of the room.

Winston and Fanny stood apart from the family, maintaining rigid poses in one corner. Side by side, the two exchanged questioning glances and discreet whispers betwixt themselves.

Phillip fidgeted in the chair next to the fireplace, while Roland stood at the mantel, pouring a liberal shot of Collin's sherry into a glass. Elenore sat beside her mother in the semicircle of chairs, patting Widow Luxley's arm as the older woman registered an ongoing list of complaints.

Galilea tried once again to use her power of sight to decipher which of them might be the guilty one who'd put the rat in her wardrobe.

Again, the images and voices in her head were distorted. Her sense of knowing had, no doubt, been hampered by her level of emotional involvement . . . with Collin . . . with this house, and its connection to her twin sister.

Left to her other devices, she could not name the party responsible for her recent perils. She could not believe either Winston or Fanny would do such a thing. And, quite frankly, Widow Luxley appeared much too old and feebleminded to be dangerous. Elenore had been so kind. Roland, while obnoxious and overbearing, had proven himself to be no more than a bag of wind. And of course, Phillip was a mere child—misguided perhaps and ill-mannered at times, but no true menace.

Just as Galilea had bolstered up enough courage to enter the library, a hand curled over her shoulder. In the same instant, a clap of thunder shook the rafters, causing her to nearly jump out of her skin.

"Galilea, 'tis only me, love," Collin assured her quickly and folded her in his arms. "I apologize if I frightened you, my sweet."

The commotion in the doorway had drawn the attention of all gathered.

Keeping one arm around Galilea, Collin flashed the assembly a smile. As he ushered her into the room, he leaned to her ear and whispered, "Rally on, my fellow soldier, into the midst of the enemy we go."

Galilea peered at him askance.

" 'Tis a line from one of my poems," he explained with a grimace. "Not my best work, I know. But I thought it rather appropriate, considering."

Before Galilea could respond, Collin seated her across from where Elenore and the widow sat in the arch of chairs. Moving to stand behind her, Collin placed his hands firmly on her shoulders.

"I shall come right to the point, this evening," he stated, addressing everyone present. "A cruel joke was played on Galilea this afternoon, and taking in to consideration that the same person may also be responsible for pushing her down the stairs, I have decided 'twas high time we got to the bottom of this nonsense."

"Nonsense? What nonsense?" Harriet Luxley asked in a clipped tone. Turning her head, she frowned at Elenore. "I've heard nothing of that woman being pushed down the stairs. What the devil is he talking about?"

Elenore opened her mouth to answer, but her mother cut her off.

"No one pushed Galilea down the stairs,

you fool," the widow spat out. "She merely fell, the clumsy twit."

"Mother," Elenore said in a soft but stern tone, " 'tis true what he's saying. I kept it from you because I knew 'twould upset you."

"Upset me? *Upset me*? Of course, it upsets me." Harriet frowned in Collin's direction. "Did someone actually see Galilea being shoved down the stairway? Or, did you simply take her at her word?"

"Mother!" Elenore injected.

"Leave her be, Elenore," Roland said in the widow's defense. "I, for one, should like to hear Galilea's answer to Harriet's question."

Roland and Lady Luxley both swiveled their heads accusingly toward Galilea.

"I can assure you," Galilea responded, slightly rising from her chair, "Upon my honor, I would not lie about such a thing."

Gently tightening his grip on Galilea's shoulders, Collin pressed her back down into her seat.

"Galilea has no call to lie," he pronounced, glancing from one to the next and daring them to disagree. "If she *says* she was pushed, she was pushed. And I'll not hear any argument otherwise."

Collin arched one eyebrow and focused pointedly on Widow Luxley. "Now, if I may proceed without further interruption, I shall continue."

He paused, leaving room for any objections.

Fixing her face with a hateful glare, the widow clamped her mouth shut.

"Thank you," Collin said to her, then went on speaking to the whole group. "First off, you should all know that I am prepared to keep the lot of you here as long as I deem necessary. Before this evening ends, one of you *will* confess to putting the dead rat in Galilea's closet today."

"*What?*" Elenore covered her heart with a hand and widened her large brown eyes on Galilea. "You found a rat in your wardrobe?" she asked in dismay.

Widow Luxley elbowed her daughter. "She probably put it there herself, you silly," Harriet said out of the side of her mouth.

"Now see here, madam," Collin remarked, taking a threatening step in Harriet's direction. "Galilea is not on trial here. I happen to be a witness to the deed. I was there when the damned thing was found. Someone had rigged the rat to swing from a string when the doors were opened."

Collin dragged his gaze over the other occupants of the room, then abruptly returned his attention to the widow. "Someone here played this nasty little trick on Galilea, and I fully intend to know *who* before anyone leaves this room."

"Really, Collin," Roland drawled, lifting his refilled glass in salute. "Are you quite certain you haven't been working too hard, old chap? A man of your learned position should surely examine all possibilities in this case, wouldn't you think? Mother Luxley might very well have a point, you know. This—" Roland gestured with his glass to Galilea. "This . . . *madwoman* was living wild in the woods before she came to the manor, for God's sake. Why on earth should any of us *not* believe she staged these little incidents on her own, simply for attention?"

Collin's jaw visibly tightened as he narrowed his eyes on Elenore's husband.

"Roland, I give you fair warning, my patience is at an end where you are concerned. I would advise you not to persist with this petty attempt to steer the subject away from the main issue. You would not care for the consequences of your actions, if you do."

A cocky, yet cynical grin cracked Roland's face. "Bold words, Collin," he remarked in a mocking fashion, then took a sip of sherry.

In three swift strides Collin met the man face to face. Jerking the drink from Roland's grasp, Collin slung the half-empty glass into the fireplace, breaking it into shards.

"Aye, *bold words,*" Collin said, staring steadily into Roland's wide-open eyes. "Bold words that I shall gladly ram down your throat if you insist on antagonizing me and insulting the woman I've asked to be my wife."

Roland reared backward, wearing a stricken expression. "Forgive me, Collin," he stammered. "I . . . I had no way of knowing you'd asked the woman to marry you. If I have offended you, or your lady, I do apologize." Squeezing his eyes shut, Roland touched his temple. " 'Twas the drink that made me say such a dreadful thing. I—"

"Be seated, Roland, and kindly keep your mouth shut," Collin commanded, though not entirely without sympathy.

Looking away from Elenore's poor excuse for a husband, Collin turned and met Galilea's admiring gaze.

As she viewed him, Galilea felt as if her heart was fluttering inches above its proper place in her chest. Although Collin had yet to say so, he had just proven by his actions that he did indeed care for her . . . and would stand against any who regarded her with disrespect. Galilea favored her handsome champion with a small smile of appreciation.

The beginnings of a smile touched Collin's own lips, then he blinked, apparently a bit embarrassed by her tender look.

Clearing his throat, he promptly presented his other guests with a furrowed brow. "Now, proceeding with this inquiry, I would like each of you in turn to account for your whereabouts early this morning.

"This is utterly ridiculous," Widow Luxley muttered, struggling upright from her chair. "I refuse to stay here and be cross-examined by the likes of you, young man."

"*Sit down,* madam." Collin's command came swift and sure. "We have, by no means, finished our discussion."

"Mother, please," Elenore put in, catching Harriet's sleeve and attempting to tug the widow down next to her.

"I shall *not* sit down." Elevating her beak-like nose, she jerked her arm from her daughter's grasp. "I am not the one who hung a bat in the woman's closet."

"A rat, Mother. 'Twas a rat, not a bat," Elenore corrected. "Now, please—"

"*Whatever* sort of animal it was, *I* certainly had no part in stashing it in her wardrobe. 'Tis that creature there—" The widow jutted her chin toward Galilea. "She's to blame for all the strange goings-on in this house. She and her alleged sister were both cursed at birth because they were born out of wedlock upon a full moon. Witches, the both of them, I tell you."

"Enough!" Collin's deep voice resounded off the library walls. "You, madam," he said, pointing to the widow, "shall calm yourself, or else."

"Or else . . . what?" Harriet lifted her doubled chin in a defiant manner. "Will you have your little witch cast an evil spell upon me? She can, you know." A gleam of madness showed in Lady Luxley's eyes. "If indeed, someone *has* done Galilea some injustice, she could well take care of the problem herself. Witches can hex people, you know . . . she can fly into their chambers in the middle of the night, and . . ."

The widow's accusations, as well as Collin's and Elenore's attempts to silence the raving woman, grew dim and faded from Galilea's hearing.

Galilea curled her numb, cold fingers into

fists on the arms of the chair. She dearly hated being the cause of the erupting argument. She moved her gaze slowly over the room as if seeing the library and the people within for the very first time.

When her eyes drifted to young Phillip, however, she noticed something extremely unusual about the boy.

He wasn't fidgeting. Hanging his head, the child sat very still and quiet. Upon closer observance, Galilea noted the lad's lower lip quivered.

In the next instant, Phillip raised his lashes, and looked at Galilea, displaying red-rimmed eyes. Then with a sudden burst of energy, he jumped to his feet and stood straight up in the chair.

"I did it!" he shouted, gaining everyone's immediate attention. "I did it! Me. *I* bloodywell put the rat in her room."

For a long moment, no one moved or uttered a word, until a sob from Phillip broke the silence.

"I'm sorry, I'm sorry," he cried out, turning his chubby, tear-streaked face to Galilea. "Please ... *please,* don't put a hex on me. Pretty please, don't. I shall never, never again—"

"Phillip, I would not curse you, child, even if I could," Galilea assured the boy. Leaning forward slightly, she spread her hands in appeal. "I'm no witch, Phillip. Surely, you can see that I'm not."

"Yes, you are! Grandmother said so."

Bounding out of the chair, Phillip ran for the door.

Roland immediately went after the child and blocked Phillip's escape at the doorway of the library. Catching the boy's ear in a vicious grip, Roland frowned down at him. "The rat, I could have excused you for, son. 'Twas but a childish prank. But to go pushing someone down the stairs is quite another matter entirely. You shall be punished severely for committing such a vile and despicable stunt."

"But Father, I didn't!" Phillip squirmed, then grimaced at the painful pinch-hold on his ear. " 'Twas not I, who pushed Galilea. You must believe me . . . 'twas not I." Phillip commenced weeping between his words. "Only the rat, Father . . . I did no more than put the rat in her wardrobe . . . that's all. I *swear* it!"

Chapter 16

Once poor Phillip had made his confession, Galilea pitied the boy. She trusted with all her heart that he'd told the truth about not pushing her down the stairs.

Everyone else in the room, however, tended to believe the child was fibbing.

When Galilea tried to speak in Phillip's behalf, her opinion was lost among the many others being spouted out at random. No one seemed at all interested in the fact that Phillip's shape and height did not fit that of the specter she'd glimpsed at the top of the stairs.

Everyone, including Collin, apparently, simply wanted the matter settled at any cost. Phillip was guilty, and that was that. All that remained on the agenda for further discussion was the proper punishment for young Phillip's crime. Galilea's protests were then completely wasted in the midst of the entire gathering's disciplinary suggestions.

Subsequently, Galilea eased her way toward the library door and slipped from the room without notice.

* * *

'Twas almost two full hours, Galilea would guess, that she sat in the chair, alone in her chambers, awaiting the verdict they would press upon poor Phillip. She'd not bothered lighting the lamp but rather passed the time in darkness, staring through the rain-splattered window at the jagged bolts of lightning cracking the night sky.

She expected the knock at her door when it came.

Rising from her seat, Galilea crossed her chambers blindly, anticipating opening the door to find Collin standing in the corridor.

'Twas Elenore though, poised in the low-lit hall, clasping her hands tightly against her waist. The woman's face was a portrait of misery. "Galilea, I . . . I should like to speak with you, if I may."

"Of course, Elenore." Galilea reached out and briefly touched her elbow. "Please, come in."

Leaving the door open for the slight illumination from the hallway, Galilea strode to the bureau and lit the lamp. As a soft yellow glow filled the room, she turned and smiled at her newly found stepsister.

"Please do sit down, Elenore. I've been waiting to learn what's to be done with little Phillip. I pray his punishment will not be too harsh."

Making no comment, Elenore settled in the chair next to the window.

Noting Elenore's level of distress, Galilea

strode to the door and closed it, then seated herself on the edge of the bed.

Galilea maintained her silence patiently, allowing the other woman to lead the conversation.

"Galilea, I do not know what to say," Elenore began. Her gaze flitted about the room, skipping to Galilea's at brief intervals as she went on. "I am so ashamed of what my son has done. I can hardly believe him capable of such wicked misdeeds. I know Phillip's no angel, but . . ."

A glistening came to Elenore's eyes, and she swallowed hard.

Galilea stretched out her arm and laid a hand upon Elenore's sleeve. "I understand, Elenore. You needn't go on this way."

"But, I must!" Elenore insisted rather sharply, disengaging her arm from Galilea's touch. "Phillip has done a terrible thing, and I feel responsible. I *am* his mother, after all."

Galilea would have given the woman a comforting hug had she thought Elenore would not reject it. As it was, Galilea withdrew her outstretched hand and straightened her posture, wondering if Roland might not be responsible for Eleanore's abhorrence to being touched.

"Elenore, regardless of the majority opinion this evening, Phillip was *not* the one who pushed me down the stairway."

Elenore's large brown eyes steadied on Galilea's.

"The person who shoved me was much

taller. 'Twasn't Phillip. He's much too short and—" *Round,* Galilea bit her lip to keep from saying.

"Plump," his mother substituted in a loving tone. A sob laced with laughter escaped her. "Phillip is plump," she added with an upward curve of her mouth and a sniffle.

Galilea shifted her weight uncomfortably, making the mattress creak. "Oh, well, I wouldn't say—"

"Yes, you would, and so would everyone else. Phillip is . . . *plump.* I cannot deny it. He does indulge in sweets far too often."

Elenore's gaze drifted to one side, and her smile faded.

"Thank you, Galilea," she said softly, "for absolving my son of at least one of the crimes. I could not bear to think he would—" Clipping off the end of the sentence, she peered at Galilea once more. "I do not excuse the child, you understand, for placing a dead rat in your wardrobe, but 'tis such a relief to hear he is innocent of . . . any other wrongdoings."

Galilea nodded, then frowned worriedly. "Tell me, Elenore. How did poor Phillip fare?"

"Not well, I'm afraid, but it could have been worse if Collin hadn't interceded." Elenore closed her eyes a moment and took a deep breath. "Roland wanted to hang the boy by his heels," she murmured.

"And?" Galilea prompted, needing to know what was to be done with the child.

Elenore reopened her eyes and smiled.

"Phillip's to weed the gardens each afternoon until every single flowerbed on the estate is cleared. 'Tis a chore that should keep him quite busy for the next few months. A stern, but just punishment, I think."

Galilea sighed, grateful Roland hadn't influenced Collin's judgment. Knowing what little she did of Elenore's husband, she suspected Roland might have wanted to have the boy publicly flogged.

Still, weeding the entire garden seemed too large a task for such a small child.

"But, Elenore," she said, then wrinkled her nose. "To work *all* the gardens appears to me, well, to be much too severe. Couldn't Phillip merely weed one or two of the worst flowerbeds? The rat was not all that big . . . *nor* terrifying, actually."

"Careful Galilea, you shall end up shamelessly spoiling him, as I already do." Elenore's smile brightened for a split second, then she sobered her expression somewhat. "Phillip does deserve his penance for frightening you. As his mother, I shall expect him to follow through with his proposed punishment courageously and hope that in the process he will have learned his lesson."

Galilea nodded, deciding for the time being, she should give up her plea for leniency. She made a silent promise to herself, though, to broach the subject again at a later date.

"Galilea, before I go . . . 'tis something I should like to ask you, if I may."

"But, of course, Elenore," she said. "Ask whatever you will."

Concern etched Elenore's features. "Please tell me you haven't give up your quest to aid our Lizzie."

Galilea smiled softly. "Collin and I are determined to learn the truth."

"Good. I feared you might have given up, with all that's transpired. 'Tis reassuring to hear you haven't. Lizzie deserves to rest in peace."

Bracing her palms on her knees, Elenore smiled again, and pushed up out of the chair. "Well, I really should be going," she said. "I . . . thank you, Galilea, not only for sharing the truth about Phillip, but also for trying to help poor Elizabeth's troubled spirit. I do so hope you succeed in sending our Lizzie to her rightful place in heaven."

"So do I, Elenore . . . so do I." Galilea looped an arm through her stepsister's and walked her to the door.

"I am glad you stopped in to see me, Elenore," Galilea commented as she reached for the doorknob. "I was fretting over little Phillip and wondering how he'd made out."

Elenore stepped across the threshold, then pivoted and grasped both of Galilea's hands in her own.

"Do take care," she whispered. "Whoever pushed you down those stairs . . . I fear, it could be the same who might have harmed Lizzie. Please, trust no one, Galilea. Not even Collin."

Galilea tilted her head. "Not trust Collin? Surely, you jest, Elenore. He's been aiding me with my quest to find Elizabeth's murderer."

"Has he?" Elenore arched one eyebrow. "They do say the best place to steal your enemy's secrets is in the midst of the enemy camp."

"Elenore, Collin is *not* my enemy." A bashful smile tightened the corners of Galilea's mouth. "In fact, he's asked me to marry him."

"Yes, so we all heard him announce in the library," Elenore remarked dryly. "Are you seriously considering his proposal?"

"Why . . . yes, actually. Yes, I am." Galilea lifted her chin a notch once the words were out. In her heart, she knew she was doing more than simply "considering" Collin's offer. Indeed, she'd already planned on accepting—although not until now did she realize she had made the decision to do so. She inhaled deeply, needing to verify her resolve verbally once more. "Yes, Elenore, I *am* going to marry Collin," she stated with conviction. "I just haven't told him, yet."

Elenore's expression showed anything but happiness at the news.

"Galilea . . . perhaps I speak out of turn, but I do so as a friend and sister." Elenore peered over her shoulder, then catching Galilea's elbow, steered her just inside the room. "I pray, do give this proper thought," she said. "I mean, what do we really know about Collin MacLaine? Hardly anything, except that he came here from London."

"I know things about him," Galilea protested. "I know he's kindhearted . . . and generous . . . and brave . . ." Galilea's words trailed off, and once again she fell victim to the silly grin she'd been getting lately whenever she thought of Collin.

"I can see that he's charmed you. You do but glow as you speak of him." Elenore smiled in spite of herself, then reached up and brushed a wisp of hair from Galilea's face. "And I will admit, he is quite handsome, and *most* charming, but . . ."

Galilea grasped her hand and squeezed it. "Elenore,please be happy for me. I love him. And . . . I truly believe he feels the same about me."

Elenore tugged her hand free, lifting it to the base of her throat. Her gaze wandered to one side. "Has it not occurred to you that he may have been sent by your mother?"

Galilea squinted at the other woman, disbelieving she had heard her correctly. "My . . . *mother*? For what reason?"

"I know not," Elenore said with a shrug. "London *was* the actress's last known address, and since Collin came from the city . . . well, perhaps your mother sent him to inquire about her daughter's welfare . . . or something."

"And do you suppose she also arranged for Collin to win Luxley Manor in a card game?" Galilea tucked her chin, and put her hands on her hips. "Not likely, I'm thinking. Elenore, it makes no sense."

Elenore gave way with a short breathy laugh. "That does indeed sound a bit far-fetched, doesn't it? I must be overly tired this evening," she said, rubbing her temple.

The smile lingering about Elenore's lips wavered again. "All the same . . . well, call it woman's intuition, if you will, I still suggest you tread with caution in this matter of the heart, dear sister. Collin MacLaine plays the cards, if you will recall. He gambles, Galilea. 'Tis how he obtained Luxley lands. It doesn't appear he kept very savory company in London, now does it? For all we know, he might have fled the city for some sort of criminal offense."

"Oh Elenore . . . I do appreciate your worrying over me and my situation." Galilea bordered on embracing her stepsister. Because of Elenore's earlier withdrawals though, she refrained once again from doing so. "Please, do not fret so on my account. I am certain you are wrong about Collin. I cannot imagine him—"

Elenore stopped her with a raised hand. "Say no more then, Galilea. I shall trust your judgment concerning the man. Simply promise me you will be most watchful of everyone in this house, and I shall be content."

After a slight hesitation, Elenore stooped and pressed a brief kiss to her cheek. "I could not bear to lose another sister so soon after finding you," she whispered, then turned abruptly and stepped into the hall. "Good night, Galilea. Sleep well."

* * *

Galilea climbed wearily into bed shortly after Elenore left although she did not fall fast asleep. For a spell, she stared at the ceiling, pondering Elenore's parting words.

Why on earth Elenore should suspect Collin of treachery was beyond Galilea's comprehension. While Collin might not have always been exactly cordial, he *had* been more than generous with the family.

Galilea had no doubt that Collin MacLaine, her husband to be, was a wonderful man in all respects.

Even so, 'twas rather bothersome that Elenore should not share the same opinion of the man.

A soft breeze floated through the window, lightly lifting the curtains and grazing Galilea's too-warm cheeks. To be quite honest, she cared not what anyone else thought of Collin. She loved him.

She . . . *loved him.*

The sudden admission produced a wondrous glow in the very center of Galilea. Smiling ever wider, she rolled over and hugged her pillow tightly. She loved Collin MacLaine. 'Twas no *ands, ifs,* or *buts* about it. She loved him dearly . . . and she *was* going to marry him.

And now that her mind was made up, she could hardly wait for morning to come so she could give him her answer.

Galilea sailed off to sleep in a euphoric mood. In the midst of her sweet slumber, however, her pleasant dreams took a sharp turn down a disturbing path.

One moment she danced with Collin in the meadow. In a column of golden sunlight, the two of them waltzed through the field of wildflowers to the tinkling sound of Galilea's music box.

The next moment, in the blink of an eye, Galilea stood alone in the cold, black void of a nightmare.

Hands stretched out of the darkness, pushing her back and forth. Then, one by one, the shadowed figures surrounding her were illuminated by an eerie green glow.

Winston . . . Fanny . . . Roland . . . Elenore . . . Phillip . . . Widow Luxley . . . and Collin.

With frowning faces, each stepped forth in turn, all of them closing in on her . . . continuing to shove her to and fro. Their mouths moved in unison, echoing a single word. "Witch," they chanted over and over again. "Witch . . . witch . . . witch . . ."

"No," Galilea cried out, but her voice could not be heard. "Collin, tell them. Tell them I'm no witch!"

Collin broke from the circle of her tormentors and glided closer and closer, until his face was merely a breath away from Galilea's.

"Elenore's right, you know," he said, his voice sounding as if it came from the far end of a tunnel. "Your mother sent me. Did you hear me, Galilea? Galilea . . .

". . . Galilea, wake up."

The whisper pierced Galilea's eardrum. Her eyes flew open to find someone stooped beside the bed, a face on the pillow next to hers.

A scream rose in her throat, but the cry was stifled by a large, warm palm closing over her mouth.

"Shh, my love, 'tis only me."

Collin lifted his head above Galilea's, and a ray of moonlight slanted across his features.

"Collin? Whatever are you doing he—"

He pressed a finger to her lips, silencing her. "Keep your voice low," he murmured, then helped her sit up in bed.

"Collin, what is it?" she asked in a whisper, heeding his advice. "What brings you here at this hour? Is it Lizzie? Have you learned anything more?"

"Nay, 'tis you I'm concerned with at the moment, Galilea." Collin peered intensely into her eyes. "The manor, I fear, is not a very safe place for you. I do not like the accusations the widow made about you this evening. The old biddy's likely to stir up a witch-hunt. Now hurry and gather the things you'll need, my love. I'm taking you away from here for the time being. I can take no more chances on someone doing you harm here."

Galilea searched his face for some feasible explanation. "But—"

Collin planted a swift kiss upon her lips. "We've no time to debate the issue now, Galilea. Get up and fetch a few clothes. I want to leave while the rest of the household sleeps. That way, we shan't be followed, and no one shall know where you are, save me."

Elenore's warning came to mind, but Galilea's faith in Collin rose defiantly above her apprehension.

With only the slightest amount of hesitation, she climbed from the bed. Scurrying about the room quietly, she promptly bundled her piddling belongings, then met Collin at the door.

"Come," Collin whispered, after peering up and down the hallway.

Folding his large hand around Galilea's fingers, he led her along the dark corridor and did not slow his pace until they reached the foyer.

As they slipped out the main door of the manor together, neither Collin nor Galilea noticed the lone figure standing in the shadows at the top of the stairs.

Collin moved in the opposite direction of the castle toward a thick line of trees, trekking across a muddy section of Luxley land that Galilea had never explored.

Glancing over her shoulder, Galilea noted the manor was swiftly blending into the dark horizon and would soon disappear from sight altogether. A chill skimmed her arms. 'Twas a cool dampness in the air left over from the storm. She could at least be thankful, she supposed, that it had stopped raining.

"Collin, where is it you're taking me?" she asked as they approached the heavily wooded area.

"To Lord Luxley's hunting lodge. Here now, watch your step." Collin swiveled and placed a hand at the base of Galilea's spine, helping her over a fallen log. "The old place hasn't been used in years, I'm told. 'Tis nearly hidden completely behind a grail of overgrown shrubbery and climbing ivy. There're traces of a trail left here somewhere . . . ah yes, here it 'tis."

The full moon shone through the branches overhead, sparsely lighting the path infested with grass and vines.

Of a sudden, Galilea's scalp tingled. Then a powerful foreboding rushed at her from the depths of the forest and struck her like a strong gust of wind. All the air left her lungs and carried a small gasping sound past her lips.

The sensation jarred her, halting her footsteps. She squeezed Collin's hand, stopping him as well.

"Galilea, what is it?" Collin caught her shoulders, and she braced her hands against his chest.

"Collin," she whispered, gazing up at him. " 'Tis where I was born, the hunting lodge. I know the place. I've *seen* it. I can tell you what it looks like inside and out."

"Galilea, how is it you could remember such a thing? You were but an infant when—"

"The knowing . . . 'tis back, Collin." Galilea's eyes strayed from his a moment. "I'd lost it while in the manor. No matter how hard I tried, I couldn't see, hear, or feel anything. But it's coming back. I sense it."

Collin embraced her, pressing her cheek against his chest.

"Do you not wish to go to the lodge?" he asked, his breath coming warm against the crown of her head.

"But I *do,*" she answered, pushing an arm's length away from him. "*I must.* I . . . cannot say why, just now. But, there is a reason I *have* to go there."

If Collin had any more questions, he kept them to himself. Wrapping a protective arm about her waist, he guided Galilea onward down the twisted path toward their destiny.

Chapter 17

As Collin and Galilea emerged into a small clearing, the rustic lodge loomed before them. 'Twas as Galilea had pictured it in her mind, only battered by time and left in poor disrepair over the passing of years.

The modest lodging would have appeared abandoned indeed had it not been for the smoke curling upward from the chimney. Nearing the entrance, a slight glow of lamplight became visible between the cracks in the tightly drawn shutters.

Collin paused just outside, and while he fumbled inside his pocket for a key, Galilea lifted her gaze to the sun-bleached antlers of a noble woodland beast hanging above the arched doorway.

"Ah, here we are," Collin commented, placing the key in the latch. The heavy wood door creaked loudly in protest as he shoved it open. "Come inside, Galilea, and warm yourself."

Galilea moved as if in a dream across the threshold. Blazing golden flames danced in the fireplace, casting wavy shadows upward to the rafters. Various mementoes of Lord Luxley's hunting days lined the oak-paneled walls. Among the trophies were stuffed birds, such as owls and pheasants, and an obviously prized boar's head. A dusty collection of long guns was displayed over the fireplace. Much higher above the mantel, closer to the lofty ceiling, the mounted head of a twelve-point buck stared glassy-eyed upon the intruders.

"I see Winston's tidied up a bit," Collin said, walking further into the room. "And look, he's left some wine, as well." Collin gestured to the table where a bottleneck protruded from among other contents in a basket.

Galilea strolled to the table and, lifting a corner of the gingham cloth covering the basket, peeked inside. "I thought you said no one else would know we were here."

"Winston, I tend to trust." Moving up beside her, Collin tilted his head to catch her eye, and smiled. "He's too damned straightforward to be dishonest, or haven't you noticed?"

The sides of Galilea's mouth twitched upward. "He is a bit stiffly starched at times, isn't he?"

"Stiffly starched, I believe, is too mild a phrase to describe our Winston." Collin reached for the wine and examined the bottle. "Regardless, he's a good man, even if he *doesn't* care a wit for Scots."

Collin popped the cork then tugged two goblets from the basket.

"It has been a most trying day," he said

while he poured the wine. "I, for one, could use a nightcap. Will you join me?" he asked, offering her a glass.

Galilea's fingers brushed over his as she accepted the goblet from him.

For a matter of heartbeats, Collin kept his hold on the glass stem.

Galilea lifted her eyes to his, and her pulse quickened.

"Collin, there's something—" she began.

"Galilea, I need to—" Collin blurted out in the same instant.

Both paused, waiting for the other to continue. The fire crackled in the moment of silence. The two of them exchanged a bashful smile.

Collin cleared his throat and let go of her glass.

"You first," he said, grasping his own goblet. "You were about to say?"

Galilea lowered her gaze by degrees to the red wine she held in a tight grip. "Collin, I've come to a decision concerning your proposal of marriage," she said quietly. "I have considered it quite thoroughly, and have—"

"Wait." Collin's face appeared suddenly pale. Setting down his glass, he took Galilea's goblet from her and placed it on the table next to his. "I . . . there's something I must say before you give your answer . . . something I should have said while on my bended knee. But fool that I am . . ."

Collin clasped her hand, and with his eyes sliding closed, he lifted her fingers to his lips.

'Twas a sweet, tender gesture, a soft kiss that lingered on, his breath growing warm and erratic against her skin.

Galilea stood motionless, staring at him, longing to reach out and stroke his silky hair, yet too weak to lift a hand to do so.

When at last Collin raised his head, his adoring gaze went straight to her heart.

"Your face is like the sun, Galilea," he whispered in a deep husky voice, "that rises and sets upon the horizon of my soul. When you walk into the room, I cannot breathe . . . I cannot think. I can only . . . *feel.*" Lifting her hand once more, he rubbed his jaw lovingly back and forth across her knuckles as he spoke.

"I . . . have never experienced such emotions . . . never known feelings such as these existed—not until *you* came into my life. 'Twas as if I walked the world half deaf, dumb, and blind, Galilea . . . not clearly seeing or hearing all the beauty that was there before my very eyes all the while. In the spring, when the wildflowers bloomed, I passed by the fields without ever noticing their vibrant color. I never inhaled their sweet fragrance—not until you stood amongst them."

Collin paused, searching her reaction, his mouth slightly open as if he strove for his next thought.

"Collin." His name slipped from Galilea in a breathless fashion. She struggled for appropriate words. "I . . . I—"

"Please. Let me finish, Galilea." Collin's

fingers tightened around her own. He blinked, then fastened his gaze firmly upon her chin. "I . . . I realize you must have reservations about me. God knows, you should have. I am no saint, nor do I claim to be. Rather, a starving poet with little to offer you, except my loyalty and my name."

Closing his eyes again briefly, he raked a hand through his hair. Then he raised his lids, and his gaze met Galilea's steadily.

Her heart pounded achingly against her breast as she watched him kneel once more before her.

"I could not fault you for having the common sense to refuse me. But, if your answer is nay, then I would ask you to reconsider," he said, grasping the sides of her skirt in doubled fists. "Pray, give me time to win your favor, Galilea. I want you alone by my side for all eternity. If I cannot have you, then I shall die a lonely man—for I shall pledge my love to no one but you."

Galilea's throat constricted, and a single tear rolled down her cheek. Leaning forward, she folded Collin in her embrace, clasping his head tightly against her abdomen.

"I am yours, and you are mine, Collin," she murmured, lifting a strand of his hair and letting it shift through her fingers. "Now, and for all time."

Collin buried his face in the folds of her skirt, and he wrapped his arms around her thighs in a fierce hug.

They remained thus for ever so long, locked

in the mutual hold . . . basking in the glow of the firelight, and each other.

Rather abruptly, a deep throaty laugh erupted from Collin, shaking his chest. Re-adjusting his grasp on Galilea, he came to his feet and lifted her high into the air.

Galilea squealed, and braced her hands upon his shoulders, then burst into giggles herself.

"Collin, you fool," she gasped. "Put me down before you hurt yourself."

"That would be a difficult trick, since you weigh no more than flea," he replied, then whirled in a circle, letting her glide down the length of his body. Once she'd landed aground, he hooked his hands around her waist. "Ah, Galilea, you know not how happy you've made me."

"No happier than you have made me," she said looping her arms loosely about his neck.

"Now to business," Collin commented with an obviously feigned look of contemplation. "Personally, I think we should recite the vows of holy matrimony within the month. No, inside a week . . . or two, at the most." He furrowed his brow. "Would tomorrow be too soon, do you think?"

Galilea's lips parted as she stared up at him. "Surely, you jest."

"Nay, love. I do not." Collin traced her mouth with a fingertip. "Right now, tomorrow seems much too far away, as is."

"Collin . . . you do appear to be most serious here."

"Oh, I am."

Galilea focused on the hollow at the base of his throat, and she rubbed her thumb back and forth over his shirt collar. "Collin, a wedding is the most important day of a woman's life. I . . . I want it to be special."

"As do I, but—"

"But there are preparations to make," she said interrupting him. "Things to do—"

"Galilea?" Collin curled a finger beneath her chin and raised her face to his. "I shall marry you wherever, *whenever* you say. But I warn you, I shall no doubt become a dreadful bear if you make me wait too long." One corner of his mouth crept upward with a lazy grin. "Now . . . with your permission, I should like to kiss you—just so I'll know this is no dream."

Galilea tilted her head back and arched toward him, flattening her breasts against his solid torso.

"Permission granted," she murmured, then closed her eyes and presented her lips.

A quivering breath escaped Galilea as Collin's mouth brushed gently over hers. A hungry need for more of him stirred inside her . . . made her cheeks burn hot. Standing on tiptoe, she clasped his neck more securely, and promptly applied a bit more pressure against his lips.

Encouraged by her amorous mood, Collin tightened his arms about her with an urgent tenderness and deepened the kiss, savoring the sweet taste of her . . . teasing her mouth open with the tip of his tongue.

He was unprepared for her response.

Galilea gave herself to the kiss, pressing into him, moving him backward until his thigh bumped the edge of the table. Her charm was more powerful than any magic potion ever could be.

Half-crazed by her aggression, he slid one hand up and down her spine, while the other dipped lower and cupped her backside. Without their lips ever parting, he twisted and lifted her, seating her upon the table.

When Galilea locked her legs around him, a groan came unbidden from somewhere deep in his throat. She claimed his mouth with an untamed recklessness, and he rose to the occasion, matching her enthusiasm.

By their own accord, Collin's hips moved in a lazy figure-eight against Galilea.

She followed suit, driving him to the point of insanity . . . making his head swim.

His pulse beat far too fast. A fire low in his abdomen burned ever brighter, hotter moment by moment. His flesh was all too willing . . . his spirit, *God,* was weak.

"Gal-Galilea," he muttered breathlessly, forcing his mouth from hers. "I . . . I think we should—"

"Nay, Collin." Galilea's silky voice flowed through him like warm buttered rum. With a sleepy smile, she grazed a fingertip back and forth across his lower lip. "Do not say we must wait for our wedding night. Have we not exchanged vows already in our own way?"

Collin swallowed hard. "Aye, but—"

"Hush then, my precious. For *I* cannot wait. I have never in my life experienced such a rush of pleasure all at once. Loving you is simply delicious, and I want more." Ducking her head, she peered at him from under her brow, her green eyes twinkling bright. "And there *is* more to it, isn't there, Collin? I can sense that there is, but I can't exactly—"

Collin covered her mouth with his—all honor gone to hell. He kissed her once, twice, and again, then paused just long enough to whisper, "Aye, there's more," before forging again his lips to hers.

Collin trailed his fingers down her dress, unfastening the tiny buttons one by one.

Galilea tugged his shirttail from his britches, and they parted long enough for her to hastily pull the garment over his head.

Undressing each other in a frenzied fashion, they sank to the floor, kissing and caressing all the while.

Galilea gloried at the exquisite feel of Collin's hands moving over her with such tender urgency. Tremoring from his touch, she arched her breasts against his palms.

His tongue dipped sweetly into her mouth, and heat flowed into her, setting her insides ablaze. She glided her fingers through his hair . . . over his shoulders, his chest . . . his flat firm stomach . . . and lower, exploring the silky smoothness of his skin. Swept along by this marvelous new ecstasy, she could not hold Collin close enough . . . or tight enough.

An onslaught of emotions rampaged through Collin. The magic of Galilea's hands roving over every inch of him made him break into a cold sweat. The power of her innocent eagerness made him physically tremble. She wrapped her essence around him like a warm blanket on a cold day, and he sailed a sea of pleasure.

Driven by a need bred of madness, he rolled Galilea onto her back and aligned himself over her. Pushed far and away past the point of restraint, Collin took her mouth with a burning desire to draw her breath into his lungs. His passion broke loose with a vengeance, his pulse pumping hard, pounding in his head, in his veins. A fever took him and when he could hold back no longer, he pressed himself into Galilea.

Galilea curled her nails into the flesh of Collin's back and arched upward as her abdomen swelled with the fullness of him. Sliding her arms tightly around his neck, she stilled his heated body, hugging him close.

Their hearts thumped hard, one against the other.

"Galilea," Collin whispered into her mouth.

"Shh," she murmured, nibbling his lower lip.

Galilea stirred beneath him, raising her hips to his.

Collin groaned, low in his throat. He began to move with slow, lazy strokes. With a great need to expose his overflowing love for Galilea, he strove for an easy, sensuous pace.

Yet Galilea responded by picking up the rhythm. With her fingers playing along the contours of his hips, she rocked upward, giving Collin no choice but to follow her lead. Burying his face in the pillow of her hair, he plunged harder, delved deeper, until he raced ever closer to her soul.

Galilea moved to the tune of Collin's body, bathed in a luminous sensation that spread outward from the point that bonded them together as one. She soared higher and higher, as if spiraling toward the stars. Her heart folded around the closeness she shared with Collin, and she reached for some nameless treasure . . . a bliss beyond all else . . . a crowning glory that she somehow knew waited ahead.

With a sudden desperation, she clutched Collin's arms, feeling his muscles flex beneath her fingers. Her intense blend of pain and pleasure grew and grew . . . until it burst inside her . . . and a warm pulsating glow slowly drained into her limbs.

Collin plunged forward one last time and, with the final force, cried out her name. For an endless moment, he shuddered. Then his body relaxed completely atop Galilea's, and he nestled his head between the soft mounds of her breasts.

In the dusky purple shadows preceding dawn, Collin slipped his arms from around Galilea.

She stirred from sleep as she felt his weight leave the mattress of the bed they had ended up in—somewhere amidst their frantic night of lovemaking.

"Collin?" she murmured drowsily. Batting her eyes open, she found him hastily dressing.

At the call of his name, he paused in the task of buttoning his shirt to stoop and press a quick kiss to her lips. "I must get back to the manor, love, before I'm missed."

Galilea reached out and caught his shirttail when he turned from the side of the bed. "Not yet, Collin. Please . . . stay a bit longer."

Dropping onto the edge of the mattress, Collin gathered Galilea up in his arms and kissed her good and proper.

"I wish I could," he whispered, dragging his lips from hers. "Soon, my sweet . . . *soon,* I shall leave you nevermore. But until we've settled all this—"

"Go then," Galilea told him with a smile and gave him a gentle shove—for she knew if they lingered in the embrace much longer, she would not allow him to leave at all.

Collin rose from the bed and swiftly slipped on his jacket, his tall form outlined in the gray shades of dawn creeping into the room.

Once dressed, he hesitated beside the bed.

Galilea braced a palm against his chest when he reached for her again.

"Go now, Collin. My kisses will be waiting for you when you return."

Collin took a backward step, paused briefly, then strode to the door.

At the threshold he pivoted, facing her once more. "I shall be back by nightfall to collect those promised kisses," he said. A fleeting smile passed over his lips, then his expression turned serious. "Galilea . . . if, for some reason, I do not show this evening, contact Winston. Understand?"

Galilea rose upon one elbow. "Is there some reason you wouldn't be back?" she asked.

"Wild horses could not keep me away, my sweet," Collin replied with a wide grin. "I love you madly, Galilea," he added, before he slipped out the door.

Chapter 18

Galilea could not contain her happiness that morning.

Although the lodge appeared no less dreary in the daylight, she puttered about the interior, dusting and straightening, and humming to herself. She wanted everything to be perfect when Collin returned.

Pausing as she made the bed, Galilea smoothed her hand over the pillow where Collin had laid his head. She could still hardly believe she was to become his wife.

Impossible dreams were becoming reality.

Collin MacLaine loved her. And he had not only told her so, he had shown her in the greatest manner a man could show a woman.

Galilea smiled again with the memory of the exquisite passion they had engaged in. Twice again, in the course of the night, Collin had reached for her as they had slept side by side. Twice more, he had taken her to the edge of heaven.

Galilea sank onto the bed, and all thoughts of cleaning deserted her. Touching her fingertips to her heart, she remembered the feel of his hands upon her, and her eyes slid closed. How she loved him. How she ached for his return . . .

She could not say how long she sat there, pondering the miraculous effect two people could have upon one another . . . basking in the wondrous glow of love.

She might have remained in that blissful state for the remainder of the day—had a strong foreboding not rushed forth to seize her.

Galilea's eyes flew open. The room looked somehow different . . . the wood paneling not so brown with age. The very same bed she sat upon was across the room . . . and a woman lay within, writhing with pain.

Galilea tried to stand, yet her legs would not lift her.

She was helpless against the horrific vision. It mattered not whether her eyes were open or shut. The scene took form quite clearly, drawing her into the midst of it. 'Twas as if her spirit soared across the room and entered the woman on the bed.

Galilea *felt* the intense pain . . . heard herself scream in agony.

An old woman's snarling face popped into view, hovering close above Galilea's.

"Shut yer trap, ye lit'le tramp." The hateful woman all but growled. "Just see ye push when I tell ya, mind ya, or I'll smack you silly again."

From some source beyond herself, Galilea realized that she was witnessing her own birth . . . through the eyes of her mother.

Powerless to do otherwise, Galilea relived

the torture and humiliation her actress mother had endured in order to give her and Lizzie life. She felt the tightening of her abdomen and bore down when she was told, gritting her teeth as she did so.

The nightmare continued.

But in the end, after all the degradation and sharp contractions, Galilea also experienced the joy of a mother gazing lovingly upon the small, pink faces of two baby girls.

Galilea's arms stretched out for the children, just as her mother must have done.

And she ached inside, just as her mother must have, when the mean old woman refused to let her hold the babies.

'Twas then that Galilea noticed for the first time the thin girl hovering nearby—a much younger Fanny.

As Galilea looked on, she watched the midwife shove one of the children into the girl's arms and whisper instructions that made young Fanny's face blanch white.

Knowing full well what Fanny had been told to do with the baby, Galilea cried out in protest.

The midwife whirled around, and Galilea's head snapped with the crack of the woman's palm against her face. Once again the mean-spirited woman stooped over her, her dark beady eyes piercing Galilea's.

"Now, ye lissen up 'ere, missy," she said, the words hissing from between her rotted teeth. "Lady Luxley, wife to the man 'oo bastarded your accursed children, bid me tell you one thing—Yer *never* t' come round 'ere no more, or else the one brat left livin' will be done-away-with as well."

With those last words of warning, the vision shattered into pieces like a mirror breaking.

Galilea found herself once again, sitting on the edge of the bed. Drenched in perspiration, her limbs shook uncontrollably. She hugged herself and rocked slowly back and forth . . . and soon the trembling subsided.

Collin reached the manor just before dawn. Moving quietly up the stairs, he crept down the hall, past the closed chamber doors, toward his own room.

Once inside his chamber, he let his breath out slowly, grateful his entrance had not disturbed the sleeping household. Warmed by the memory of his blissful night with Galilea, he loosened his cravat as he crossed the room.

When Collin sat down on the edge of the bed to remove his boots, a low crackling sound caught his attention. Furrowing his brow, he lifted his pillow and found a crumpled note stuffed beneath it.

Collin opened the wadded paper and frowned at the contents.

I know who killed Lizzie.
Come alone to the castle ruins at daybreak.
Wait beside the white handkerchief.

The childlike scrawl was almost unreadable, making it impossible to decipher whether the message was written by the hand of a man or woman.

Regardless, Collin had little more time to consider the matter. The first rays of light were already streaking through the curtains of his window.

Rising from the bed, Collin made haste and left the house by way of the servant's entrance.

The round golden sun was just rising above the horizon when he climbed the hill. He may have been too late for the meeting, he realized, shading his eyes from the brightness.

As Collin started toward the castle, he saw a small patch of white on the outlying grounds surrounding the castle. Changing directions, he strode toward the object, finding upon approach, that it was indeed a handkerchief placed carefully on the grass.

He stooped beside an open sinkhole and picked up the white square. Rubbing the linen between his thumb and forefinger, he noted the handkerchief belonged to a man. Initials were embroidered in light gray on one corner. As Collin squinted to make out the letters, he heard a sound behind him.

The vision in the hunting lodge was not the first upsetting sight Galilea had ever experienced, although it was much more disturbing than all the rest of the frightful images put together.

Even so, she *had,* in the past, developed a

method of calming herself after just such an episode.

Fastening her mind on some pleasant recollection, she would close her eyes and take slow, deep breaths. While not working quite as effectively as usual this time, she finally managed to pull it off.

When she had focused solely on Collin, the procedure eventually brought her the peace she sought.

Afterwards, Galilea spent the afternoon outside, doing her best to thin the fortress of weeds around the old lodge. 'Twas a hopeless endeavor, she well knew. Still, it kept her busy whilst she waited for Collin.

As the day stretched into evening, an eerie premonition of pending disaster crept upon her. She was pulling stray grass from the narrow rock walk that led to the door when the nape of her neck began to tingle.

Galilea squinted up at the darkening sky, and her heart doubled its normal rhythm.

Filling her lungs to their full capacity with the sweet woodland air, she dropped her head and continued her work.

She refused to acknowledge even the remotest possibility that the feeling was a prediction of Collin being harmed. She would not dare think it. Before she finished weeding the walk he would come, she assured herself.

Aye, Collin, would be there any time now. And tonight, he would hold her in his arms again, and kiss her . . . and love her . . .

Galilea's sight blurred slightly for a moment, and when her vision cleared, she spied a trickle of blood dripping from the tip of her finger.

Turning her palms up, she noted both hands were equally damaged, scratched and cut, no doubt by the sharp blades of grass she'd been jerking from the rock walkway.

As she stared at the tiny flecks of red, the crimson color grew in size until it blanketed her entire gaze.

And the sensation of doom evolved into full-blown alarm.

"Collin," she whispered.

Coming swiftly to her feet, she turned in the direction of the manor . . . and a chill skimmed her arms.

"Oh, dear God," she murmured beneath her breath. " 'Tis . . . *Collin.*"

Galilea ran with the speed of wings toward Luxley Manor, out of breath and stumbling by the time she reached the servant's entrance.

Pausing just outside, she braced a hand against the door frame and peered into the kitchen.

'Twas a stroke of luck to find Winston puttering about the room, fixing himself a hot buttered rum.

"Winston," Galilea called softly.

The old butler flinched, then looked over his shoulder.

"Oh, mistress," he said in a hushed tone, rushing in a worried fashion to open the door.

"You're not to be here. Why, Master Collin would have a fit if he knew—"

Catching hold of the butler's crisply starched lapel, Galilea pulled herself just inside the kitchen.

"Winston, where is he?" she asked on a note of desperation. "Where's Collin? Is he here?"

Winston tucked his chin and peered at her hand twisted into his jacket.

"Why, no, mistress. I thought he was with you."

Galilea's gaze drifted to one side, and she fell limp against the butler.

Winston caught her by the elbows before she sank to the floor.

"Why, miss, you're fairly shivering. Come and sit down," he said, guiding her into a chair. "I was just about to have a cup of hot rum. I shall fetch you some as well."

Galilea gripped his sleeve as he started to step away. "No, Winston . . . 'tis Collin. He's in trouble . . . in *pain*. I can feel it."

Winston's expression went flat. He stooped and grasped her shoulders. "He's in trouble, you say? Are you quite certain?"

Galilea's eyes slid closed, and she pressed a hand to her heart. "I *feel* it, Winston. He's . . . *hurting*."

"Where? Where is he?" Winston fingers clenched down harder upon her shoulders. "Can you see him?"

Galilea squeezed her eyes tighter shut and furrowed her brow in concentration.

"No," she murmured around the knot that rose in her throat. She shook her head sadly. "I don't see anything but darkness. I can't—"

"You must try!" Winston shook her slightly. "Try harder, mistress. If Master Collin needs our help, we must find him immediately and—"

"Why on earth should Collin need anyone's help?" Roland inquired. Stepping further into the kitchen, Elenore's husband raised an eyebrow. "Winston? I demand to know what's going on here."

Winston swiveled on his haunches and frowned at the man. Galilea leaned to one side in the chair, peering around the butler.

"Well?" Roland folded his arms across his chest and set one foot to tapping. "I'm waiting, Winston."

Galilea and Winston exchanged wary glances.

Roland's mouth twisted into a sneer. "I'm growing weary of this little guessing game. If something's happened to Collin MacLaine, by all rights, I should be told."

Winston pushed up from the floor, and squared his shoulders.

"Mistress Jones believes he may be injured," he stated with a lift of his chin. "I too, am of that opinion, sir."

Roland strode forward and, stopping beside Galilea's chair, glared down at her. "And would this, by any chance be something you know for a fact? Or, is it simply a figment in that pretty little head of yours?"

Galilea raised her gaze to his and held it steady. "I *know*. When the feeling is this strong, I am never guided in the wrong direction. Collin is lying somewhere out there hurt, possibly dying . . . while you insist on standing here debating the issue, Mr. Cameron."

A cynical grin creased Roland's thin lips. "Precisely what would you have me do about it, Mistress Jones?"

"Form a search party." Galilea rose from her chair, and thumped Roland on the arm with the heel of her hand. "Gather some of the tenants . . . and bloody-well *look* for him, you pompous jackass!"

Roland brought his head down abruptly, so close to Galilea's that he came only a hair away from butting her like a goat. "Now, see here, you little twit, you've no right to talk to me in that tone. I'll have you know—"

"Here now, that's quite enough of that," Winston blurted out, stepping between the two and shoving them apart. "There's no need for name-calling. We should be thinking of Master Collin, not squabbling amongst ourselves."

Galilea widened her eyes on the wise old butler.

"You're right, of course, Winston," she said, then ran a hand over her face and shifted her gaze to Roland. "Forgive me, Mr. Cameron. I did indeed lose my composure."

Roland gave his jacket a tidying tug and elevated his nose. "I shall accept your apology just this once, Galilea. But do see you hold your nasty little tongue in the future."

Galilea swallowed her favored reply. She would have liked nothing more than to knock the man down a notch in a war of words. But now was not the time.

"I shall," she said a bit too sweetly, then dropped all pretense of being cordial. "About that search party—how soon could one be organized?"

Roland cocked his head to one side, viewing her as if she were insane. "A search party?" He laughed. "You can't be serious."

"Oh but I am."

Winston stretched his head over Galilea's shoulder. "I believe we should do as she says, sir," he put in.

Roland frowned profusely at the butler. "You're as mad as she is, Winston. I'm not about to round up the tenants to go trotting off on some wild-goose chase. We've no proof anything at all has happened to Collin."

"But, sir—"

"But nothing, Winston." Roland glanced back and forth between the two. "I'm sure there's nothing to worry about. Collin is no doubt around here somewhere."

Winston straightened his posture and clasped his hands against his waist. "Then might I suggest we at least search the premises, sir?"

Roland pressed his lips into a tight line, then sighed.

"Oh very well. We shall split up then. Winston, you check the grounds. Galilea, you look upstairs. I shall search in the wine cellar and on the first floor."

Roland glanced about the kitchen and frowned again. "Winston, where's Fanny? She could certainly help."

"Gone to market, sir," Winston answered with a lowering of his brow. " 'Tis Tuesday, if you recall, sir. Fanny always goes to market on Tuesday."

"So she does." Roland shrugged. "I suppose it shall just have to be the three of us then."

Galilea climbed the stairs and went straight up to the third floor. She knew she would not find Collin there.

In fact, she was fairly certain, if he had been anywhere in the manor, she would have sensed his presence from the first moment she had entered the house.

'Twas Lizzie she hoped to locate when she stepped into the corridor of the unused third floor.

Galilea walked promptly into Elizabeth Luxley's old bedchambers. Stopping in the center of the room, she turned in a slow circle, seeking the presence of her long-dead twin sister.

Several moments passed before a light buzzing sound reached Galilea's ears. Peering over her shoulder, she caught sight of a movement in the darkest corner of the room.

Galilea pivoted and narrowed her eyes on a

wavy shadow that faded in and out. Stepping closer, she could barely make out the form of the little girl.

Lizzie's image was so dim and transparent that one might have passed right by without noticing her.

Galilea stretched a hand toward her twin sister. "Lizzie, I need your help. Please . . . please, Collin's missing and—"

The buzzing that came from Lizzie rose in volume, elevating to the point that Galilea could recognize the noise as an urgent string of whispering.

Galilea furrowed her brow, trying to distinguish the message Lizzie tried so hard to convey. But the words were garbled, in very much the same way as when Galilea had first heard the whispers.

Then, a few audible sounds broke free from Lizzie's moving mouth.

"Cold and dark . . ." she wailed pitifully. *"So cold . . . so cold . . ."*

The words trailed off into nothingness, and Lizzie's pale image flickered brighter, once, twice, then she was gone.

"Lizzie, wait." Galilea attempted to follow her into the shadows. "Please . . . come back."

A weight settled on Galilea's shoulders as she turned and left the room. She had counted on Lizzie's aid in finding Collin. Poor Lizzie, it seemed, had problems of her own.

Halfway down the stairs to the second floor, Widow Luxley could be heard ranting.

Heading down the hall toward the widow's

room, Galilea saw that the door to Harriet Luxley's chambers stood wide open.

"I shall not calm down!" the widow shouted. "It has been one thing upon another ever since that wretched madwoman came to this house. 'Twouldn't surprise me a bit to learn that . . . that *Galilea creature* did away with Collin MacLaine herself."

Despite the rudeness of entering a room without permission, Galilea marched down the remainder of the hall and sailed directly into Harriet Luxley's private chambers.

She came to an abrupt stop just inside, noting the whole Luxley brood was gathered there as well.

Lady Luxley reclined upon a mountain of pillows, pressing a wet rag to her forehead. Elenore sat on the edge of the bed next to her, while Phillip bounced around on the mattress by the footrail. Roland, of course, was also present, and had no doubt related Galilea's worry over Collin's disappearance.

All heads turned Galilea's way upon her entrance.

Straightening her spine, she tilted her chin toward Harriet Luxley.

"How could you possibly believe I would do anything to harm the man I love?" she asked, letting her gaze drift over the others as she did so.

"Because you're a witch." Harriet lifted herself upright from the pillows. "An evil, wretched woman who knows nothing about *love*."

"Witch, witch, witch," Phillip chimed, bouncing ever higher on the end of the bed.

The blunt accusation took Galilea aback. She opened her mouth to protest, but the widow cut her off.

"See? She cannot deny it." Widow Luxley smiled smugly. "Look at her, Roland. She's as guilty as sin. I say we send for the proper authorities immediately."

"Mother!" Elenore shifted, staring wide-eyed at Galilea. "I don't think—"

"Hold your tongue, Elenore," Roland commanded, and his wife complied. "Mother Luxley's right. We should turn her over to the authorities for questioning, I believe. Collin *is* missing. How could she have known that, if she wasn't involved in some way?"

Once again, Galilea was struck speechless. She looked to Elenore for support, but her only ally sat motionless with her head bowed.

"No," Galilea said in a hoarse whisper, as she started to back out of the room. " 'Tis not true . . . I would never hurt Collin. I love—"

In three swift strides, Roland reached out and caught her securely by the arm, halting her retreat.

"Lock her in her room, Roland," the widow suggested, her eyes twinkling with a strange glow. "Then fetch the constable from the village."

Chapter 19

Galilea attempted once more to pick the lock of her chamber door.

Once again, she was unsuccessful.

Tossing the hairpin across the room, she took to pacing back and forth at the end of her bed.

No matter how hard she tried, she could not see Collin in her mind's eye. She could only *feel* him. He was growing weaker by the hour.

And she was caged in this damnable room with no way to help him.

Flopping down on the edge of the bed, she ran her hands over her face, letting them rest at the base of her throat.

Where was Winston? Where was Fanny? Surely, one of the two would aide in her escape. Sitting here doing nothing but waiting for news of Collin was driving her to the brink of insanity.

With a deep sigh, she reclined on her pillow, folding her hands behind her head. Her gaze strayed to the glowing lamp atop the bureau. A moth battered itself against the globe, determined to fly into the flame.

'Twas late, Galilea suspected. Just how late, she could not guess, for each minute she had spent locked in the room had seemed endless.

Rising from the bed in a restless fashion, she strode to the window and opened it. Had they jailed her in Collin's room, she could have climbed down the lattice. As it was her window was much too far away from the sturdy wooden grillwork.

Galilea peered up at the bright full moon hanging in the night sky . . . and wondered if Collin could see it from where he was.

Her heart constricted at the thought of him alone and injured out there somewhere.

Why couldn't she see him? Why did she only see darkness? Why hadn't he made an attempt to send her his thoughts . . . to tell her his whereabouts? Was he unconscious? Or . . . ?

Nay. She would not even think it.

Spinning around to face the door again, Galilea focused on the brass latch. She had to free herself. But how?

With wooden steps, she moved to the bed and crawled into the center of the mattress. Drawing her knees to her chest, she lay upon her side, staring unseeingly at the suicidal moth. Her brain worked furiously, gathering plan after plan of escape . . . then discarding them one by one for some reason or another.

Her head began to ache in the process, and she closed her eyes to ease the dreadful pain in her head . . . and in her heart.

Soon exhaustion overcame her, pulling her down into a deep pit of slumber.

A loud screech woke her some time later, causing her to bound upward in bed.

Magus cawed again from the window sill, demanding her attention.

"Magus," she murmured with a smile stretching her lips. She edged off the mattress and started toward him, but the crow cried out one last time, then flew out the window and into the night.

In his wake, upon the sill where the bird had sat, something glinted in the moonlight.

As Galilea drew nearer the window, she recognized the glimmering object as the locket that Magus had brought her at the castle ruins—the battered bit of jewelry that had once belonged to her twin sister.

When Galilea picked up the small silver heart and held it in the palm of her hand, Lizzie's last words came back to her. *Dark and cold . . . so cold . . .*

Galilea closed her fingers over the locket, and suddenly she *knew* where Collin was.

Without further adieu, she glanced about the room, searching for something heavy enough to bash the lock. Before her gaze landed on anything suitable, a light rap sounded at her door.

A key clicked in the latch, and the door creaked open to expose Elenore standing in the hallway.

"Hurry," she whispered. "Mother's sleeping, and Roland and the others are still out looking for Collin."

Stuffing the locket into her pocket, Galilea made a hasty exit.

"Fortunately, the constable was off visiting his brother in London," Elenore told her, catching Galilea's arm and dragging her swiftly along the corridor. "He won't be coming round till tomorrow. I'll help you hide until we can—"

"Elenore, I know where Collin is."

Stopping at the top of the stairs, Elenore turned and stared at Galilea. "You do?"

"He's in the sinkhole at the castle ruins," Galilea paused long enough to blurt it out, then made a move to race down the stairway.

Elenore caught her elbow. "Galilea, you're not thinking of going out there all alone? Perhaps we can locate some of the men looking for Collin and—"

"Collin's hurt, Elenore. I haven't the time to waste. I must go to him now," she said.

Lifting her arm from the other woman's grasp, Galilea took to the stairs again.

"Then I shall go with you," Elenore called out behind her. "We will need to fetch some rope and a lantern from the shed."

The full moon cast an eerie glow over the ruins as Galilea and Elenore trudged up the hill toward the castle.

The closer they came to the sinkhole, the harder Galilea's heart beat. Collin *was* there. She sensed it with every part of her being.

As they approached the wide yawning in the ground, Galilea noted the boards had been removed.

"I cannot see a thing," Elenore remarked, holding the lantern above the deep dark pit.

"He's down there somewhere," Galilea insisted. Cupping her mouth she lowered her head into the hole. "Collin?" she called out, hearing the name echo over and over again.

Goose bumps rose on Galilea's arms at the lack of response.

"He's there, I tell you," she said to Elenore. "Toss the rope in and hold it steady. I'm going down."

"Galilea, you can't." Elenore's pale features displayed horror in the wan light of the moon. " 'Tis far too dangerous to even consider doing such a—"

"Stop it, Elenore. I'm frightened enough already." Galilea added a feeble smile to the harsh words, then she laid a hand upon her stepsister's shoulder. "I *must* go. There will be no talking me out of it. Don't you see? Collin *is* there, and he needs our help. Now, please, just hold the rope."

Elenore nodded reluctantly. Setting the lantern on the edge of the sinkhole, she wedged her feet against the surrounding rocks and gripped one end of the rope.

"Thank you, Elenore," Galilea said, then lowered herself into the wide, dark cavity.

A cold musty air swirled around Galilea as she descended. The rope grated her hands. It seemed forever before her feet touched solid ground.

"I've made it," she cried out. Looking up, she saw Elenore's face bathed in the soft yellow glow of the lantern far above, the stars in the sky framing her head.

"I cannot see you," Elenore called back. "Are you all right?"

"All is well, Elenore. I'm going to see if I can find Collin now."

Going down on all fours, Galilea crawled into the black void, feeling her way along blindly. The hard surface beneath her was ice cold and gritty. The smell of mold and mildew was overwhelming.

She had not gone far, when she heard a slight groan coming from her left. Stretching out a hand, she leaned in the direction of the faint moaning, and her fingers grazed a solid form.

"Collin?"

"Ga-Galilea?"

The voice was no more than a weak whisper, but 'twas Collin's voice, all the same .... and the most beautiful sound Galilea had ever heard.

Moving closer, she wrapped her arms around him, nearly covering him with her body. "Collin, you're shivering," she said, holding him tighter in an attempt to warm him.

"Gal-Galilea . . . don't trust . . . "

"Shh, Collin, my love. Don't try to talk. We're going to get you out of this dreadful place soon." Galilea brushed her hand through his hair and pressed his head to her breast. While his skin was cool and clammy, his forehead was sizzling to the touch. "I must leave you for a moment, Collin. I must go back and have Elenore fetch the others to help."

"No, no . . . " he muttered as Galilea laid him gently aside. "Don't . . . don't trust . . ."

Unable to bear his feverish pleading, Galilea moved quickly, and hastily returned to the wide opening where Elenore waited above.

"I've found him, Elenore," she shouted. "I've found Collin."

Elenore's face appeared unnaturally bland as Galilea peered up at her. The golden light from the lantern made her features seem hard and harsh.

"Is he alive?" Elenore asked in a bizarre monotone.

"Yes," Galilea answered, then laughed because it felt so good to say it. "Yes. Yes, he is . . . but Elenore, I fear he's ill. Please hurry and find Winston and Roland. We have to get him out of here as soon as possible."

Elenore rose slowly to her feet and stood on the edge of the sinkhole, staring down at Galilea.

'Twas then that Galilea noticed she had the rope coiled over one shoulder.

The hair on the back of Galilea's neck stood on end. "Elenore? Why . . . why have you pulled the rope up?" she asked, though in her heart she already knew the answer.

"Because you'll not be needing it." Elenore's voice went flat and dry. She knelt beside the hole again. "You and Collin have each other, don't you?" Elenore smiled in a strange fashion at that point, and one by one, began sliding the wooden planks back in place across the opening. "What else could you possibly need, Galilea? You . . . and Lizzie, you have it all."

"Elenore." A breath rushed from Galilea as she said the woman's name. Panic rose high in her chest while she watched the sparse sky above her disappearing.

Keep her talking, instinct urged Galilea.

"Elenore, wait," she said, then paused and moistened her lips. "Please . . . I . . . I don't understand. I thought we were friends, you and I. *Sisters.* Remember? You said . . . that I was like the little sister you lost. Like—"

"Lizzie." Elenore paused with the last board poised above its place. Wedging her face between the narrow space, she snickered. "Just like Lizzie. Pretty. Sweet. Daddy's little darling."

Elenore wrinkled her brow in a pained expression. "*I* was Daddy's girl," she whimpered, "until Lizzie came along. Lord Luxley adopted me, you know. He loved me just as much."

"I'm sure he did, Elenore."

An awful notion suddenly dawned on Galilea as she eyed the woman above with pity. She braced a hand against her midriff, contemplating the possibility that Elenore might have had something to do with Lizzie's death.

Before Galilea had a chance to question her, Elenore stretched out across the beams covering the sinkhole and began softly weeping.

"I . . . I n-never meant to hurt Elizabeth," she said between sobs. "Truly, I didn't. 'Twas . . . 'twas an accident, really. Truly, it was. But . . . but, they would have never believed it. They would have said I'd done it . . . on p-purpose . . . out of s-spite . . ."

A teardrop fell between the slats, striking Galilea on the back of her hand. The small spot of moisture glistened in a sliver of moonlight. Galilea's throat tightened at the sight of it.

"I believe you, Elenore," she said, gazing upward. "Please, tell me how it happened."

Elenore rose on an elbow and peeked through a crack in the boards, her large brown eyes shining in the glow of the lantern. "You won't tell?"

"Not if you don't want me to, Elenore." Galilea made an X upon her chest, though she doubted that Elenore saw her do so. "Cross my heart and hope to die," she said earnestly.

Elenore sniffled. "I . . . I simply wanted her to trade lockets with me, that's all. Father had brought us each one home from his trip to London. Mine was oval, and hers was in the shape of a heart. Elizabeth always got the prettiest presents . . . the prettiest ribbon . . . the prettiest tin of sweets. It wasn't fair."

A short span of silence followed as if Elenore had lost her train of thought.

"No, of course, it wasn't," Galilea commented, prompting her to continue. "But . . . Lizzie didn't want to trade, did she?"

"No." Another shuddering sob broke from Elenore's throat. "I . . . I brought her here, intending to take the locket anyway. Sh-she was wearing it. But . . . Lizzie backed away when I reached for it . . . and she . . . she . . ."

"She fell into this hole," Galilea said quietly, finishing the sentence for Elenore.

A flood of melancholia washed over Galilea at the thought of little Lizzie falling into this deep dark pit. How terribly frightened the poor child must have been.

"You left her here, didn't you, Elenore? You simply walked away and never told a soul she was down here." Galilea could not hide the bitter ire in her voice. She couldn't help but wonder if Lizzie would be alive now had Elenore gone for help that very day.

"You're going to tell on me, aren't you, Galilea." Elenore stated rather than asked, all traces of her weeping gone for good.

Galilea quickly changed her tune. "No, Elenore. I promised I wouldn't. If you'll just let the rope down, we can discuss how best to handle the sit—"

"Liar." Elenore slammed the last plank over the remaining open space, shutting out the moonlight . . . and sealing Galilea and Collin in a tomb of darkness.

Chapter 20

Groping through the dark tunnel, Galilea made her way back to Collin. He groaned as she sat down beside him and carefully positioned his head in her lap.

"She's left us, Collin," Galilea murmured, though she doubted whether he heard her in his condition. "She's left us here to die."

Collin stirred a bit, and she combed her fingers through his hair, noting he felt even warmer than before.

A great weight pressed down in the center of her chest. Surely, someone would think to check the sinkhole. Then again, perhaps they already had searched the area. Collin would have been too weak to answer their call. And Galilea doubted whether anyone but the "madwoman of the meadow" would have actually lowered themselves down into the pit.

She should have waited for Winston. Perhaps, had she taken the time to go out and find the butler, she and Collin wouldn't be in this predicament.

Galilea pressed her spine against the cold stone wall and tilted her head back. Sitting here fretting about what she should have done or didn't do wasn't going to fix the matter.

A light breeze floated through the air, fluttering the wisps of hair that framed her face.

Galilea raised her head slowly, paying closer attention to the distant sound of wind coming from somewhere further down the tunnel.

A small smile curved her lips. A touch of hope grazed her heart.

There had to be an entrance . . . *an exit* . . . another opening of some sort for the small current of wind to pass through the tunnel.

Good old Ollie. He'd not neglected her study of nature's science. Now, perhaps, one of his teachings that she had deemed rather useless, albeit interesting, until now, might just be worth all those long evening lessons.

"Collin," she said, shaking his shoulder. "Collin, there may be a way out of here, after all."

Collin shifted in her lap and mumbled something unintelligible.

"Did you hear me, Collin?"

"Hmm." Collin reached up and cupped her breast. "Mmm . . . Galilea," he whispered.

Galilea ducked her head and peered hard at him through the darkness. "Collin, are you awake?" she asked.

There was a short pause. "I . . . think so," he answered, his voice still not very strong. "Galilea? Are you really here with me?"

"Yes, my love," she said, brushing a lock of hair from his forehead.

"Then I must be dreaming again." Collin attempted to lift his head, but with a grunt let it fall back into Galilea's lap. "Ahh, I think I've cracked my skull."

" 'Tis a nasty bump on the back here," she told him. "I can feel the swelling. But, I believe you'll live—if I can get you out of here before we both starve to death."

" 'Twas Elenore, Galilea," he said in a rush, as if suddenly remembering what had happened. "I received an anonymous note offering an explanation of Lizzie's death. I was to come here, the note said, if I wanted answers." Reaching up, he wrapped his fingers around Galilea's forearm. "She came out of nowhere, Galilea, and shoved me. Did she do the same to you?"

"No, you were my lure here, Collin. After I came down in search of you, Elenore pulled the rope up. She has us boarded over as well, I'm afraid. And has left us for dead."

Collin moved his fingers over Galilea's face in much the same method as a blind man would. "Are you all right?" he asked. "She didn't hurt you?"

"No. She didn't have to. I fell into Elenore's trap on my own. Not to worry, though," she added. "Other than being a bit cold and quite hungry, I'm very well, thank you."

"You're hungry at this hour?"

"I was too worried about you to eat supper." Galilea stroked his jaw gently. "Now that I've found you, I'm famished. Can you walk?"

"Nay, I don't think so. I believe I broke my ankle when I fell."

"Well then, I suppose I shall have to fetch you help on my own."

"Don't tell me," Collin said, and Galilea could envision the half-cocked smile upon his face. "You really *can* fly. You're going to swoop up out of that hole and—"

Galilea slid her hand over his mouth, and she felt his grin grow wider against her palm. "Don't be silly, Collin. I'm going to find the other opening."

"The other opening?"

"Well there has to be one. Don't you feel the draft?"

"Now that you mention it, I do," Collin said thoughtfully. "But 'tis so faint, Galilea. What if the opening is too small to crawl through?"

"Then I shall make it bigger." Galilea dropped a kiss upon his cheek. "Will you be all right alone for a short spell?"

"Well, I *am* afraid of the dark, you know." Collin's hand snaked up her bodice and dipped into her chemise. "Perhaps you should stay here and keep me company for a bit."

"Collin, stop that," she said, giving him a sharp rap on the knuckles. " 'Tis not the time, nor the place."

Regardless of Galilea's rational opinion, a fuzzy warmth circled her heart and grew brighter, encompassing her entire torso. "However," she added a bit breathlessly, "'twould be most proper, I think, to thoroughly kiss me good luck."

Galilea took the strength of Collin's kiss with her as she groped her way through the tunnel of blackness. Running her hand along the cold rough surface of the corridor wall, she put forth every effort to unite her gift of the knowing with Collin's love—faithfully believing the combination would be an unstoppable source of guidance.

The harder she strove for the sixth sense, however, the farther away from her reach it seemed to float.

Apparently, some time after learning the truth about Lizzie's death, Galilea had lost her grip on the power of unnatural sight. 'Twas as if some door in her mind had closed, sealing off the mystical knowledge.

Nevertheless, she forged blindly onward, telling herself she must now rely on the special instincts that God above had given everyone . . . reminding herself, as she fought the dangling cobwebs in her path, that Collin was depending upon her to find the way out.

Another hour or so passed and the main corridor split off into several others. The tunnels twisted and turned until Galilea could not say in which direction she traveled.

After running into numerous dead ends and still being unable to locate the source of the draft, Galilea finally conceded defeat.

Promising herself that she and Collin would no doubt eventually come up with another solution concerning their entrapment, Galilea attempted to backtrack her steps.

She moved slowly down the particular corridor she believed would lead her to Collin again, praying all the while.

As time went on, and after several occasions of running into solid walls it became evident that her prayers had gone unanswered.

At the point of frustration, she came to a complete stop and stood locked in a darkness that prevented her from seeing her hand in front of her face.

But Ollie had not raised her to be a quitter. "Quitters never win," her wise old friend had told her time and again.

Galilea closed her eyes a moment and took a long, deep breath that lifted her shoulders.

Pick a course of action, a small voice inside her prompted. *Don't just stand here in the dark doing nothing.*

'Twas simple reason speaking . . . common sense. But good, sound advice.

Galilea latched onto the next thought that entered her mind.

"Collin!" she yelled with all her might. "Collin, where are you?"

The words echoed down the length of the surrounding tunnels, rebounding off the cold stone walls. *Where are you . . . where are you . . . where are you . . .*

Galilea's hollow sounding voice circled back to her, then trailed off to an end.

In the stillness she waited for an answer.

The anticipated response of Collin's ready reply did not come.

Instead a great rumbling sound surrounded her.

The floor beneath Galilea shifted, distorting her balance. The ceiling above her groaned. And a great crash sounded in the tunnel just ahead.

A rush of dust and debris flew at Galilea, knocking her backward. Her breath left her body as she landed against the hard surface of the corridor floor. Rocks rained down upon her, causing her to automatically cover her head.

'Twas over almost as quickly as it had begun. Galilea laggingly rose to a sitting position, and blinked several times before she realized what had happened.

The passageway had collapsed somewhere just ahead of her. The vibration of her voice when she'd called out for Collin must have triggered the cave-in.

Shivering, she crawled forward, sliding her hands over the crumbled fragments. When her fingers glided upward over a huge blockage of stones, she realized in horror that she no longer had a path to follow.

Behind her loomed a dead end. Before her, her way back to Collin . . . had been completely closed off by a pile of rocks.

* * *

Time dragged endlessly on for Galilea, with only the cold damp darkness to keep her company. A day had passed, she gauged . . . more or less. In Galilea's ragged state of mind, she could not say for sure.

The thick air grated against the inside of her lungs each time she inhaled. 'Twas becoming increasingly hard to breathe. Other than a few bruises here and there, she had not been seriously hurt. At least, she didn't think so.

Still, her muscles had grown stiff and ached with a chill. She had exhausted her strength with her useless attempts to dig through the debris.

She was so tired that she could not think anymore. Curling into a ball against the barrier of rocks that separated her from her beloved Collin, she slid her eyes closed, ready and willing to let her soul drift where it would.

Just on the edge of blissful slumber, a fierce whispering pierced Galilea's eardrum, causing her eyes to fly open.

A shining column of light illuminated the space around her in a soft golden glow. She squinted, shielding her eyes from the brightness with a hand.

Lizzie stepped from the light in what appeared to be solid form. Wearing a serene smile, she floated forward, the distinct, nontransparent shape of her body outlined in a silver aura.

"You mustn't sleep, Galilea," she said very

clearly, her smooth childlike voice void of the earlier warbling. *"Don't be afraid. Hear me, you must fight to stay awake. 'Tis not yet your time. You must go on."* Lizzie brightened her smile to a glorious degree. *"You must live for both of us."*

Collin paused, bracing his weight against the makeshift crutch again. The sturdy stick he'd come across while crawling through the tunnels had made his progress a bit easier.

Peering into the black void ahead, he frowned. He only hoped his slow but sure advance would be fast enough.

His heart stirred in his chest once more. He had to find Galilea. He had heard her call out, but before he could answer, something akin to the sound of thunder had rumbled through the underground caverns.

Collin shifted his cane, and limped forward with purpose, the pain in his ankle minor to the one that rode his heart. If there *was* a God, surely that supreme being would not take Galilea from him so soon.

Forging ever onward along the pitch-black corridors, Collin prayed in his own pagan way that if indeed God did exist, He would be merciful. If not for Collin's own sake, at least for Galilea's.

Several hours later, Collin halted his steps again, trying to determine which damned tunnel he should take this time. He could halfway ignore the throbbing ache shooting up his leg. 'Twas the panic rising in his breast that he feared most. For he knew to think rationally he must stay calm.

When Collin limped around the next bend, a pinpoint of light became visible far ahead of him in the tunnel. Oddly, he moved toward it without hesitation.

The light grew to the size of a small melon as he approached it, and when he came within its circle of illumination he could plainly see 'twas no ordinary lantern.

Collin swallowed, both fascinated and somewhat frightened by the hovering globe of light. While he stood staring, the thing moved ahead of him just a bit, then paused . . . then came back . . . then moved a tad farther into the tunnel. 'Twas as if the ball of light was urging him to follow . . . as if—

A tingling scurried up the length of Collin's spine. He smiled tentatively. "Lizzie?" he whispered. "Is that you?"

The globe brightened for a split second, indicating, as far as Collin was concerned, that indeed it was the mischievous little ghost.

Collin's grin grew broader. "Show me the way, my Wee Lizzie. Lead on."

Galilea stretched her eyes wide. Struggling with the heaviness of her lids, she hugged herself and rubbed the chill from her arms. *I cannot sleep . . . I must not sleep.* The phrase rolled over and over in her weary brain. She must not fall asleep. Lizzie had said so.

Collin was coming. *Someone* was going to find them. She knew that much, even without the aid of "the knowing". Galilea had faith in Lizzie's presence.

A scratching . . . clacking . . . grating sound reached Galilea's ears. At first she thought it might be the chattering of her own teeth. But when she stilled her shivering for a moment, she could tell the noise was coming from the other side of the rocks that blocked her exit.

"Galilea?" Collin's voice vibrated through the stones.

"Collin!" Galilea flattened herself against the wall that separated them. Then with haste, she began to dig frantically, clearing away as many of the smaller rocks as she could.

Working together on opposite sides of the stone enclosure, they soon broke away a space large enough to reach through and clasp hands.

"Galilea," Collin said, closing his fingers tightly around hers. " 'Twas Lizzie, *she* showed me where you were. "Galilea, I *saw* her," he added excitedly. "Well, actually I saw—"

"Hullo, down there . . . down there . . . down there . . ." Winston's voice echoed into the maze of tunnels, circling round and round. "Buck up, Master Collin. We'll be down to fetch the two of you directly . . . *directly . . . directly . . .*"

Less than half an hour later, a swiftly fashioned gurney was lowered into the sinkhole.

Galilea pressed a kiss to Collin's forehead and tucked the blanket beneath his chin before the men above began pulling him upward.

Winston stood beside Galilea, bracing her up with a sturdy arm. The two of them tilted their heads, watching Collin's ascent from the dark hole.

As Collin's gurney reached the lantern-lit surface, Galilea's gaze met with Elenore, who stood on the edge of the opening peering solemnly down into the pit.

"Elenore," Galilea murmured, then pressed her lips into a tight line.

" 'Twas she," Winston said softly, leaning to Galilea's ear, "who told us where to find you, miss. The search party heard her screaming, and we found poor Elenore some hundred yards from the house. Pitiful, she was. Ranting and raving that she had been attacked by Wee Lizzie and a black crow."

"Did . . . did she say anymore about Lizzie, Winston?" Galilea glanced at the butler, his features barely visible in the dim stream of moonlight.

Winston ducked his head. "Aye, mistress. She admitted she'd left poor Wee Lizzie down here, and she had known where she was all the while we searched for the child."

Galilea wanted to ask him more, but the gurney had been lowered again and was waiting to take her to join Collin.

"Here, mistress, let me help," Winston offered, guiding her onto the flat board stretched between the ropes.

"Thank you, Winston. For everything."

Galilea leaned forward and kissed the old butler's cheek, making him blush. Then she folded her fingers around the rope and tugged lightly.

As the gurney rose, Galilea looked up, and fastened her gaze once more on Elenore's painfully pinched expression.

Despite all she'd done, Galilea's heart went out to the poor demented woman.

Elenore moved forward, twisting her hands at her waist, and met Galilea as she was helped from the gurney.

"I'm sorry," she blurted out, her voice wavering from an excess of weeping. Reaching out, she grabbed Galilea's hand and squeezed it much too tightly. "I'm so sorry, Lizzie," she repeated, looking Galilea straight in the eye. "You can keep the locket. I shan't try to take it from you again. I promise I won't."

Roland stepped up behind his wife and closed his hands gently over her shoulders. He met Galilea's gaze above Elenore's head.

"You were right, Galilea. My wife does need my attentions," he said, wearing a sincere expression for the first time since Galilea had met him. "I feel partly responsible here. Perhaps, had I not neglected her so much, you and Collin might not have been put in this danger."

Galilea looked to Elenore again, who now stood staring wide-eyed into the distance.

"I have convinced Mother Luxley not to pursue the charges of witchcraft. In exchange, I would ask you not to mention Elenore's involvement in what happened here this evening to the constable. We shall be leaving for the townhouse in the city within a few days," Roland remarked, as if he had read Galilea's thoughts. "I'm told there's an excellent doctor in London. I have every confidence that she will recover this malady . . . with time and loving care."

Roland gave Galilea a genuinely kind smile. "Best of luck to you and Collin," he said, then turned his full attention on his wife. "Come, Elenore, 'tis time to go."

"Wait." Galilea reached out and caught Roland's sleeve as they turned to leave. "I have something I'd like to give Elenore."

Pulling the silver heart locket from her pocket, Galilea pressed it into Elenore's palm. Then grazing the woman's cheek with her fingertips, she smiled at Lord Luxley's adopted daughter. "For you, Elenore," she whispered. "From me, and Lizzie."

Elenore's eyes brightened at the sight of the glimmering locket in her hand. Raising her large eyes to Galilea's, her mouth curved upward. "Truly? I may keep it?"

Too moved to speak, Galilea merely nodded, and she folded Elenore's fingers closed over the heart-shaped locket.

Galilea spent a quiet moment watching Roland and Elenore walk away arm in arm. Then she peered over her shoulder to where Collin lay on the ground with the doctor bowed over him.

Moving swiftly in that direction, Galilea lowered herself to her knees beside Collin.

"Will he live long enough to marry me, Doctor?" she asked, her gaze roving lovingly over Collin's face as she smoothed the hair at his temple.

Collin's silver-blue eyes twinkled as they met hers. "Nay, Doctor. Answer me, first," he said, then lifted an eyebrow at Galilea. "Would tomorrow be too soon, do you think?"

The gruff old doctor rolled his eyes at his patient. "Aye, he'll live," he muttered, then grasped his black bag and rose to his feet. "I'll be back to check on you in a few days time. See to it you rest well until then," he concluded, then left.

With a lazy smile, Collin reached out and trailed his fingers down Galilea's arm. "Read my mind, Galilea," he said in a husky voice.

Galilea didn't need her sixth sense to know what the smokey change of color in Collin's eyes meant. " 'Tis not rest you're thinking of, I can see."

He tugged on her arm, and Galilea reclined beside him, noting some of the tenants were gathering their lanterns and were beginning to leave, one by one.

"Tell me our future will be bright, Galilea," Collin said into the dwindling commotion going on about them, his voice sounding suddenly sober. "Tell me what I feel for you in this moment will never waver."

Galilea searched his questioning face for a

long moment, then she lifted her gaze to the dark towers of the castle ruins.

"I cannot, Collin. Since I've lost the knowing, I am as blind to the future as you are." Galilea took a deep breath, then lowered her eyes by degrees to his again. "Does that make you love me less?"

Collin curled a hand around the back of her neck and brought her face to his. "I would love you with or without the powers," he said against her lips. "If we must move blindly into the future, then so be it. But we shall do so together."

In that fragment of time when Collin's mouth closed over hers, Galilea felt as if her heart merged with his. And she was not afraid anymore. Not of love. Not of facing the future without the aid of her special sight. Not of anything the world might pit against them.

Not of *anything*.

Epilogue

Galilea stood by the master bedroom window, admiring the spring gardens below. The late afternoon sun cast a radiant glow over the blooming flowers of every imaginable color, showing off Winston's efforts to their fullest.

'Twas a picture-perfect sight, and quite proper that the day was so glorious—on this, the six month anniversary of her wedding.

A light breeze fluttered the curls about her face and lifted the scent of roses into the air. Breathing in the sweet fragrance, Galilea smiled with contentment. She had found her place after all the years of searching.

An exchange of squawking and chattering drew Galilea's attention to the high branches of a tree in the yard. There, Magus pranced and preened along the leafy limbs, paying court to a pretty female crow. Her old friend, Magus, it seemed, had found his own true love.

The chamber door opened behind her, and Galilea peered over her shoulder. Her smile broadened at the sight of Collin. He'd been in the fields again, overseeing the restoration of the manor and its grounds, working side by side with the tenants. He set Galilea's heart afire with his disheveled hair and sweat glistening on his face and bare shoulders.

Galilea stretched her hand out to him. "Come and have a look, Collin. Magus is smitten, I believe."

"Is he now?" Collin asked with a wide grin as he moved to window and slipped an arm around her waist. "So am I," he said, kissing her neck. "I see you are already dressed. You look beautiful."

Tilting his head, Collin observed the two birds's flirtatious dance along the limb. "Well, it appears old Magus may be a proud papa before too long."

Collin shifted his gaze to Galilea's, and he rested a hand upon her rounding abdomen. "There're two things at least that Magus and I have in common. Both fathers-soon-to-be, and each of us loves you madly."

He pressed a kiss to Galilea's lips, then stepped back and wrinkled his nose. "I smell of sheep. I'll clean up and be ready to leave within a half hour. Are you all packed?"

"Yes. I cannot wait to see London again," Galilea answered, watching him strip off his work clothes. She was still a bit mesmerized by the beauty of his body. She had a sudden urge to glide her hands over the sleek contours of his chest, but she knew the action would lead to making love and consequently would make them arrive in London much too late. To avoid further temptation, Galilea focused her attention out the window once more, then asked, "What time do you meet with your editor tomorrow?"

"Ten o'clock," he said, his voice trailing off toward the wardrobe on the other side of the room. "We meet with the investigator I've hired to find your mother at two."

It had been Collin's idea to attempt to locate Galilea's mother while in London. Galilea had agreed, figuring her mother was another puzzle piece missing from her past.

Galilea heard the splash of water as Collin washed, and she could not resist a peek in his direction. "I'm so proud of you, Collin," she commented. "Just think, I'm married to a published poet."

Collin dragged the towel down his face, revealing a lopsided grin. "I owe it all to you, love. It was the piece entitled 'The Fairy-Queen' that caught the publisher's eye." Grabbing his clean shirt, he stuffed his arms into the sleeves and moved forward to drop a kiss upon her forehead. "You inspired me," he said with a wink.

Galilea quirked the corners of her mouth upward and reached out to button his shirt. "Aye, but that was before I started growing fat. I daresay, I shan't be much of an inspiration when I begin to waddle in the next few months."

Collin lifted her chin with one hand while grazing the fingers of his other back and forth across her swollen stomach. "You are not fat,

Galilea. You are blossoming with beauty as you carry the weight of my son."

Galilea peered lovingly into his steady blue-gray eyes. " 'Tis no son I carry, but rather a girl child. I have no doubt."

"A daughter," Collin murmured, searching her gaze worriedly. "I've no experience a'tall with little girls."

Galilea trailed her fingers down the front of his shirt, continuing to fasten the buttons. "I don't believe you'll require much, Collin. All you have to do is love her."

"And that I will do with all my heart." A smile formed on Collin's lips. "What shall we name her?"

"Why, Elizabeth, of course." Galilea's fingers faltered on the buttons, and Collin caught her hand in both of his.

"You still miss Wee Lizzie terribly, don't you?" His softly spoken question came out as a statement.

"I simply wish I could have said good-bye," Galilea whispered.

Tears misted her vision but, blinking them away, she smiled at her husband. "You should finish dressing if we're to make it to the inn in time to catch the coach," she stated, giving him a little push in the right direction. "If we miss the coach, there won't be another until tomorrow. And you've promised to take me to the ballet tomorrow evening, remember?"

"How could I forget?" Collin twisted his mouth as he went to the bureau, picked up his cravat, and looped it around his neck. "You've reminded me every day since we received the letter from my publisher inviting us to London."

While Collin concentrated on tying his necktie, Galilea turned and stared out the window again. She didn't want Lizzie's memory to intrude upon her happiness. Yet she needed some sort of closure . . . a final farewell.

The wind picked up, blowing through the window with a suddenness that made Galilea catch her breath. The sound of a child's laughter, carried by the breeze, reached her ears, drawing her attention to the tall hedges at the far end of the garden.

There, upon the path that led to the family cemetery, stood Lizzie, her long blond curls fluttering about her shoulders.

Galilea tried to speak, but her throat tightened around the words.

A golden glow outlined Lizzie's form as she looked up at Galilea and raised her hand in a silent wave.

Galilea raised her own hand in response. "Good-bye, Lizzie," she said beneath her breath. "Thank you . . . thank you."

In a matter of seconds, a tall, white-haired man stepped from behind the hedge and took hold of Lizzie's hand. He turned his head and gazed up at Galilea just long enough for her to recognize him as Lord Luxley. Lizzie's father. *Her* father.

Lord Luxley gave Galilea a brilliant smile

that went straight to her heart, then he led Lizzie away, and the two figures faded.

"Damn," Collin muttered. "Galilea could you help me with this blasted thing?"

Galilea swiveled from the window to find Collin cursing his cravat. Moving swiftly to his aide, she brushed his fumbling fingers aside and tied the scarf neatly.

"There," she said, then raised her lashes to meet his gaze. She wanted to share her experience of seeing Lizzie one last time with him, but before she could do so, his mouth closed over hers, driving all thoughts of anyone but Collin from her mind.

His kiss left her breathless and dazed. "I love you, Galilea," he murmured against her lips before he stepped aside to grab his jacket.

"And I love you," Galilea replied, taking in the width of his broad shoulders in his suit coat.

"Come," he urged. "We're off to London."

Slipping an arm around her waist, Collin guided her to the door. Just short of exiting the room, he bent to Galilea's ear. "With any luck, we'll be the only two passengers taking the coach this evening," he whispered suggestively.

"Aye." Galilea lifted an eyebrow. "And at the moment, Collin, I do believe we *are* the luckiest two people alive."